Ariel Dorfman

HARD RAIN

Translated from Spanish
by George Shivers
with the author

readers international

The title of this book in Spanish is *Moros en la costa,* first
published by Editorial Sudamericana in 1973 in Argentina
© Ariel Dorfman 1973

First published in English by Readers International Inc,
Columbia, Louisiana and Readers International, London.
Editorial inquiries to the London office at 8 Strathray
Gardens, London NW3 4NY, England. US/Canadian
inquiries to the Subscriber Service Dept, P O Box 959,
Columbia LA 71418-0959 USA.

Cover illustration, *When It Rains Everyone Gets Wet,*
by Jaime Azócar
Cover design by Jan Brychta
Printed and bound in Malta by Interprint Limited

Library of Congress Catalog Card Number: 89-64272
British Library Cataloguing in Publication Data
Dorfman, Ariel, *1942-*
    Hard rain.
    I. Title   II. Moros en la costa. English
    863

ISBN 0-930523-77-6 Hardcover
ISBN 0-930523-78-4 Paperback

Preface to the English Translation

Hard Rain was written during the last months of 1972, in the middle of one of this century's most fascinating, and tragic, social experiments: the revolution known as the Chilean peaceful road to socialism. Two years before, in September 1970, Salvador Allende, supported by a coalition of leftwing parties grouped together in the Unidad Popular, had won a plurality in the Presidential elections and thereafter become the first Socialist in my country's history - and in fact, the first in the world - to try to build socialism using non-violent means. Until then, all revolutions had been based on the principle that, before one could attempt to radically reform an unjust economic and social structure, the working class and its allies had to replace the prevailing institutions with new structures. Allende and his followers believed that Chile, because of its stable democratic tradition, could initiate those deep alterations while keeping and even extending the freedoms associated with democracy, and without touching the military that had, until then, been the guarantors and enforcers of the status quo.

Enormous changes were initiated in all walks of life, mainly in the economy: the State gradually took over the most important centers of economic power, nationalizing foreign-owned natural resources as well as large industrial and banking complexes that were controlled by a local oligarchy, and expropriating vast tracts of land, which were handed over to the peasants.

The people who, from time immemorial, had been the owners of Chile did not easily accept this assault on their wealth. Allende's policies met violent opposition: strikes, sabotage, civil disobedience, murders, economic blockades

v

and boycotts, attempted coups. As would be proven conclusively later by the U.S. Senate investigating committee chaired by Senator Frank Church, and was at the time certainly suspected, the counter-revolution was financed and directed (a process called destabilization) by the Nixon administration, using the CIA. By the end of 1972, it was clear that the Allende government was fighting for its life.

I wrote this novel while, outside in the streets and among the people of Chile, a battle raged for power, a battle to determine not only who would prevail in the country but also who would get the chance to tell its story, to write its history. *Hard Rain* expresses, on one level, the extraordinary optimism and energy of those who dreamt of sweeping away oppression without killing their adversaries while at the same time subtly revealing, at another level, the fear that it would all end disastrously and that we would be the ones to die. A preface such as this one is certainly not the place to analyze what the novel means or even what it desired to communicate, but it is safe to say that in these pages the reader will find clues both to why the revolution failed and what was so magnificent and joyful about the process of so many marginalized and excluded human beings suddenly becoming the protagonists of their own destiny. What is clear, almost twenty years later, is that this fictional universe - if I may so call it - was subject to many of the same pressures, constraints and new explorations that the country itself was undergoing. Everything was being questioned at the time in Chile - not only the economy and the political system, but the deepest core of human relations, sexuality, culture, thought, art, the narrative structure itself - and *Hard Rain,* I believe, must be understood as part of this process of collective and personal self-examination as well as an attempt to reflect it.

Violence, like a hidden wind, blows through the narrative voices. It would eventually come to the surface in the hard reality of historical Chile. Less than ten months after I completed the text, a military coup brutally ended our experiment. In it, Allende and thousands of other patriots died; the reforms that had been instituted were drastically reversed; the bodies (in this novel and in everyday Chile) that danced and meditated and loved and painted walls and doubted themselves and reached out to the future were tortured, jailed, persecuted, exiled.

The liberation that the novel promised turned out quite differently, as the circumstances of its very publication show. The day it was sent to the printer in neighboring Argentina, instead of celebrating the occasion, its author, having seen his own books burned on television, was going into hiding. In fact, the first public service that *Hard Rain* performed for me was not to inform the world, as I would have liked, of how near Paradise Allende's Chile had been, but rather to help me get out of the Inferno that Chile had become. By the time it was published, I had taken refuge in the Argentine Embassy in Santiago, along with 900 or so other frightened people. When the Pinochet government refused me safe conduct out of the country, the novel itself came to the rescue. It had won a major literary prize, in Buenos Aires, and the Argentine chancellery was able to press the Chilean generals to allow me to leave the country, suggesting that it would be embarrassing for such a work to be circulating freely while its author was denied that same right. A short time later I was given permission to travel to Argentina, the first stage of what was to be a long exile.

It is symbolic that this novel appears in its first translation ever, this one in English, now that my exile is finally over, now that we have returned to democracy in Chile. Being part of a movement that had been so ferociously crushed, I had never been particularly attracted by the idea of new editions in Spanish nor of agreeing to translations when more urgent political and literary endeavors seemed to be necessary. Now, after so many years spent in the exhausting struggle against the Pinochet regime, it is time to come to terms once again with my own past. I am proud to be able to give readers a glimpse of the wonderful, confusing Chile that preceded that horror, a Chile that, in the terms described in this novel that I love so much, will certainly never again return.

This text is not exactly the one that Spanish-language readers could acquire in December 1973. I have changed the title (originally called *Moros en la costa,* which literally translated would have been something like *The Coast Is Not Clear*); but, more significantly, I have shortened the book somewhat. I intended to do the cutting myself before the novel came out, but was unable to, first because of the constraints of the Chilean situation (who cares about editing the niceties of a novel if you think you, your family and your friends may all be killed tomorrow?) and later because it was neither possible nor plausible to receive proofs at the embassy where I had taken refuge - where I could hear people being shot just on the other side of the walls as they scrambled to try to get in.

The reader can rest assured, however, that I have avoided the temptation to rewrite the text. It is as prophetic and as blind, as hopeful and as anguished, as fervent and as experimental, as it was when I first hurriedly wrote the words, not sure whether I should be taking time out from the revolution to tell its story. Now I am glad that I did.

In its original incarnation this novel was for my wife, María Angélica, to whom I have, since then, offered several other books. If I may be allowed to re-dedicate it now, I would like it to be for all those who died for freedom during the Pinochet years, for all those who, represented in some strange way in these pages, never lost hope that we had the right to tell our version of history, all those who were silenced but somehow still speak to the future.

Ariel Dorfman
May 1st, 1990

viii

HARD RAIN

HARD RAIN

"Aquí estamos otra vez,
y que fue, y que fue."

"Here we are again,
we can't be stopped, we can't be stopped."

(Street cry of the Left for decades in Chile)

"A hard rain /
is going to fall."

Bob Dylan

Dare to do it.

All you need are a body, a killer, and a detective. Perfect first ingredients. Season well with a few other characteristics (a list of suspects, limited to residents and visitors who had access to the closed space where the crime took place; authorities who feel bewildered and impotent; a criminal who threatens to strike again; a detective who is emotionally involved in the case; an explosive atmosphere) and we've got ourselves a first-rate mystery novel.

In spite of the fact that *Con-centrations,* a narrative by Arístides Ulloa, a young Venezuelan who has lived in our country since 1967, exhibits the subtitle "Mystery Novel" prominently in blood-red letters on its cover, the reader's doubts, and more importantly those of the critic, with regard to this classification begin to be justified even before the end of chapter 1. By the end of chapter 2, a deeper puzzlement has set in.

In a Nazi concentration camp the body of a Jewish woman has been found. Death by strangulation. After lengthy interrogations establish that the guilty party is no doubt one of the prisoners, it is decided that the aid of the Gestapo will be sought to carry out the requisite investigation. The chapter ends with the arrival of Captain Heinrich Geerhardt, "in whose grey eyes there was a glimmer of something distant and weak that some would have called fear."

The reader's surprise can only be compared to that of the guards of that extermination camp. What sense could there be in murdering a woman who in another 48 hours would have died in the usual and proper manner in the gas chambers? Is it worthwhile to pursue the killer and can that individual act be defined as murder when it simply anticipated and hastened an execution which had already been scheduled? And why are the Germans concerned with finding the responsible party, when he's going to be eliminated, along with all the other prisoners? In the worst case, in a matter of a few days; in the best case, in the very next group.

It is true that the murderer succeeded in suspending executions for twenty-four hours, while the investigator searches for the guilty party, but after this brief postponement the slaughter will go on as usual, even though it means eliminating witnesses, evidence and murderer. If that was the purpose, we have to agree that the means have far exceeded the desired ends. It's also possible that someone hated that woman so intensely (or, as one of the agents suggested, loved her so much) that he wanted to snatch her away from her executioners.

But more than anything else it appears to be an absurd gesture. Why are the Nazis so interested in finding and judging *one* murderer, when they annihilate thousands of prisoners every day? And especially considering that these actions taken in the name of "justice" unfold in an atmosphere of incredible misery and cruelty, where those who make up a human vegetation that was fluid, transitory, floating, a wagon-load of animals, phantoms, suddenly have acquired individuality and a personal voice, a specific weight, as if the fact that one of them had killed another restored to all the right to be seen. Generally, the act of murder calls attention to the precariousness of normal, peaceful existence, that of human beings who live and die of natural causes. Here, on the contrary, "as if it were endlessly raining beneath the sea, as if someone were trying to explain the difference between Mozart and Bach to a deaf person, as if you picked up an hourglass in order to see the sun better", that outburst of destruction appears to be a unique and exceptional act of sanity in a madhouse where the patient must suddenly treat and care for the doctor. Someone has become normal. He must be found.

Beginning with the second chapter the reader's bewilderment deepens further. From the very first words (the heavy lust of the sun, thought Quiroz, overwhelmed by the freedom with which his legs obeyed orders. Even the corpse will be sending out a greeting. That above all. Then, to look for a way to escape.

"I want to see the victim," said Quiroz, staring tranquilly at Colonel Ceballos. "I understand it's a woman."

"What about the prisoners?"

"I'll talk to them later, Colonel, if that's all right with you"),

we understand that the scene has moved to another extermination camp, located now in the middle of a torturous South American landscape, which might be Haiti, Paraguay, Brazil or Venezuela, where the same murder has occurred, a woman strangled at precisely the same time (two o'clock in the afternoon). Although the victim has another name (Ana García instead of Gerta Rosenfeld), the vital statistics of both coincide almost exactly, at least on a formal level. The same is true of the testimony of the jailers, the alibis and the confusion of the suspects, the peculiar physical layout of the barracks, which blocks visibility from one of the control towers, and the mud which still bears the deep scars of a struggle for survival.

The continuity of plot is evident. What occurred in Latin America is an exact replica and at the same time a prolongation of what happened in Dachau or Auschwitz.

But in this split ocean of time, where the symmetry itself emphasizes and accentuates the grotesque unreality ("like two monsters who believe they are in front of a mirror every time they look at each other," words that go through Quiroz's mind as he questions a pair of twin girls, identically deformed and pathetic), it is the detective who provides the element of change. Because Gerardo Quiroz, far from being an agent of repression, is a famous criminal lawyer incarcerated in another prison in that country for having joined the national liberation movement. He hasn't the slightest doubt that as the regime becomes more repressive and less concerned with international "public opinion", he will also be moved to a camp like this one, where people disappear and are never heard from again. The methods of mass extermination are, of course, less sophisticated, technically inferior to those used by the SS in Germany (after all, it's not for nothing that we're underdeveloped), but their brutality and efficiency leave no room for envy.

The underlying competition between these alternative investigators, the contraposition of attitudes, psychologies, motivations, moral conduct, are what lend the plot its dynamism. Who will unravel the tapestry first? The revolutionary, who must escape that prison in order to proclaim to the world the extermination that is taking place, or Captain Geerhardt, who will see in the capture of the murderer conclusive proof of the superiority of the Aryan race? For the Nazi, conscious that Germany is falling back on both eastern and western fronts, what is at stake here is the war itself, German efficiency and discipline, the very foundations of the Fascist State and of any legal order that would be eternal.

"I need a few more hours," he told Colonel Macher, and in spite of everything, his voice showed a slight loss of control.

"Impossible."

"That word does not exist for us, Colonel. Think of the joy with which that Jew will die, his last thoughts as he agonizes, laughing at us all the while. Colonel! We must postpone resumption of the executions."

This fanaticism, this emotional rigidity, the moving force behind his search, is also the source of his weakness. He knows that to solve the case, he must somehow identify with the unknown strangler. But because he despises both the victim and her murderer, the Captain cannot carry out the investigation with the necessary calm and objectivity.

16

Quiroz, on the other hand, is too close to the prisoners. It's like pursuing myself, "someone is sending me a message through this woman with her neck crushed, someone is moving his lips on the other side of the fog and I can't hear." His sympathy for the murderer grows throughout the search. In that act of contempt for the routine by which destruction is legitimated, a condemned man is expressing his faith that men are in control of their lives, right up to the savage and lucid frontier of their own extinction. Someone who is playing at the very door of the oven, rebelling against the mass anonymity of death, assuming control of his own skin and lungs, when everything is about to dissolve. But to admire the killer and to share his point of view naturally constitute an obstacle to finding him, because that tends to obscure the tracks, ignoring the most compelling signs. Besides, Quiroz's mind does not function calmly. He is suffocated by hot waves of fury and disgust, as the suffering, the misery, and the purulence that compose the physical and moral quagmire of that concentration camp become entwined with his calculations. In spite of all that, he has proposed to carry out his task, since he thinks it possible that he will be freed (he has demanded certain guarantees) and that his exile from the country offers the possibility of carrying on the struggle, and of coming back sometime later. And even though the murderer is going to be killed in any case (whether individually or collectively when the firing squads and the mass graves in the middle of the jungle resume), Quiroz is corralled by uncertainty; he isn't sure whether perhaps the best course might be simply to declare, I did it, I killed the woman, and then take his place there in the line with those awaiting the order to fire, and then to fall with his brothers, to fall.

The two protagonists then could not be more different, and yet both followed an almost identical line in their investigations, using similar reasoning, methods and technical procedures, and also making the same mistakes in reconstructing the murders. In their respective chapters, each one depends on the evidence uncovered by the other, with the result that whatever the effects of the discovery that is claimed, they advance in a single, methodical direction, each one unconsciously collaborating with his counterpart, like a relay race in which one begins where the other leaves off, not knowing that the one handing him the baton is his most bitter rival and mortal enemy. As they follow the continuous and uninterrupted thread of their activities, oppressor and oppressed, Nazi and revolutionary, are involuntary allies.

Although these two, in alternation, monopolize most of its chapters, the book is more than just a counterpoint of the two. Several sections (six or seven, and especially the last two chapters of the novel), add other characters and twists of this "cosmic detective", in a fragmented fashion, and these also contribute, piling up material, evidence, trails, like an unknown vagabond who suddenly turns up in the line of a church soup kitchen and then continues on his way the next morning. The function, the situation, has not changed. It is simply one more splinter in the mask of the main character, carrying on the work of Geerhardt and Quiroz, but only fleeting across the reader's consciousness, bearing with him other concentration camps in other parts of the world, more mass executions, more torture, more death.

There's the Yank, investigating a prison camp in Vietnam. We find him floundering precisely at the moment when his own fatigue and all the brutality surrounding him will no longer allow him to serve his country, however much he repeats to himself those time-worn phrases: "patriotic duty", "my country, right or wrong", "America, love it or leave it".

Or the black leader in Rhodesia, who sees in his charge an unquestionable demonstration that whites are incapable of successfully carrying out the task and that he "of that race dressed in the color of night, the dark lion in the sun's core

18

when it is penetrated", will overcome them on the turf of Western logic itself. He has no illusions (this distinguishes him from Quiroz) that the exploiters of his people will fulfill their promise to free him if he manages to identify the murderer. ("What kind of honor are you talking about?" said Nyagaro. "The honor of men who violate our women? An honor based on whips and guns bought with money extracted off our backs? What good is their word?") But he will search for the killer in any case. For higher reasons, political reasons. And therefore he asks his fellow prisoners to cooperate. We can't give them the advantage by behaving like animals; this just reinforces their concept of us as barbarians. It's not that we're against violence. But we'll use it against them, not against each other. Murder is also condemned by our law and when we find the one responsible we should punish him ourselves, in accordance with the traditions of our people.

Nyagaro's indignation is not shared by the skeptical detective, full of irony, who investigates a strangling among a group of women, all condemned to death, in a French prison. He actually feels a fierce loyalty toward that proud but mad attitude. "I wish you could share with me that sense of security you have in the world and in yourself, unknown murderess, the confidence you had to commit such an act in a place like this." And floating through one chapter there's even a Spanish corregidor in Peru in the eighteenth century, who with his foreign laws confronts a group of Indians, on the point of being executed for their participation in a rebellion against the Viceroy. The psychological panorama of the novel is enriched by the amazement the Spaniard feels as he confronts that culture so different from his own, one which, as an enlightened man, he can admire despite his prejudices.

But the fundamental point is that the lives of these investigators are all truncated lives, a night spent with a masked woman, a half-finished statue seen through the window of a speeding train. We will never know how they resolved their problems, the parabola finally described by their lives, how they rebelled against, were transformed by or accommodated themselves to these new experiences. Will that clean-cut, circumspect, honorable and eminently fair Englishman, who is slowly discovering the inhuman scars of colonialism in a concentration camp near Bombay at the end of the nineteenth century, denounce the situation? Or will he become accustomed to it, making himself an accomplice by his silence in order not to stir up the garbage in his own life? Or what about that slave detective who has lost all sense of his own dignity and who thinks only of abandoning ship, his mind bursting with plans of escape, interested only in survival, terrified of having to die like these others, ready to betray his best friend if necessary, but don't go on torturing me, don't kill me. Will that man achieve his purpose? Will he allow himself to be carried along by his own misery and his own fear until he becomes his captors' accomplice?

We never know the answer. We are given hints, possible outcomes, secret objectives that float lazily through the individual mind. At the end of the chapter, as we bid him farewell, that fragmented detective is frozen and becomes pure potentiality, refracted and annulled and answered by the echoes and the acts of the other protagonists, his continuation, prognosis, parallel and heirs. He has involuntarily delegated his rights of choice to other men of whose existence he hasn't an inkling, with the same blind certainty with which we bring a child into the world, confident that he will never commit suicide, or we write a letter full of useless advice to the great-grandchild of our great-grandchild.

It's as though each one of these detectives, in order to delineate an immense mural, had to use the clumsy hands and the Daltonian eyes of apprentices and rivals. Not one of them, therefore, including both Quiroz and Geerhardt, occupies a privileged place, one that is sufficiently per-

20

manent and eagle-like to impose a clear and decisive direction upon the collective life that, without knowing it, they are immersed in. To put it another way, not one of them is seated at the controls. Through what others did or failed to do, we will guess at all the routes, deviations, missteps and mistakes. Like gods who must be judged by the actions of their worshippers twenty centuries later, we will discover the most likely solution. Something like a group of old women, during the long, hot afternoons of magnolia blossoms and settling dust, gossiping about the promising future that had awaited George, if it hadn't been for that fatal case of pneumonia when he was twenty-two, or what might have happened to William, if he hadn't been swept off his feet by that hussy.

The reader, then, must be paid over-time, or at least get a bonus. He must superimpose the successive and individual voices of a chorus that manages to sing together only at some distant point of their own imagination. It is evident that beneath this formal game of variation and continuity, adopted, so it seems, from the techniques employed by Cuban writer Alejo Carpentier in his short story "Similar to the night" and also by the Chilean writer Renato Fardo (pen name) in his *Which of These Roads Leads to Rome?*, there lies the notion that all men are really one man, that Geerhardt and Quiroz and all the others are facets of a single personality, one Man who is searching for truth, using all the means and the mirrors and the personalities within his reach, trying on first one mask and then another in order to realize his selfhood, to glimpse, trembling at the bottom of a well that contains no stars, his unique, true and eternal face. Each detective would exist to the extent to which he participates in the repeated universal archetype, the human being as Detective, like a compass that creates its own north in order to be able to orient itself, and the revolving and oppressive action in which each of them particularizes his own dilemma is only an appearance, an illusion, a dream, "that I was the reflection in the water," one of them thinks, "and not the eyes that observed it."

It is clear that the structure of the novel confirms this kind of interpretation. We are often absolutely convinced that we have here a line of paper dolls cut out by the same scissors from a paper that was folded ten times, even though we are never abandoned by the narrator's secret urgent sense (as well as our own) that reality must be something more than an anguished accumulation of multifaceted consciences that happened to have coincided in a plot structure that both transcends and links them. The tension increases, therefore, as we approach the end of the novel, when we find ourselves facing that moment when they will have to decide which road to take, when one of them will have to remain with the microphone in his hand and the rest can only sit passively and expectantly in the bleachers.

There are, of course, common traits which join all these protagonists. Each of them, in spite of contrapositions and rivalries, must find the murderer. They see in that search something more than a police action. It is also a *personal* struggle to pull a dove out of the most hidden recesses of the darkness, a struggle to impose order and meaning upon a reality that is sinking into its own delirium and spinning into chaos. All of them trust deductive and inductive reasoning as the instrument by which the human being must orient himself in life. They all realize that here too their manhood, their ability and their solitary strength are being tested: their selfhood will be revealed in all its magnitude and meanness as it confronts a problem which has a fixed deadline for its resolution. One can succeed, or one can fail; that is all. Strangely, all of them feel that their lives have not produced the expected fruit and that now, facing imminent death, they have been given one last chance to carry out their personal and inscrutable destiny.

This temptation of the characters, their individualism, the affirmation of their own personality as a cramped muscle in

22

an exhausted body, the celebration of themselves as living and winning, finds its extreme incarnation in the next to the last chapter, in one of the personalities, which, on purpose, we had not mentioned earlier. With all the evidence in hand, and not knowing how it's going to turn out, unable to put together a single, intelligible picture with all the evidence and counter-evidence, all the confusing testimony, calculations of the time of the crime based on the state of the victim's digestive processes, only an hour before the fatal deadline when once again the gas chambers, the guns, the electric chairs, and the death by starvation and thirst will go into action, we read with shock the name of the detective chosen by the author to unmask the mystery, the one who will drive the final rivet into place and make the last connection in the plot.

Will it be the Gestapo captain, the Latin American revolutionary, or one of the others?

None of them. We are dealing with no less a personage than Hercule Poirot, the famous creation of Agatha Christie. We listen in astonishment to his implacable deductions, the magic thread of his analysis, the sharp clarity with which he structures the evidence, the skill with which he eliminates the rubble of false trails.

One would think, and such is our first intuition, that this figure is a pop element of the kind that are very characteristic of many of the continent's young writers, for example Juan Agustín, Reynaldo Arenas, and Juan Menguant, one of those pranks by which they attempt to transgress the literary Mount Olympus.

Nevertheless, Poirot's presence is in no way arbitrary. It is a pole to which all the detectives have been moving internally. He is a companion that has been guiding them from the very beginning of their investigations. Because here, Christie's detective is the complete technocrat, a veritable calculating machine who does not even bother to embarrass himself with questions that would only muddy the

23

waters of the investigation. Poirot, there in Algeria, supported by French machine guns, has no interest in matters of justice or injustice, nor is he attacked by any doubts as to the sense of inoculating a dead man or of combating a plague that attacks only the dead in their graves. For him, the only thing that matters is solving the mystery. It's all a matter of an algebraic equation, whether men or numbers, and a rigorous, logical process can resolve it, as long as you don't insist on introducing alien, extra-scientific factors, emotional tangles, ethical recriminations, and political quagmires. "Therefore, I, Hercule Poirot, by sheer intelligence, have finally managed to resolve this matter. Because from the very beginning I realized that the murderer himself had set this trap for me: that I would allow myself to be entangled in problems and perspectives that had nothing to do with what is essential. The victim. The murderer. Here we have the only elements that need concern us."

Although he shares Geerhardt's coldness and lack of compassion for and interest in the prisoners, Poirot, unlike the Nazi, does not have a cause or an ideal (however terrible and perverted these may be). His is merely an empty esthetic, and it is this which will surely be successful in this battle, between the murderer and myself, messieurs, mesdames. Anything else is merely decorative. Poirot reduces man to a robot, a mercenary in the service of his own refined technique. The alienation of all the other partial detectives in the Myth of the detective is revealed as what it really is: the inhumanity of a technological society, egotism singing its praises in the desert of Hiroshima and Nagasaki.

And if Poirot's neutral and rather mechanical appearance has been possible, it is due to the fact that all the other protagonists carried the germ of his presence within themselves all along, a driving force and an objective, linked to that common denominator, a tangential territory in which Quiroz and Geerhardt can brush against each other and perhaps subscribe to certain partial agreements. Poirot was the bridge that linked those dissimilar destinies, the quintessential detective, the reduction to the lowest common denominator, a man who lives only to investigate and who has succeeded in repressing any emotion, memory or desire which does not serve that end. It is for this reason he was chosen to uncover the name and the face of the unknown killer; it is he who will bring together all the incomplete points of view and join all the efforts of the others into one beautiful synthesis.

But the author will not give him that satisfaction, for he will also cut short that spectacular paragraph in which the detective is about to reveal the identity of the guilty party.

We enter the final chapter.

Who will be appointed to close the circle? How will all these divided and fragmented existences culminate? What was the reason that motivated such a sterile murder? What reward or punishment await the detective and the murderer? What trail will we be offered in order to understand the peak or the precipice toward which all are moving?

The author will not answer these questions, leaving Poirot with the last word fossilizing in his dry mouth. The detectives, each one of them, will remain in the last place we saw them, on the brink of taking the definitive step, not knowing exactly what they will do.

Because, at the end, we find ourselves in a small border town in the south of Chile. The snow-covered road makes it impossible for anyone to enter or leave the valley, where a murder has been committed on an *hacienda*. As the chapter begins, the policeman has guessed who is responsible for the crime, but has decided not to reveal the culprit, even if that action results in his being tried and expelled from the service. Instead, he simply receives all the day's reports, the accusations, the usual parade of alcoholism, poverty, exploitation, ignorance, deaths from the cold and from hunger, the inhuman swamp into which the inhabitants of that society are sinking - mental retardation, abortion, child abuse, abandonment of the old, exploitation of peasants, fraud against the Mapuche Indians, poisoning of dogs, the heartbreak of the single mother who loses her child, a knife fight between gangs in a saloon.

And with that the novel ends. With a detective who refuses to continue the investigation, who has no interest in finding, arresting or punishing the guilty party, absolute passivity, in contrast to Poirot's frenetic shrewdness. The moral seems clear: the world itself is a concentration camp, and those really responsible, the true criminals, are not the ones we insist on searching out and denouncing and prosecuting, this man, this woman, at our side.

We cannot help but feel that this ending is somewhat contrived and arbitrary. Its effect is to simplify a novel that until that point had had a complex and well-drawn plot. Unfortunately, it reduces all the different alternatives to a mere outline, transforming the images of guilt, death and freedom, which had been interwoven in the preceding chapters, into a rather commonplace symbol. But one must also admit that the presence of this detective who would rather confront the system itself and not its cast-offs and/or secondary effects, was being set up in all the other protagonists. Because just as the temptation to solve the case, irrespective of its consequences, with satanic pride, has gnawed at them all and culminated in Poirot's reasonings, they have also lived, especially Quiroz, with radical doubt as to the meaning of their search, and, ultimately, as to the meaning of their own profession, the endless questioning to search out the true causes of a death and not just the hand that by accident has been found pulling a trigger or squeezing a neck. It is the prisoners, those rags without a body, those blind-bee eyes, the persecuted and the defeated, the back of the indomitable Vietnamese man, the Guatemalan's malaria-ridden frame, the flaring eyes of a small Jewish child, the colonized burning themselves in Africa and India, the silence from the last cell in European jails, the flood of sadness in factories, the wall pressing against your back the instant before the rifles fire, needles jabbing at genitals, this is the backdrop of hunger and threats which has never disappeared from the novel. In contrast with the Poirots who understand concentration as an act of thought, isolated within their exalted mental refuges, there are those who have concentrated on multitudes across the wide and sickly surface of the earth, those who come together as prisoners searching for a simple gesture of solidarity, an extended hand, the brotherhood of struggle.

Furthermore, we do not believe that Ulloa, by forcing his detective to take leave of us with a symbolic and redemptive act, making himself a co-participant in and even co-responsible for the sufferings of the condemned of the earth, has solved (or even wished to solve) the problem unilaterally.

As we said earlier, each one of the detectives remains free to try other routes. However silent they may be, and however much the fact of closing the book may make that policeman a representative of the rest, his decision does not necessarily bind them. The author affirms his own personal preference, but in doing so, he does not annul all other possibilities; he does not erase the Poirots, the Geerhardts, the Quirozes, the Nyagaros. He doesn't even assure us that the final attitude is the correct one (if Quiroz had adopted it, for example, it might be interpreted as àn empty, infantile gesture, wasting a life that should have been saved for the revolution). The other lives and problems are still valid, are still unfolding daily all over the world, and it is the reader's task to imagine the trajectory that each one must follow, given the impulse that we had observed in him. The author helps the team that he likes, but he is no referee, and he does not alter the final score. He makes no pretence that the better man wins, but rather shows that within the reality and the truth that he tries to reveal one can observe a tendency

27

toward progress, a movement forward.

And therein lies the stylistic and narrative unity of the work, which could have been scattered and dispersed, like a conqueror who does not know in the name of what king he is claiming the land, but who goes on planting his flags on new continents. Parallel to the detectives' search, the novelist also throws himself into a rather vacillating and uncertain excavation of the ruined temple of his own art, placing himself tensely at the heart of each word. Like Quiroz, Ulloa is radically doubting his own work. He has no idea if it makes sense to send up prayers, to write, describe, transcribe; he is uncertain whether the world is really the way he is describing it, an extermination camp where the masters have almost all the arms. He doesn't know whether literature has any reason for being in the face of exploitation and of death sentences, whether long-range or short-range. Because if his last protagonist chooses silence and renunciation, if he chooses to separate himself from all collaboration with a world of pale, white hemorrhaging, an incorporeal and unreal world, then what right does his creator have to invent a novel, to choose the word and the full and enthusiastic expression of his own personality, to combine sounds and syllables and meanings which not one of those prisoners, of those eternal agonists, will be able to read? Does it make any sense to use the resources of a Borges, the labyrinths, the double personalities, avatars and crossroads, the lucid moments in which a man knows who he is, to use the spiraling time of other Latin American narrators, to work a metaphor, to correct and balance a verb, if mass murder, the invisible wall of exploitation and death are still going on?

In an interview given to the weekly, *Tiempo Indefinido e Infinito,* the author confessed he had conceived of his novel while in a Venezuelan jail and that, later, as an exile here in Chile, he decided to carry his experience through, "while choosing the destiny that seemed most appropriate to me, as

I waited to determine the most creative way I could participate in the revolution. Perhaps the fact that it was the fruit of a period of relative inactivity, with regard to politics, explains a certain degree of skepticism, some doubts with respect to death, for example, that never bother me when I am living an active political life, but seem to filter through as soon as I face a typewriter."

Perhaps this sense of discomfort, almost of guilt, may explain the language of this book , which juxtaposes a certain narrative sensuality, a highly charged and heavy undercurrent, with the black and white sharpness of the dialogues, the way a pharmacist, despite his own illness, would fill prescriptions with absolute accuracy. Words provide the battlefield in which the confirmation of his own art and any doubts with respect to it, in which suspicion and cooperation, face each other off, with no love lost between them, just as the detectives themselves do, summing up in this way the form in which he wished to express the kaleidoscope of geographies, customs and cultures by means of which we witness the savage and drunken music of a universe where human beings exterminate each other.

He has found a style which is sharply mysterious, one in which we find juxtaposed the sense of what is unreal and dreamed with the certainty of the undeniable solidity of everyday reality, that is, the Detective and the prisoners, the concentration camps and the Murderer, the human heart in the midst of doubt. No wonder, when they asked him to define the way in which he felt life, Ulloa said, "Imagine that a swarm of mouthless, hungry ghosts suddenly invaded a soda fountain and ordered hot dogs, with everything, *a la americana,* and with plenty of chilli. That's life."

...And that's all I can tell you about the birth of Donoso's *The Obscene Bird of Night*. Nevertheless, if I may be permitted to abuse the privilege of having this tape recorder, which the Center for Documentation of the National Institute of Culture has provided, and knowing, as I do, that very little has been told about the crisis and collapse of traditional narrative in Chile during the decade of the seventies, I think it might be well to state here a few previously unknown facts about that period, even at the risk of having them attributed to the senility of a dull old novelist. Much of the information I have provided is part of the public domain, offered in fact, by Pepe Donoso himself. And how many interviews haven't been given by Jorge Caballero Muñoz, explaining the meaning of his break with his own literary evolution in *But You'll Do It/Tomorrow/ Yes, If...* On the other hand, the case of Hernán Iriarte Arriagada is part of intra-history, my own inner reserve. Those who hear this recording will probably not know who I'm talking about. They'll never have seen his name in any anthology, not even in the bibliographical indices of the Center for the Study of Chilean Literature at the University of Chile.

Hernán Iriarte Arriagada had written several short stories that were distributed among a few "intellectual" friends, as well as a couple of dense essays that were commented upon by even more restricted circles. Then, it must have been around 1964 or 1965, overnight we learned that he had taken off for the University of Kansas, and from there he sent back cryptic messages, suggesting that he was working on a masterpiece, a work that would open up new vistas for the Chilean novel (which, according to what he had read in a copy of *Ercilla* that reached him, was suffering from the furious attacks of cannibalistic and semi-literate young writers). We thought that this was just one more effort that would never bear fruit, like *Revolution* by Carpentier or *Bird* itself, by Donoso, Mother Hubbard without so much as a cupboard.

In August of 1970 I met Caballero Muñoz who told me in passing that Hernán was returning, with his novel finished and tucked away in his suitcase. I didn't pay much attention to the matter. We were in the middle of the Presidential campaign and I was already at that time working out the details of *The Hero's Nightmares,* not sure whether Allende was going to win in September, and wondering if the "peaceful road to Socialism" could even work. The next to the last chapter of *Nightmares* shows, additionally, that those presentiments and questionings were never entirely silenced - nor should they have been.

In any case, the arrival of Iriarte at my little house at dawn on the fourth of November was a tremendous surprise. I was just returning from the Alameda, where we had been celebrating Allende's inauguration as President, and what do I see but a real scarecrow of a figure with long hair standing in my doorway flanked by two suitcases, apparently waiting for me. It was Iriarte. He explained that he had just arrived. On the same plane as Julio Cortázar, he added, with a smile that clearly came from somewhere else, and that only later would I understand fully.

I invited him in, and I made up the sofa as best I could for him to sleep on. Anyhow, I was astonished that among all the acquaintances he had, including his own relatives, he had chosen me for his first visit. I was quite a bit younger than he, and we had had a series of verbal run-ins - largely because of political differences, and that was back in 1958, can you believe it?

"Don't go to any trouble," he told me. "I'm going back tomorrow."

"Going back?"

"To Kansas," he said. "My wife and kids are there."

31

"Do you already have your ticket?" I asked.

"Yes. Why?"

"Because all the airlines are booked solid for the next month. All the fascist scum are in a panic to get out. Some of them will come back, once they've sold all their little dollars. I've got an idea for a story about that. Told from the point of view of a maid who they take along as far as Mendoza so they can get more money out."

"Oh, yeah," he said. "The scum. Yeah, I have reservations."

I didn't want to push him on his future plans (wisely, as it turned out), about whether he intended to spend the rest of his life in Kansas, or whether maybe the popular victory in the elections might also have changed his plans.

"It's just a short visit," he observed, with that usual damned irony of his. "I came just to see you, to talk to you."

"To me?"

"Yeah. You're the only, well, Marxist friend that I have, and I wanted to come and talk to you, and, well, to show you something."

"You came from Kansas?"

"I stopped off in Buenos Aires first; I had to talk with the people at the publishing house, Sudamericana. I'm going back tomorrow . . . Besides, I have enough money. I can afford to pamper myself."

At that moment there passed through my mind all the really useful things that could have been done with that money Hernán was so casually spending, but naturally I didn't let on that I gave a shit.

"It's worth it," he continued. "Even if you can't understand why, I can tell you, it was worth it. It was enough just seeing people here tonight. I mean, I was right to come."

"You came to see the people."

"No, I came to see you. To give you this."

He stood up, opened one of his suitcases, took out a

complete manuscript and handed it to me.

"I withdrew this from Sudamericana. They were furious. They already had it ready to go, but fortunately they still hadn't sent it to . . ."

"It's your novel?" I asked.

"I want you to read it," said Hernán. "Tonight, César. We won't have another chance."

I looked at my watch. It was 2 a.m. I calculated everything that awaited me the next day: work, Frei tying the Presidential ribbon on Chicho, a meeting with colleagues in the Ministry of Education, helping to paint a wall with colors and birds and raised fists.

"You've got to do it," said Hernán. "I've never asked you for a favor. Now I'm asking you." I almost told him to go to hell. I mean, what with the work we faced after General Schneider's assassination, and the drunken revelry that came later and then all the days of persistence and planning, what with meetings with CUT, the labor union, and with having to quickly catch up on everything we had left for another day, when there'd be some free time, a day which would never come, of course, I really did almost tell him to go to hell. Him, the University of Kansas, the whole jet-set clan that would blessedly take him back there, his wife, the damned manuscript. What the fuck did they think they were doing here! There was so much to be done, and Hernán Iriarte Arriagada shows up, damn him! And he wasn't begging me. He was telling me. It was imperative. And after all, there was a matter of a certain amount of curiosity on my part to know what had brought him all the way down here, and there was a certain amount of consideration too.

"OK. I'll read it. . . And what then?"

"You'll see," he told me.

"If you want," I suggested, glancing at the title: *Outside,* "you can sleep, or read . . . or do whatever you want," I cut myself short. No thanks, he would stay right there, without doing anything, really just watching me while I read, which

33

didn't turn out to be quite as unpleasant as I had thought. I wasn't bothered by the way he looked at me; it was more like the way a father would stay in the room while the doctor examined his new-born child.

From the moment the wild, hot saliva of his conscience awakened him, from the moment that something inside him overflowed, biting hard and deep, he knew that everything had gone wrong, that he was screwed from the beginning, from that first mad-dog moment inside his head, ever since then. "Everything's gone wrong," you told me. "Everything must have gone wrong," I told you. "I'm screwed."

Naturally I was familiar with the tendency of a lot of European and Latin American writers to portray the human being as victim, an alienated, passive creature, trembling on the edge of nothingness, carrying the heavy burden of the written word as if it were a cancerous tumor of life. A world of beachless waves, almost waterless and sea-less waves, and it goes without saying, waves devoid of swimmers.

But, incredibly, Iriarte's novel pushed the frontier one step further, opening up a territory that one would have suspected could not even exist. It explored the extreme (and the Extreme Unction) of a human being dissolving without managing any more control over reality than being its disfigured and useless witness.

We may suppose that the year is the future, say, 1980. Commander Bert Haggard of the U.S. Air Force is travelling in a space vehicle, en route (another supposition) to the stars. The duration of the odyssey: 5000 years. The Commander and his crew have been placed in suspended animation, a way of freezing the human body and causing it to sleep for millennia, until they reach their destination, when they will be awakened automatically, and will be able to populate another constellation with a new and better version of humanity. But plans (especially scientific plans) do not always turn out in the way expected. Because as soon as the Commander awakens (and the novel begins), he realizes that he is not feeling, smelling, hearing, tasting, not becoming aware of the weight and proximity of things, not breathing, not warming up his stiff muscles, nothing. Except for endless thinking. Space has disappeared; his body is no longer there with him; all that remains of reality is successive and elastic time, the lineal and successive company of himself, the thread of a mental voice which is the only evidence of his existence.

The first thing that occurs to him is that the voyage has reached a successful end. All he has to do is wait for someone to come and help him get up. For some time (understanding that time is measured by the duration of phrases in his memory), he simply reviews the immediate tasks that await him.

But it turns out that no one comes. Try as he will to order his eyes to open and his feet to move, try as he will to mobilize his auditory senses, there is no sign whatsoever of any outside presence coming to his aid. At this point he's beginning to worry a little. The idea dawns that "something is going wrong", and the possibilities of what might have happened are beginning to trouble him; some of those possibilities are comforting, others are less so.

It may be that he has awakened before the others, since he is the Commander after all, and that they'll come later to free him.

It may be that the spaceship has just taken off only a couple of minutes ago, and that five thousand years of travel and of total awareness lie ahead of him before he reaches his faraway destination in the galaxy. Perhaps the mechanism has malfunctioned, his body has entered suspended animation, but through some error, his mind continues working. An error? But what if it's an act of revenge by one of his enemies? Some bizarre punishment that's been prepared for him? Or an experiment by the Psychiatric Section of the Intelligence Agency, one of those that he himself witnessed during the Vietnam War being carried out on the prisoners?

Measuring the effect of such isolation on the mind of a human being, constructing theoretical models for the circuits that have suffered deviations in cybernetic schemas. He remembers being told one night by Dr Foreman when they were talking about problems with robots that only an analysis of normal human beings who are cracking up can help us in our efforts. Schizophrenics, the mentally retarded, and paranoiacs are no use to us, Bert. We must work with clean, healthy minds, right? And, of course, that is impossible, so we're stuck in the next phase of the program. But he can't be pinned down in some laboratory, with all his sensory organs being monitored. We aren't living in some barbaric age, deep in the caverns of collective madness.

And what if the technical failure in the aircraft has affected the whole crew, all thirty of them? And what about the three other interstellar rockets accompanying them? Are they all incommunicado, unable to know if the same thing is happening to each of them, muzzled there in their beds of ice and crystal. And when they finally reach Alpha Centauri, will they all be mad? Or will one of them have survived the crossing and still be able to summon up enough strength to perform a few functions at the control panel and save them all? Or will they go on like this forever, until they finally disintegrate in space, or will they continue there, indestructible, right up to the apocalypse, when the sun, the secret star they are looking for, expands and overheats in the non-existent inner walls of the vacuum, and . . .

But that kind of thinking is not good for you. You're a commander in the U.S. Air Force; you're in complete control of your faculties and your emotions. Don't allow yourself to be influenced by images of corruption and defeatism.

But what if he were not in the space ship? Deprived of all connection with the world of objects, he has no way of knowing where he really is, nor even the date, the hour, the instant. What if this is really death? Because one would suppose that the memory of the death agony itself would still be with him, but he remembers nothing at all like that.

How can he find out if there was some kind of accident? How can he find out if some counter-order was given from Earth and they're going to return to the third planet, and all these are just passing effects?

Nevertheless, his faith in technology, in his own intellect, and in the ability that enabled him to rise from the poor foothills of Appalachia, to study in the university and to enter the armed forces and fight in a war in Southeast Asia, always overcoming the most adverse circumstances and material limitations, always moving up the ladder, leaping toward success, motivated by the desire to triumph, to arrive first, to jump the gun, and then NASA, and then the Apollo flight and STAR FOR DEMOCRACY, an ultra-secret plan to populate our system in the great cosmic beyond, so that even if Communism manages to dominate the earth and destroy the foundations of our institutions, a plan that has been unfolding, believe it or not, since the Korean War and the earlier Red victory in China, even if that can happen, we will have an empire in other constellations, it will be our Universe, even if they do have the earth, so that our country's flag will fly over infinity. This is a battle in which eternity is at stake, so let God be our judge, good luck. Yes, Mr President, thank you very much, Mr President.

I'm trying to remember the exact details of Iriarte's novel, but many years have passed, really, and that night I read only until dawn, with those seemingly lidless eyes of his contemplating me from the sofa. I'm trying to be as faithful as possible. That's why I'm following this order which is so formally chronological. I'm trying not to miss any detail of the meanderings of that mind, caged inside itself.

The astronaut managed, I remember, to reaffirm all his convictions and put aside any doubts, as he reconstructed - almost drunkenly, to be sure - his entire past, his own personal history. Nevertheless, in the middle of these mental wanderings there were again intense explosions or at other times more subtle intrusions of bewilderment, imaginings of other possibilities, resentment and feelings of impotence, which are inevitable when you're immobilized in the throes of a fever that never lets up and when there's no mouth through which to introduce medication, nor veins in which to inject an antibiotic or a transfusion, and despite all his efforts, more and more cracks appear in his morale.

In the past, in many and subtle ways, there had already been foreshadowings of this situation, a suspicion that everything was not exactly the way it was being presented to him.

I've often contemplated the sky. And the dawn, you tell me. The dawn, sure, of course. Lying in my bed, trying not to awaken my two brothers, I contemplated the clear, jaguar sky and the howling light and darkness that danced from the window to the street below, until finally the outside light slowly went out. My eyes squinted shut in pain for just an instant, but it was hard to know if the lids were really closed or not. So I pressed them really tightly, so that I could imagine different colors and shapes and movements - just the way you're telling me now - yes, just like now, with shadowy characters unfolding their lives on that innermost screen of the membrane that covered my eyes. Mama was there. Go to sleep, she told me, I guess, because if she had really been present at that moment, that's what she would have said. After that, animals and friends and a kaleidoscope of candies that I almost never had, so it was natural I fell asleep. But sometimes I remembered that I had to open my eyes again, just the way the rules of the game stipulated. There was the darkness, gnawing at me like the black and rotten tooth of an ogre. There were no colors in that world, nor parents. Not even a snail's shadow at mid-day, not even the dark blue of underwater caves, nothing, just pure, uninhabited darkness. Naturally a shape, a fluttering silhouette reappeared almost immediately, the green filtering fingers of a near-by tree, faint lights like sounds tired of having nobody to hear them, and the foot of the bed. I kicked at the covers, to see if I could see how they fell. But there was never enough light for that.

And do you remember whether the darkness went away, you ask me? I remember, I tell you.

Were the newly-weds in the house across the street making love? Was the student preparing for his exams? Did you catch a whiff of the pale mold that covers your room? The moon was probably out, you answered me. And what if there is no moon? The stars, then. And what if there are just clouds, and some hand that hates pastels has painted every last stellar space a dark gray, and in the process has chained the sun to the suffocating short circuit of a pillow?

You were young back then.

Agreed.

Somehow, you tell me calmly, the light will get through.

Maybe it comes from the big cities. And Papa and Mama won't let anything happen to the big cities. You were old enough to know that all you had to do was reach the light switch and electricity would do the rest in some miraculous way, the warm breath of color would awaken your brothers and they'd give you a sound thrashing. Cities can't die. Papa and Mama were a guarantee, no hydroelectric power plant would dare disobey Papa; Mama probably cast flirtatious glances at the moon. Do you remember? Hey, listen.

Yes, I told you, triumphantly, my little nose held high, Papa and Mama won't let anything happen to the big cities. And now you really did fall asleep. You really did. Right.

But the more Bert remembers of his past, the more he is assaulted by doubts. In fact, as he tries fruitlessly (as though in this way, suddenly, taking his sleeping body by surprise) to see, to hear, to (Move it, I tell my fingers, but there are no fingers, there's no forearm, no shoulders, no neck, no nerves, nothing to receive an order or to transmit it, nothing to move or to be moved, no fingers, just words), he begins to doubt the Earth itself and whether this past he is relating to himself in order to prop himself up in the face of his own fragmentation is really his past at all. Certain conflicts arise, certain variations, in the versions of his own past.

In fact, he begins to confirm that there is not now nor has there ever been any other reality than this one, even though he constantly tries to rationalize and is attentive to any sign that someone has discovered the imperfection in the ship's mechanism and will carry out a rescue.

In order to facilitate and to bring on such an eventuality, he tries to describe minutely any object that comes to mind, a perfume, a stain on a shirt, his wife Helena's hair comb, his daughter Carmen's laughter, but every image is obscured and darkened; he cannot affirm the existence of anything. He is losing all certainty that the world or even Bert Haggard has ever existed.

Yes, a punishment, but one of much greater scope and dimensions. It is God who is submitting him to this test. All he has to do is discover the sin, the guilty moments, then repent and escape this purgatory, or at least to know what this hell is all about. He thinks over his life once again, not to discover any signs of his success, but rather to get a handle on his mistakes and failures.

He vacillates between justifying his actions and a raging and destructive self-criticism. How can I find out if there's something that can save me, if there's anyone who can examine me periodically in order to evaluate my advances? Does it make any sense to be humble, to accept that I won't be able to win? Or is it better to scream, like a deaf-mute who's been castrated – just in case the vocal cords work?

Or my life back then was the same as it is now. It's simply a matter of other stories and other faces that must be invented, just to fill the time. He tries to remember stories which, nevertheless, always end up in situations of death, prison or paralysis. Stories of children who haven't been born yet or are still-born, except for their brains. Stories of

40

tailor's mannequins in the great designing houses that will never again open their doors. Stories of men who try to fill a river with stones from the shore only to realize in the end that they will have to start over again, because now the river is the shore that must be filled. Stories of old people who deny the existence of their grandchildren and who are stoned as a proof that those grandchildren really do exist and that once they're murdered can no longer answer the question, don't you see, we exist, don't you see? Don't you see? And many other stories that I no longer remember very well. Iriarte had spun dozens of fables and myths into that section.

You always prided yourself on being a rational man who measured and calculated even the amount of emotion required to achieve your purposes. Now, alone there with your mind, you tell me, like always.

You were always a great actor. So great an actor that your costume ended up being indistinguishable from your street clothes. Now you keep trying out all the roles, all the roles and all the characters in the human race, whether great or small, hell, maybe that's the way you allow them to exist, maybe I'm God and in that way the world begins retroactively.

Let's see if you can imagine and dream even a little finger that will press the button that will release you, go ahead, imagine that button, and that will be enough to make the rest of the universe exist, speedily reconstructing itself.

Why do you always stay in the cruelest and bloodiest intersections of human history? Why does all that slowly spin around your memory? Why is it that the fragments that heat up my perception are all collective and individual crimes? Maybe you're paying the price for all human beings. Five thousand years is plenty of time to save mankind, to be the little rabbit the archangels need, to hear the circular confessions of the inquisitors.

You're the chosen mouthpiece; you will be the representative; everyone will be judged by the way you repent for the sin of having lived. Now you're turning back, back from the arrogance of thinking that there is any meaning in this chance act, in this loose screw in the ship, thinking that you might be the central figure in something, the focus of some privilege, some glance from on high.

"Are you afraid to open your eyes? To stretch your arms?"

"No. Of course not."

"Ah, you are afraid."

"Cut it out!"

"Maybe you don't want to wake up?"

"Of course I want to. What do you think I've been trying to do?"

"You always said that all anybody needed was will power, that it was you against the world. Don't talk to me about cowards, you said. Not to me."

"Yeah, I think I said that."

But it might also be some test of your loyalty, an investigation that someone's conducting to find out if you can be entrusted with this mission to the stars, whether you may not be a communist agent.

Since he can't kill himself, can't even move or communicate or prove that he's dead or alive, or fully remember his past, the best thing to do is just try to extinguish himself in an immeasurable whiteness, from time to time testing to see if it is possible to move, to see whether his blood is circulating again. But he's invaded by thoughts and objects; naming the universe, that's the solution. Table, bed. What is a bed? A bed is . . . Machine, wound. What is a Coca-Cola, Mr President. Vietcong, orgasm, cat, bird, glempfill. . . Glempfill. What's that? But it turns out that invented words, disconnected syllables can be as real and full-bodied as those that the reader recognizes as actually pertaining to an object from daily life. Bert Haggard has no means of buying, of gauging, nor of normalizing.

Or perhaps mathematics can be a dike against the absurd.

42

Extrasensory communication with others.

What is the human capacity for boredom?

How many times can he repeat the story of his life?

He might never have existed, Mama, Papa, why precisely that night? Why didn't they return a little bit later to go to bed? Why couldn't that burst of semen have been diverted, or why couldn't the encounter have been with some other spermatozoid? But not me. No, never, not me.

It's all the machines' fault. We depend on them.

Everybody's like that. They're like that on earth too. They just don't know it. We've always been like that. I've always been like that. There's no way to silence the black lightning flashes of galloping passion and insanity. They come out of the nothingness and they disappear; I can't control them. This is what I am and nothing more, a sheet on which someone is projecting a movie that was never filmed.

Also floating through his mind, ever more incoherently and fantastically, there is a long sexual relationship that never produces a child, the real and potential traumas of his being with women, a son who will come to awaken me, who will rescue the treasure and kill the dragon.

Thus ends the first part.

I stood up to get a glass of water.

Hernán's expression did not change. For some reason that I couldn't fathom back then, I sat down again without having turned on the faucet, without a drink of refreshing liquid in my parched throat.

"I've finished the first part," I told him. And then added, inevitably, "Now I'll go on to Part Two."

I can barely remember the second part. I think it started with the words: I don't know how long I was rambling like a crazy man.

I hope it's been five thousand years, five thousand years minus a few minutes.

The break between the two parts was a source of

consternation to the reader, to this reader, to be exact, this poor César Roccafitto. How long could that poor sap go on suffering? Even the miserable certainty that sustained that stampede of words had ended, as if we could guarantee that we could resuscitate a cadaver by torturing it.

Because now he's lost even the vague notion of date and temporal movement that had never failed him during the previous phase.

Perhaps he was delirious when they opened this bed at the end of the journey; perhaps six thousand years had already gone by when we arrived at the edge of Alpha Centauri.

Where is Bert? Let's look for Bert. Bert is crazy. How is Bert? Bert is crazy. Look at Bert. Look at this madman.

"He must be cured," says Helena. I'm sure it was Helena who pronounced those words.

But all to no avail; it was impossible to help you. They closed the box, while you went on screaming, or you continued silently, with a mongoloid smile on your lips, reviewing stories and more stories in the dark night.

The one screaming is Bert.

I'm better now. Why don't they come?

Or have they given me up for dead.

Others will come. You won't be able to keep them away. What will happen when the army of insects begins to interrogate the meadow of your memory? What will happen when there's nothing left but the thumbs of midgets, when the court has condemned you to the midget's thumbs?

Actually, the second part of the novel was more difficult than the first part, because Bert was not all there; you might say he went off on tangents, everything a jumble. I was very tired and, I must confess, I skipped some pages. The hope that it's all a dream, and that in reality it turns out to be something else, someone at the very edge of unconsciousness in front of a broken mirror in a Saigon bar, a drug addict sprawled in a gutter just before the last dose, a woman with

44

her back broken after being raped by soldiers, the first instant after birth, when a human being forgets everything that preceded, as if this were the River Lethe, and in every moment of agony and of resurrection, like the circling ducks in an amusement park shooting gallery, it would be necessary to repeat this process, the true story of what happens to men and women in the eternal reincarnation, and that's why there's so much sadness and misery, so little real happiness in the world.

Oh, just to be able to evoke a little bit, even if it were just a shred, a speck of sunlight!

Because it all could have happened in a minute, that's all; it could be just one regular night's passing that we don't remember when day breaks.

There's no doubt that at that moment Iriarte achieved his maximum esthetic power: Who knows, it was insinuated, if all of us don't go through exactly the same thing every minute of every day in some permanent underground of our souls?

But it doesn't last long. There's no way to stop the parrot that is scratching at my mind.

Suddenly they really do come looking for him. He stands up. Congratulations. Joy. Let's get to work, said the Commander.

But it was sheer imagination, a merciful lie.

The reader believed it as much as Haggard himself did.

This means that from that moment on anything can happen; they really can free him and we'll never be truly sure whether that's real or not. We'll never have sufficient proof that it hasn't been imagined by this man who always scorned the environment, history, and reality; we'll never know whether what happens to him is anything more than self-delusion.

Wasn't this punishment, perhaps, inevitable? If not him, then some other person must pay for this journey to the stars; somebody has to pay a high price for this expansion of the empire. The more you progress, the more you must suffer, the greater the cost. One's country is not an easy mother.

You're trying to impose meaning where there is none.

I don't remember the end of the novel very well; it's a shame really. I'm not even sure I finished it. It was extremely long, and as you can well imagine, I was exhausted.

No doubt its language was very different from the language I've used in reconstructing the fragments that I do recall. There was an alternating use of "I", "you" and "he", but very different from Carlos Fuentes' or Michel Butor's use of the same technique, as if the protagonist were constantly attempting to conjure up another person with whom to carry on a dialogue, and thus to present an alternative. Third, first, second, always circular, plural, the sawdust with which one narrates oneself.

On the other hand, the extreme introspection which he achieved, the radical doubt about the outside world, reminded me that his good friend Caballero Muñoz, at that very moment was working on *But You'll Do It/Tomorrow/ Yes, If...* But Iriarte's work allowed a fundamental ambiguity: it was not clear whether it was intended to be a portrait of what we might call "contemporary man", of alienation in science, in the city, in metaphysical blindness; or whether, on the other hand, it portrayed the internal collapse of the North American mind, corroded by a point of view in which the hatred and desire for revenge of an outcast, a marginal being, had installed themselves; Hernán Iriarte exercising his Latin Americanism by means of the torture imposed upon the oppressor, the imperial soul. Was it Purgatory that Haggard found himself in, or was it Hell? Was he suffering because he was a human being or, because in his life as a human being he had been a son-of-a-bitch, living inside a shitty body in a shitty country? That unreality, those words that approached the very edge of nothingness, like birds without even a sign of wings - Was it all an

46

existential or a political allegory? Was it possible that all the political consequences and connections were not even desired? That they had simply infiltrated the text against Iriarte's own wishes? Was it because he had emigrated to the States during the Vietnam War that his story transcribed the increasing awareness of racial minorities, the beginning of student agitation, that he had felt the impact of rebellions which, in his homeland Chile, had somehow not touched him? And besides, why give it to *me*? Why did I have to be the Bert Haggard who read and suffered that decomposition, that nakedness? It was high time for me to go to bed, since tomorrow. . . At some particular moment, I no longer remember when, I handed him the stack of pages.

He accepted them from me unenthusiastically. He stood up and handed them back to me. "You didn't read the whole thing," he told me, with no note of recrimination in his voice, as if he were a newspaper reporter telling of an accident.

"You're quite a writer," I told him, just to say something. Besides, it was true.

But Hernán hadn't come to fish for compliments.

"It's enough that you read it," he replied. "Even if you can't finish it. I don't need more than that."

"That's quite a job," I told him. What an effort he had made! I mean taking Beckett's literature to extremes that not even Beckett could have imagined! Poor Latin Americans. *Other-directed.* Imitating and exaggerating. That's us.

And something else, I added, something more than dependency. Struggle. Yes, struggle too. So, with that, I had something to talk to him about and I felt less uncomfortable. Here in Latin America people have to be guided by cultural models they don't feel entirely belong to them, and they imagine that only by deforming them can they elevate them. It's the anguish of underdevelopment, being the monkey on the sidelines as absolutely the only way of being, of someday finding their own way. It's part of the process: guarding your

47

own lie, reproducing the tape, but at a higher speed. As if our death and the ghost we are going to become had to be lived by us before we're even born, so that we have a right to birth and to having a mother and to the air we breathe.

I said something like that to him.

"That's not a bad image," he said. "It applies to the novel."

And his cheeks flushed a little.

"Where are you going to publish it?"

He didn't answer me right away.

"César, you have to believe me, I didn't want to write it. It was something I couldn't avoid. I no longer believed in literature or in anything else. It was just there and I had to finish it. Years had gone by since I first got the idea for the situation. I had already invested too many hours not to prove to myself that I was capable of finishing it, that it wasn't just another excuse. The idea's a good one, isn't it? Never mind. It's better if you don't answer that question. It's done."

"It is good," I told him. "Of course I do have some observations."

"Keep them to yourself. I'm not interested. Life is strange . . . Look, I sent it to Sudamericana Publishing Company. They were going to publish it. Then, well, in September Unidad Popular took power."

"Not power. The government," I corrected him. A bad mistake. What the fuck! At that hour, just before dawn, it was no time to go into the differences between having the executive and having full state power. Poor Hernán wouldn't grasp the idea of dual power in his whole fucking life.

"So I think it's better not to publish it," he said. "It would be like becoming Bert Haggard myself."

Shit. I hate it when reality and fiction begin to mix.

"But even Haggard tried to defeat silence with words," I said, valiantly playing along.

"It depends on what words," Iriarte took up the game.

"In fact, as some demon inside me that had possessed me for months made me type, another part of me was gradually losing interest. But let's suppose that most of the time I was debating with myself, César, I was dying to tell that story, to survive in . . . in that flow of language."

I couldn't restrain a yawn. What the hell! It was almost dawn.

"So you'd like to come back here," I told him, hoping that he would say yes, and that way I could fix his bed and get my drink of water. "To join the revolution, if I'm understanding you correctly." I was not understanding him very well at all.

"*Nyet,*" he answered. "I don't have the balls for it, to tell you the truth. The only important thing I've done in my life is in this manuscript, the only remaining copy of all my efforts, and I could care less whether I did it or not, I feel absolutely nothing for this novel. . . I like comfort, I get along well with my wife, I adore the kids. I'm weak, I'm afraid, and it's too late to change."

"It's never too late," I had to say to him, with the usual etceteras, but really, taking a good look at it, for Iriarte it was too late, and that was that.

"I'm going to support you from a distance. I'll organize solidarity committees. Or maybe I won't do anything. But I can do something for Chile: not publish this garbage."

And now he shot another melodramatic metaphor at me. "When a child is going to be born deformed, and you have the chance for an abortion, and the abortion fails and makes the kid even more bloody and monstrous in the bargain, the only choice remaining to you is to give birth to the kid and then put a bullet through its brain, César, before you learn to love it, before you get all caught up with Saint Francis of Assisi, Mahatma Gandhi and the vegetarians. You have to destroy it as soon as possible."

Waking up all of a sudden, I realized that something unusual was happening here.

"You were that impressed with the people in the streets tonight?" I asked.

"Long before that. That crowd, all that solidarity, just confirmed it . . . Look, it's no accident that I wrote this precisely between 1964, when I left, and 1970, when I came back. If it were 1964 now, of course I'd publish it and be damned proud of it. But I waited too long. It's no longer the right moment. It would make no sense. I was born a little too late, just as if Bert, up there in that rocket, suddenly remembered to give a kiss to a woman who had stayed back there on earth and that he would never see again." He talked like that for a good while. He said his public, the rich, were leaving the country in those trips I had spoken to him of. Sooner or later he would write for those Chileans living in Mendoza, he had already been doing it, but without realizing it, all this time. Mendoza was always here in Chile. He said he had wanted to write the great twentieth-century novel, a fable that would express all the anguish of the age. But even if he had achieved it . . .

"You say you don't have the balls to stay here and join the struggle," I interrupted him. "Stop fucking around. Let Kansas go to hell, and join us. All the professional people have got to come back." But it was more out of a feeling of ideological obligation than any real conviction on my part. Nothing was going to convince him. I was so worn out by then I couldn't light my own fire. How was I going to shake him out of his stupor?

"I've kidded myself long enough, César. I'm going back. That's it. What'll happen? I'll feel endless nostalgia for the novel I never published. I'd always feel incapable, always wanting to describe and express the revolution others are building and I'd end up just imposing my own pessimism on it. I'd rather keep quiet, show that I'm in touch with the philosophy of my own novel, take a lesson from my character. There are no reasons for things. Why cause myself more pain and anguish?"

"But don't you think others could learn those lessons, that it would be worthwhile to publish it?"

"No, I don't think anybody can understand it. I think I have to do the same thing I did with all the other copies back in the United States. The only thing to do with this novel is to burn it."

And with that, he grabbed it out of my hands and set it on fire right there. The tape's coming to an end, so I have to hurry. The next day Allende assumed the Presidency. Iriarte left in the afternoon. I didn't go to see him off at the airport. I wrote to him once or twice, but he never answered my letters. I never knew what happened to him.

ROUGH DRAFT OF AN ARTICLE FOR THE NEW ENCYCLOPEDIA OF CHILEAN LITERATURE, FROM ITS ORIGINS UNTIL THE YEAR 2018

JOSEFINA DE LEON, nun, also known as "Saint Teresa of the Revolution".[1] 1940-1972. Only work, published posthumously, *Story of a Potato.* (Editorial Teoliberación). The many imitations which followed justify calling her the originator of the literary genre called "the material epic of the invisible", one of the mainstays of the literature that emerged out of the Chilean revolution. Two events actually anticipated and prepared the way for this magnificent creation. The first was the Latin American Conference of Christians for Socialism, in which Mother Josefina was a prominent participant. The other, perhaps the spark which definitively set in motion all the Marxist nun's potential, was the publication of the novel *Interventions* (*vide* Del Fierro, Manuel). This event, which passed unnoticed by the two wings of bourgeois criticism of the time (*vide* Alone, and Valente, Ignacio, pseud. of Ibáñez Langlois, José Miguel), had profound repercussions upon the nun's literary output.

The truth that *Interventions* revealed is that a liberating perspective could take place anywhere, at any time. All you needed to do was to assume that intimate perspective that was hidden in Chilean reality, the new interests that until now had found no other voice than the incessant, albeit secret,

---

[1]"It was Jaime Quezada who gave her that name," says Federico Schopf in his *Memories of the Generation of 1970.* "We were with Arístides (ed. Ulloa), on our way back from Concepción, and Jaime had just read some verses by the nun, published in *Trilce*. His words blended with the sound of the train and it suddenly seemed as if the rails were speaking, but I would swear that it was Quezada and not Ulloa, as Lihn insists.")

material transformation of reality. It was the struggle for the right to make a name for oneself in the center of each object. While certain tendencies arose that warned of the paternalism of such attempts, and others labelled those efforts as "petit-bourgeois opportunism, oblivious of Lenin's insistence on a proletarian literature," the creative wave that surged forward under the inspiration of *Interventions* could not be contained. In the realm of perception it was the equivalent of all the marches, movements and organizations. "More eyes for Chile," Skármeta shouted, during the cultural marathon in the Alameda in April 1973, "and more breath in every word in the land."

On the other hand, Josefina de León found her niche in a certain kind of literature that had intellectual roots, especially *Pools*, 1971, by Esteban Monreal (*vide*). The action developed there was one which Monreal had established theoretically in his *Essay on the Waters* (1969): the world as a secret network of unity. To make connections among the different zones through which the face of reality apparently showed itself, it was enough to follow the thread of a single image, in this case, the image of the water in Santiago's pools during the summer of 1970-71. With nothing more than a bathing suit one could trace the thread back to the loom and from there back to the weaver who would then point the way to another transfiguration of water, where the author could then chat with the boatman who at four in the morning was making sweet *cuchuflines* with his father, while his uncle worked on repairs at the waterworks, and the water...etc., an entire novel, one sentence, with the obvious purpose of showing that the only truth in the universe is the senseless movement of scrambling, swimming, resting, drying off, filling and emptying pools, and a series of other metaphors that are interspersed at various moments, thought up by who knows which one of the shipwrecked minds.

53

Josefina de León's work shows Monreal's stylistic influence, but we must look for another context to illuminate its meaning. As the title of her epic states, it is the story of a potato. From the transported seed to the mashed potatoes which it becomes for the nourishment of a family. Of course, the lives that touch it are unfolded like branches at each step in that potato's growth: peasant farmers, truckers, middlemen, shop owners, housewives, etc. But much more than this is found in the solid fluidity of the existence of a living thing. The truck had to exist, the highway for the truck, tires, cement, and around each new object another network of workers and tools (both passive and active) is produced, all forming slices of life, illuminations of objects. The whole economic process that produces and makes possible the utilization of the potato. And linked to that process is the emotional jumble, all the human beings who surround each act. There are even those who, without focusing sufficiently on the passionate and apocalyptic language of the work, have called it a "biological novel." An acceptable label, so long as we understand that the foundation of that science is the cell and its reproduction. "This story," stated Josefina to a reporter from *Los Libros,* "could have been the same, whether it started earlier, later, or even right now. It wouldn't have made the slightest difference if we had chosen a carrot, a nail, a can of linseed oil, a T-shirt or a sheet of paper. As far as the universe is concerned, you know, it doesn't matter whether you're the throat or the ear-drum."

That implacable movement from object to object, crossing all the galaxies in which human beings group themselves during their transitory permanence on earth, carries us throughout all the social strata, to some of which we return from time to time, but always through another portal. An industrialist, owner of a company that manufactures van chassis (that produces the one used by a peasant who sowed the corn that was eaten by the hen that was roasted by the owner of a restaurant where the farmer that produces the potato has a contract), eats breakfast, sticking his spoon in an egg cooked by his maid, and that egg came from a farm where the wood piled up beside the house was cut by someone by hand, and, hey, Fresia, the guy wants a potato with his sausage, and that's all we needed, the appearance of the word "potato" to find ourselves once again back on the land beside the protagonist, the woman who centralizes and unifies all the scattered energies of the universe. It's enough that at some moment in the odyssey we stumble upon a potato, and that returns us once again to the central trunk of the story. When we get back it's a little later in time, the potato has continued its development, has been planted, watered and is reaching upward toward the sun, etc.

In this way time passes. For the potato to mature we have to sally forth many times in search of the objects which make it possible and which themselves also simultaneously wither or grow. We encounter certain repetitions, the way one would greet old friends at occasional parties or on chance encounters in the street. And from there we return once again to the potato, and after a brief stay in that home, we hit the road yet again, another bounce on the trampoline embarking us on other paths, until we feel we hardly have breath to go on, more objects to describe, along with all the people associated with them, and nevertheless, inexorably, the potato continues its march, moving toward some mouth which awaits it down the road.

In this way, what illuminates each paragraph is the certainty that this world is made for work; it is the creation of men. And not because the author announces it with grandiloquent language, but rather because we deduce it as an emotional consequence of reading the book; it is the secret truth that holds the whole thing together. At every moment we can be certain that what is being narrated here is the beginning of the universe, those bright, clear mornings when everything begins again as if Zeus himself were placing each and every object in its proper place along with all the hands that will use them, like the creation of stars and of the firmament. That's the way the hands of the people would speak "if they were bells, if all their throats together formed a sea and they had a beach on which to roll up like waves." The extraordinary richness of the language, the mystical joy in the celebration of each moment as the creation of the unparalleled ability of every man and woman, sustains the sensual rapture of a world lifted by human effort, expanding endlessly, "like a mother who never tires of breathing upon her children with her lamp of love."

But if that is the central stream of the work, there is also no lack of tributaries: all the poverty, hunger, falsehood, and sickness that the production of those objects brings with it, the way an apple at the moment of sprouting might anticipate being eaten. It is evident that the fundamental revelation of existence, the bride that is every object, the bed that is found in every hammer, the air that refreshes the pale night, the unending creation of objects to serve humanity, to extend their bridges, to inspire love at their only supper, jubilation, has been lost in the very world that surrounds these objects, that is the recipient of these words. It is a degraded world (*vide* Mariano Aguirre, "The World of Degradation in *Story of a Potato*" in *Annals of the University of Chile*, number 198, 1982, tribute to Josefina de León on the tenth anniversary of her death): abysses lying between blind men, cold blows, shrieking of cats at dawn. Like a sewer, says Manuel Jofré in his love poems to the dead nun, which flows all night and rocks the cradle with its whisperings. Men - the same men who make those objects, who construct that fine presence we call reality, the manufacturers - have only a partial glimpse of that truth of which they are carriers and makers. Slave-like, they walk by the objects without seeing them, simply using them, with a hatred that is at times indifferent, with a slight polish of enjoyment at other times. Those men that hang like clothes drying on a line, dried animal skins remembering in the blazing sun everything that they were before breathing, are, each time we meet them, sadder, never hearing the magical chant by which the objects point toward a promised, frustrated land inside. (See the study by M. Elena Bascuñan and M. Elena Claro on the relationship with Ernesto Cardenal.)

Herein lies the religious, almost liturgical, message of the book. It is the combination of hope and exploitation, the growth and elevation and benefit which each object contains and the misery which that object has spread throughout the world, without really meaning to, the distance between the dream behind every object produced by human beings and what each of them could become, and the constant frustration which that expansion endures. God and the Devil fight it out over reality.

And in spite of the fact that the world into which each object falls is satanic, the potato's entire cycle, from the moment it germinates until the fatal words which close the book ("he put it in his mouth and started to chew"), belie any pessimism. There is no sadness in the potato's final sacrifice, and the reader is content that, at last, it has met such a rich and inviolable destiny. It is the consummation of the potato's meaning, as it assumes the role of Christ, the god who dies because of his love for humanity and who has been created by that same humanity in order to assure the road to social liberation. For that matter, each object must repeat this cycle; it anticipates the world of tomorrow, a world in which human beings will all be like that, like the potato, in which the joy which each hand has contributed to material reality will be returned, that is, communism, nature and society, one, manual laborer and intellectual, one, humanity and god, one, emotion and thought, one, you and I, one.

Story of a Potato, therefore, presents an inverted world, an upside down world, like so many others in Latin American literature, where human beings are the slaves of objects. But with one difference: it rescues the shoreline toward which we all move and upon which, in fact, we already find ourselves by the mere fact that we exist as part of the struggle: within the objects, along with all the effort and the seed and the love of human beings, is found the source of liberation, the material necessity for change. The object has been deprived of its mission as a small prophet, but its life, its enormous potential, its nuptials, its distance, its birth, its adolescence, its youth, everything that trembles and is day after tomorrow and

today, all of it reminds men of the way to destroy the demonic. The fault does not lie in the objects themselves, but rather in the way in which men produce them, use them and distribute them.

"It's a typically Christian, humanistic distortion of the young Marx's concept of alienation," said the scholar Jaime Poupin. "The nun can't understand economic laws, so she spiritualizes the material world."

Pato Manns, who always came to Josefina's defense after her death, answers the Althusserians: "Finally, when we throw open the blinds and discover that somebody has sealed off the windows, we experience the relief of knowing that we don't need to mourn and to blame the cement: we feel the joy of knowing that every wall along a one-way street dreams and must also be the wall of a house that protects someone from the cold."

END OF ARTICLE

COMMENTARIES
(hand-written in the margins of the last page):

Gone beyond the allotted space. Biographical data missing. Starts off well, as one would expect for a notation in a literary dictionary, but then gets lost in a language that is too lyrical, even apologetic. Unsuccessful in clarifying the Christian-Marxist problems that formed the center of the debate which accompanied the work's success. The detailed reference to *Pools* is unnecessary, since another researcher had already treated that topic. Makes no reference to the symbolic use of the colors yellow and black. We suggest that the article be rewritten or given to somebody else. It is imperative that a critique of the poet's pantheistic utopia be added, and that reference also be made to her experiments in microbiology at the Catholic University. Her use of the gerund should also be emphasized. And the bibliography should be presented more systematically, citing pages and editions.

The time had come to lie down with you, Elena, under the lemon trees and to talk about us, about how I was your comet and your orbit and how one day I would stay and then be your sun, and never again a star that comes and goes, showing itself only to prove it still existed, only to flower like ashes in your eyes and then disappear. I felt like everything we had lived through during those last weeks, and during this vacation, was pushing us together, and I was going to have to decide, to put an end to these rude visits where I'd loudly and deliriously cross your path, my face turned only to you, looking down at you, while everybody else scattered through the gardens and the mirrors of Karolina and Nancy and Juan and all the others, like a bride who stayed forever in her photograph album and so never really married, perhaps tonight, in just a couple of minutes, you were going to be, to see my only face, Elena, the one that had only to rise in the distance the way all comets do, every 94 years, speeding from solar system to solar system, filling the heavens to be disfigured and captured by some other humanity, wandering and wearing down, and for weeks not even phoning you, destroying the drop by drop flow of our relationship. But perhaps tonight, Elena, the pieces would come together.

You were on the other side of the room, getting me a drink, and I was still listening to Luciano and La Negra who were talking about the nationalization of the copper industry, its advantages and difficulties, and the need to reform the constitutional process and then I saw Juan standing right in the middle of the rug, his hands defiantly on his hips. Juan, who right from the start had pushed you toward me, who was always looking for a way to get us together. Juan, who was always offering you to me, but who now was going to separate us, organizing the rest of the night for us, and would begin to bring some order to all that life that was dispersed around the living room. You're going to screw it all up, Juan. Not now.

"Attention. Attention," shouted Juan, clapping his hands.

Not now, Juan, because right now, Luciano, something could come up with you, something I had been waiting for. I would go on admiring your way of living, the absolute security with which you turned every corner or opened a letter or repaired a bicycle, explaining what every nut and bolt was for, or explaining how to tell when a watermelon is ripe, your big hands weighing everything and your lower lip stuck out and trembling, and me, trying to pretend enough enthusiasm to keep on standing there with you, one beside the other, not touching, that's my fault, because you, of course, were interested in what I was showing you and telling you. You were so interested in everything, but I'll be damned if I cared about that bolt or about how to raise chickens. Or the time had come to share that silence of yours, Luis, curled between Lennon's voice and McCartney's, granting each of them the sacred bear of your breath, because you really did sense everything that was happening to me, who I was, just as Karolina knew it, but she could have cared less; she knew the way you know a second language, without all the nuances and variations of your native language; our calculator, Karolina, Kalculina, and you just happened to be my wife, but Luis cared enough about me to let me forget about myself; I forgot about this fear and this distrust that drive me like a hunter through the forest of other bodies, while you and I were talking, Luis, and I was trying to put one over on you, pulling a few rabbits out of my hat, rabbits with fine, soft, slippery backs, made for petting, and down below all the rabbits were hopping away hysterically, shedding their fur in the trembling light; the rabbits were a little bit mangy, Luis, and you didn't fall into the trap, you, the great magician, giving the animals back to me with their labels changed back, so that I would know that when I

61

wanted to show you the truth of who I was, you'd be ready to accept it. Maybe at that very moment when Juan was about to interfere, we were on the border, the horizon that was Luis was about to rise up and move to the point where I, the good ship Tomás, was waiting for him.

But Juan was going to be insistent; there was no way for any of us to get out of it. Maybe it was all the wine's fault, it could be, but Juan was one of those people who never use a parachute when they're falling; the wine over-excited him, as if we'd just poured an army of dogs down his throat and they had to come out somewhere - how was this man, who only looked straight ahead, or up, at the Milky Way, supposed to know that we really had no desire to do what he wanted that night, that this time the hardheaded bastard was wrong, because this ship has no captain, no bursar, no customs officer and no first mate; there's nobody to control us or organize us, do you understand? But how was he going to understand, even if he said he did. He just set himself in motion, stopping once in a while to see if we were with him, and then he would reach back and take us firmly by the hand and set sail for where he said there was land, even though there was not even a piece of floating driftwood in sight. Always onward and upward, and sometimes we fell behind and sometimes he was completely alone, ringing his bell in the night's quiet center that we had reserved for silence or for whispering, as if a house were ringing the bell inside the man who was never going to live there, and it was enough for one of us to follow Juan and everyone else would fall in behind, knowing that they were about to witness something important. But not this time, Juan. This time you were wrong. No one was paying any attention to you. Everybody withdrew deep inside himself, and I was the only one who knew that you were going to win again, that you'd end up getting your way, just as you always did.

He was going to screw us, his booming voice in the darkness splintering my plans, just as this body that everybody called Tomás was getting ready to dance, to touch, maybe finally the magic of Elena, hurled at me by Juan as if throwing you over a cliff to see if I would catch you, and when I embraced you early on in the evening in the hall your hand came up to my lips and cut off the words I was about to windmill into you and I felt the tight power of your waist and further down, what only the night before had been so far and solitary in another bed and another house, sleeping next to Juan, conquering streets that belong to no one, your tendons and a belly and the soft fragrant cleft of your neck, your sex that I did not yet know, later, later, said your fingers to my lips, later. Each body would move to the center of the party and deposit its softness, its pincers, its perfume, everybody swaying to the music so that you, who happen to call yourself Elena and I, who still don't know my name, could discover each other at last among the animal bodies of us all, culminate so many months of preparatory moves. But only if Juan didn't interfere. It was a moment for angels, or perhaps for demons: anything could happen now, now was finally later, it was about to happen.

"Attention. Attention, ladies and gentlemen," shouted Juan, and what was about to happen was called Juan, and nothing could be done about it. You needed everybody's eyes fastened on you; it wasn't enough just to screw me, no.

In that motionless pouring out of dawn anything could happen. You might actually give yourself, gringo, fucking gringo, hand yourself over like an egg that expands without breaking its shell, a baby chick that's born without breaking the egg, do you understand? Or maybe there'd be shattered shell everywhere, or we'd poach you and swallow you whole, or you might be the water we used to cook tonight, even though later it's poured down the drain, you shithead gringo. Maybe right then and there you were about to come up to where La Negra and Luciano and I were talking about politics, the revolution, structural changes and Allende, and then you'd finally tell us, Yes, I'm naked, here I am, but you

63

won't say it, gringo, and that would really be a way of salvation, putting an end to all the skirting and the sleight of hand, because you couldn't go on like that, being all soft and buddy-buddy, when in fact you didn't love anyone on the face of the earth, Carlitos, gringo, how we would have welcomed you, this land is so dark and warm, come, touch it. What a quiet welcome it was for you not to recognize that you had never been here and to stop repeating those words you never used. There's a home in every human being that we meet and then leave, and no doubt Luis is looking at me and may be thinking the same thing about me now; maybe at this moment Tomás is going to melt that hot, contraband ice of his, that links and divides us all; come, fucking Tomás; this promise that's so seldom kept, that I would show myself just as I am, that I wouldn't be afraid that the others would abandon me, when they saw what a pisspot I am inside. No, Juan, not now, because the night was about to explode, I'm sure it was about to explode; the sun was going to come up right then and there; the night was a pack of friends, men and women, all of them the feathers of a wing about to take flight.

"Attention," repeated Juan. But no one paid any attention.

You were the only one who could keep him quiet, Karolina, because while we fitted life so easily into a thousand niches and names and theories, and were enjoying colors that no one had even thought of painting, you were listening to the grass grow, and that's what it is to be green and when there's wind you move and when there's none, you're still, Karolina, and to lie with you under the lemon trees, and one day I was going to leave you, we don't get along, Karolina, but maybe I love you; to go off with someone else, perhaps with Elena, because we were two beautiful but different rhythms and things aren't going well; it's possible that at this moment I could have finally told you what for so long I had needed to tell you, even though you

64

were hardly speaking, you didn't believe in language, that we should stop being contiguous rooms in an enormous but empty house, that we should separate once and for all or I would be your candelabra again and you, my candle and I the matches and you the wick, and you, melting and covering me with your liquid wax, but you would always harden. If I only had the courage to tell you I was in love with Elena, to break down the barrier of air you had put up around yourself and from behind which you understood absolutely everything. If only I could confess to myself or to you, and then perhaps be able to find peace there beside you, both of us clean at last.

"The train's leaving. Yes, yes. It's moving out," said Juan. "Last chance to get on the train." And then, as if he were reading my mind: "Tomás!"

I could still fall asleep, I could still pretend to be asleep, while the rest of you searched for each other in the semi-darkness, among the curtains, the smoke, lamps going out beneath my eyelids, bare feet and slippers slowly scraping along around my head, but without hurting me, and I could dream about all of you, pretend to be asleep and watch you from my own mountain, as always, while Juan planned your night for you, gave you instructions, made you turn like wheels inside his handless, numberless watch.

There was still time to tell Juan to go to hell, because there was so much to do. Chile was moving toward socialism, Christ was born - so they said - nineteen hundred and seventy-one years ago, and here we were fooling around talking nonsense, when there was a new society to be built, a nation to serve, praxis, the new man is shaped under real conditions in an underdeveloped country. Exploit our guilt feelings, put us on an ethics trip and in that way save the night, not have to follow Juan where he wanted to take us, without ever forgetting that, if we were in the revolution, it was because we had followed Juan back then, that was it, preach for two hours and feel completely lucid and fine, and besides everything I would say was true, represented perfect political orientation, just coax Juan into the argument with Luciano and La Negra and take charge of the ceremony myself, intervene brilliantly to bring everything to a perfect close, when everybody else was worn out, I would be the one giving orders, because, no doubt about it, I'm good at it, real serious, a little bit like a deaf and mute and blind man, caressing his only color, and feeling like shit because, however much I help others, however much I succeed in inspiring enthusiasm, I'm not really giving all of me, I control myself too efficiently, with so much calculation in my emotion, like someone who's winning a race that's already won but who cheats a little in order to break the record. Nancy, listening so intently she's mesmerized, with her mousy little face almost ready to come out - to emerge I would have said - from its hole, with the cat outside and one chance in a thousand of saving herself. Nancy, a frozen waterfall. Maybe the night was yours, Nancy, so you could snow on it once and for all, could let yourself get wet, risking pneumonia. And Luis, thinking the same thing about me and about Tomás. Go ahead, just dare to. But it wasn't to be. It was impossible to talk about politics.

Juan had screwed me, whether I climbed aboard the train that was leaving or if I invented another train or even if I tried to get off. So that's the way it was. Anything could have happened that night, and the best thing was just to let it happen, forget the irrigation projects, the canal, the public welfare, and let the water flood the fields or find its own course, in general the name of that course was Juan; we would always be stones along his path, the alphabet in his books; if Juan had decided that he was going to be the center of things that night, then it was useless to rebel. I would be one of the cracks in his spotless white wall, and there could be no doubt that in half an hour I would be the only one left breaking out of his own sad, torn shell, while all the others would have become white walls like him, smooth and spotless; he would lead them with his magic and I would follow along behind, unnoticed by anyone, without Luis even suspecting it. Only Karolina would guess, and she wouldn't give a damn. Me, back there like a dog rummaging in a garbage can, beleaguered by the very garbage on which he had fed himself his entire life, and maybe every one of us was thinking the same thing.

Juan unplugged the record player, the song came to a screeching halt, with just a few complaints, *once there was a way to get back home,* the groove and the needle stayed there, mouth to mouth, the Beatles left voiceless, so close · and yet nothing coming out, cut off from life and electricity. Later someone would start the record again, and the song would go on as if no one had ever interrupted it, *sleep pretty darling, do not cry and I will sing a lullaby,* and maybe unconsciously or maybe fully conscious, you and I, or Karolina, or Luis, maybe the gringo, or everybody would go on dancing, or maybe Elena, or sleeping, the night especially might have dressed up like Elena, because we had to break up this relationship or make it clearer and deeper; maybe later it would be possible for the night to once again open up new alternatives, but now Juan was choosing the only one that he wanted, his alternative.

From different corners arose threats, little shouts and jabs. Antonio stuck out a tongue that was astonishingly long, but it was more or less a habit, part of the protocol, and Juan seemed to brighten with the protests.

"The train left," said Juan.

"Ciao, train," said La Negra, as she raised a hand to wave good-bye.

We all watched as the locomotive disappeared in the distance. When it was only a dark echo, Juan spoke. "Now we can begin."

And with that, not even Karolina could stop what was going to happen. I was probably pretending to go along with the rest of them, maybe that's what we all were doing, moving my body along with everybody else, so they wouldn't realize that I wasn't dancing with them, and only Juan understood, because sometimes with all that pretending we really did begin to dance.

"You could have told him no," Luciano whispered to me, angrily. "He listens to you."

Luis's wife stood up to close the door of the room where the kids were sleeping. I thought of them with envy.

"Children," Juan shouted, "I'm going to save you; I'm going to put you to the test."

But you're no priest, man, you're just a clown. Floury white, pale, full-moon face, sanguine, orangutang-like, suspended and completely stagnating in the party's parade ground, as if it had been stuck up on an invisible stake or better yet, glued on wallpaper, one more artificial flower among so many that multiplied themselves on the wall. You were going to ruin my night, Juan, and if I made the slightest effort to turn you off, - what Luciano said was true, you did listen to me - I would be the great organizer, I would be the petty god that closed the circle around himself, just the way right now we were all imperceptibly dragging ourselves closer to your magnet, that unreal scar that was your flesh, to our sorrow, but still already caught up, drawn out of our own spheres, listening to it, that head of yours totally undisturbed while the rest of your body sobbed, almost like the penis of a marionette, its hands frenetic and bubbling like a Coca-Cola from so much applauding, once more he would cancel us, he would control his surroundings down to the last detail, him, him and no one else.

I don't want to give in, Juan. I want to talk to Elena. You yourself placed me under her tree, so the apples would fall on my head and I'd learn the law of universal gravitation. Right now, yes, something was going to happen, something luminous.

"Who has the soul of a child?" asked Juan suddenly, lowering his voice, with an intensity that surprised us all, as if he were pressed against one of our windshields, trying to get in, but without breaking the glass, just fogging them up a little, little cracks of dew that later would disappear; Juan was going to buzz here inside my head or the gringo's head, he had asked in a tone of voice that was so uniquely his, if we had the soul of a child.

We didn't answer him.

"Tonight," said Juan, carefully examining every face, taking his time, "we're going to see who still has the soul of a child."

You could see the interest grow, necks relaxed, people made themselves more comfortable. But not me, Juan. Elena has now sat down next to Antonio and she's not going to bring me that drink until who knows when. Today something was going to happen. Later I'll be starting from scratch; I'll be too drunk, and I'll have to start over, hell, tomorrow I won't even remember, but I don't want to compete, Juan, that's a race that no longer interests me, and by now everybody else is inside his frame, everybody lined up and docile, and if somebody doesn't save the night for them, if someone doesn't go on humming *once there was a way* deep down inside, then the night will be lost, like a little grandmother who departs before we're able to send her a last letter, knowing that tomorrow she's going to die, but nevertheless we don't write to her; somebody had to be the guardian, so that after Juan would come Elena, I could still visit Elena.

"Who's innocent here? That's what I ask myself. Tonight we're going to find out. Enough fucking around." And he started making trumpeting noises with his hand up to his mouth, like a carnival barker, a man with a microphone: "Ladies and gentlemen, your attention please, ladies and gentlemen." For a moment it was as though we were in a circus tent, they were, I was far away by then, refusing to cooperate, the elephants would come in now, or whatever the next act was, we'd all be struck dumb by the trapeze artists, our stomachs tied in knots. "I present . . . the game of the night," like that, fast, "yes, yes, the game of the night. Who has the soul of a child? That's the question each of you must answer, but only by the end of the evening, dear *compañeros.* Nobody is being forced to play, we're not going to demand an accounting from anyone, ladies and gentlemen, but anyone who's at least ten years old can play."

And what about me, only a few weeks old? How could I play?

"Whoever doesn't want to, doesn't have to play. Who has the soul of a child? Luis? Elena?" And he went around the room like that to each one of us. "Antonio? Carlos?" laying his hand on each of us, identifying us to the rest of the audience. "Tomás?" and his hand was hot and heavy on my head, but now his hand was resting on the head of Luis's wife, who turned, somewhat startled. "Loreto?" One by one, he introduced us to society, all those other eyes focused on my face, and all of them, happy. "What about you?" he asked La Negra. "Or, you, Pecosa? Luciano? Or maybe Juan's the one. Is it Juan who has the soul of a child?" And with that, he rested both hands on himself and gave a little bow.

"Now let's understand. It has nothing to do with how old you are. We're not holding a contest. I mean, OK, OK, there may be a few who - but nobody's on trial here. There's no sentence. Let me make myself clear; it's not a matter of competition. Not one of you will know if somebody else has been more or less a child tonight. Not one of you can find out. You all could care less about that, because children don't worry about that sort of thing. Right, Tomás?"

I had to play along with him, I guess. "Sure," I answered. "They just play. They don't ask stupid questions."

"Fine, fine. The contestant's answer is correct. You're off to a good start, Tomás."

Elena appeared all of a sudden, and something in my stomach gave a start, something like a little sneeze, a baby's

70

sneeze. She handed me a glass of pisco. But she didn't stay. She went back to the other side of the room.

"Thanks," I told her, just in case, although I was sure she hadn't heard me.

Juan was rubbing his fleshy hands together, sensing his own power, the magnetism of his voice, as if we were permanently crippled and he were our crutch, wheelchair or mattress, a top-of-the-line life jacket, knowing that he could turn the night completely around. "Anybody who doesn't want to, doesn't have to play." But he didn't ask if anybody wanted to leave; fortunately, he didn't force us to declare publicly that yes, we would play. "Anyone who wants to devote himself to more interesting things," and he looked for Elena and Pecosa, as if the two of them had very interesting things to do together, it was an absurd correlation, it was just to keep from including me and Elena in the same glance. "But we, all of us, are going to play. . .game-of-the-night. Who is innocent? Who will win, ladies and gentlemen? The big game, the jackpot, the million-dollar lottery. Who will be our child-for-a-night? Who's it going to be?"

We were waiting. But Juan didn't say another word. All of us waited quietly, expectantly, for what would come next, but Juan didn't open his mouth. The silence pleasantly prolonged itself for another few seconds.

Everything led us to believe that Juan was going to continue, his voice would still control us like obedient puppets, moving La Negra from place to place, reciting instructions, adding details, precisely and exactly defining limits, prerogatives and responsibilities, turning us into passive and immobilized receptacles, upon which he would impose his always astonishing activity; always the whip, pushing us forward; we were the tides and he, the moon; he was the sea and we were the beach, but he didn't say a word. By this time he had managed to get under our skin; he had pulled us away from whatever we really wanted to do, asking

71

each one of us questions about innocence and being children; but now Juan had decided to keep quiet.

We looked at each other uncertainly. There was a kind of sensual luminosity in Juan's eyes that turned our own glances away. Luciano started to vibrate; it was as though the whole room were shaking inside his skin, with a babble of lights.

"Juan," said Elena. She's the one who understands him best. But he didn't answer. His body was a little swollen, like a drowned man who's been pulled from the sea after several days of immersion, still not decaying, but punished by the water. He had lost his train of thought, it happens to all of us; he had jumped track after his last words, following the trail of some thought that was his alone, plunging into the Atlantic, only to come to the surface in some other sea, the Pacific, for example, and demanding all the time that we follow him on land, or with a submarine detector or radar, yes, demanding that we find him when we didn't have the slightest idea where he was, what he was thinking. He expected us to be right there with him, whenever he decided to come to the surface, ready to pick up yesterday's conversation once again, just as if it were today's, always today's; for Juan every day was tomorrow.

Or was it better to go back to where we were before? Was it possible? Exile Juan to the wasteland of eccentricity, accept him as one more disharmony in a night that was growing like a tree and which had its plastic branches and its aborted seed, as well? Or just wait patiently - after all, things weren't so bad here, were they? Maybe Juan had realized that he was screwing things up; maybe that was the light of revelation that was shining in his expression; it was better to go back. He would say: Excuse me. I lost track of things. I'm a damn fool. And no one would contradict him, or somebody would take him off to one corner and talk to him, maybe I'd be the one, we'd talk wildly, the way we always did, Juan and I; maybe the night would be called Juan for me alone, and the others would have their freedom of action.

But Luis's wife was impatient. She went to the record player and moved her hand toward the plug; the Beatles were only an inch away, *sleep pretty darling, do not cry* and there we'd be again in the middle of that full night that was about to ripen, with Juan accepting the fact that he was just one more person there and not the central figure.

Then, Juan, maybe because he was stimulated, or afraid, or maybe just because once again no one was expecting it, shouted: "On your mark,". . . and Luis's wife dropped the plug . . . "Get set" . . . Elena, her interest piqued once again, shifted to a more comfortable position on the other side of the room; now she wouldn't come over until later, "And" . . .

But before we heard the "Go", I suddenly thought about hide-and-seek. We wouldn't fit under the chairs; we were too big. It occurred to me that Luciano would be thinking about a mouthful of cake, a grimy handful of candy or dirty waterpaint water, or a blackboard. Nancy looked at me with the cracked picture of a doll in the peninsula of her narrow eyes, those tiny cracks you see in a doll's face when it's old; you'd never take the plunge, Nancy. And you, gringo, Humpty Dumpty had a great fall, we could read everything on your lips now; so you're a fag, right, gringo, and just when you were about to have the guts to tell us that, just when you're screwing up your lips, smiling at me; but you know what? We don't give a damn. Be yourself, man. And there's Luis, just a mask, completely inscrutable.

So Juan was silent again. He said nothing. He was abandoning us all at the point of departure; didn't you want to be free, Tomás; didn't you want not to be controlled? Here we were on the pier while he sailed off without so much as a "see you later", and we could no longer go back to that magical moment, Juan; we were already remembering our childhood, already turning playful, like cuddly, little teddy bears, but he didn't really say "Go"; he was standing there with his hand raised like a pistol, his index finger resting on a trigger that we could all see clearly up there in the air, that - like children - we could trace easily in our imaginations, the finger resting on that trigger, but not pulling it, a pistol that we could use later to play cowboys, or cops-and-robbers, or whatever he decided we should play; he'd kill us and we'd come back to life; we'd play at doctors and nurses, or war, or play out love scenes, beneath his benevolent gaze, always pushing us to be ready. But he didn't offer us his parting blessing; we didn't hear the shot. He was standing there serenely; he had become a statue; he didn't say "go"; nobody said "go"; he'd left us in the station again, had convinced us to board the train, but the train was leaving from another platform, with the damned conductor, the mother-fucking engineer; come back and look for us, Juan; even I was telling you that; you had succeeded in pulling me out, rolling me up, stuffing me in your suitcase and then hanging me on a hook. But even I needed you to explain what I was supposed to do. But you weren't revealing a thing, motherfucker, there you were so close, but so silent. I felt like punching your face in.

Luciano was laughing. "Hey, Tomás," he whispered to me. "Tomás, Tomás."

I didn't want to hear him; I was concentrating on Juan and I didn't want to miss a single moment of the departure.

"Tomás," Luciano insisted, tugging at my shirt sleeve. That makes me sick and Luciano ought to know I can't stand to have anybody pull on my sleeve.

"What do you want?" I said, half-mad, like when Mama would call us to dinner just when one more block would finish the castle, so it's still not a castle.

"Anybody that laughs goes straight to jail." He said it rather loudly. Everybody must have heard him. Luciano became very serious, he tightened his lips so that not even a trace of a smile would appear. I felt my own lips getting stiff, and I saw that somebody was already starting to work on Karolina, softly tickling her leg. I couldn't see who it was,

74

whoever it was was hidden by Juan's erect figure, but she, my little unweeping willow, wouldn't give an inch; never-but-never was she going to end up in jail. She stubbornly stuck her finger in her mouth and started sucking on it, almost with pure delight, as if she were really enjoying that tickling hand - now almost detached from the arm, working her ankle over, as if it were floating in mid-air, it was Luis, I'm sure that hand belonged to Luis - turning it into a pacifier, or better still a saliva centipede, but she wouldn't laugh for anything in the world; her stare was glazed and empty. Hell, Karolina! How long were you going to suck that finger?

Lady bug, lady bug, fly away home. It was La Negra and Pecosa, singing in falsetto and slightly hoarse, sounding more like dwarfs playing at being little princesses than adolescents reverting to childhood at that long and lightning flash moment when they give up their virginity and accept pleasure, more like La Negra and Pecosa than two school girls. "Come on, Tomás," said one of them, with spiders and leprosy dripping from her fingers, "let's get moving." And she told Luis's wife to go look for a broom and a pan top in the kitchen and all of us would march to its drum-beat, but Loreto had her own plans, and was sliding along in another direction:

"I'm gonna look for a paper donkey," she said, ". . . and a tail."

Sure, and a napkin, to blindfold us, so that some other hairy, but tender hand, bigger than our shoulder, could spin us around, and there'd be the animal's silhouette on the wall, but no way, we'd be carried this way and that, between the spinning furniture, or maybe musical chairs, why not? I almost shouted, but I didn't say anything, just remained stubbornly quiet; we were as dizzy as hell, and the tail always ended up pinned to the chair, to the donkey's ear, or maybe once in a while on his smooth and voluminous rump, right there in the center of the universe, you win the prize, or the pin might fasten with a vengeance in Luis's eye, as he played the tambourine, sitting on the floor, or in a wild rage was beating someone up, no doubt it was me, or maybe Elena, on the floor, with immortally big sticks; and for a while the rest of them played musical instruments, drunk and excited, one, two, three, ready, set, go, everyone concentrating on his own game, and now Luis had captured an ant and was caring for it, performing experiments with it before he would kill it or obliging it to listen while he told it all about his problems with this or that teacher or learning the ABC's. I was about to tell Luis's wife to bring that napkin, or a scarf, and I almost took off my own tie, but I had already lost it, who knows when that night; I probably gave it to Liliana to tie up her hair that kept falling down; but I didn't say anything; Luis's wife had already taken off, and she'd come back with something anyhow, she was real organized that way, but a little prissy and uptight, and later there'd be blindman's buff, and then dress-up, so long as we didn't come down to the game of truth, where you lied so much it ended up sounding like the truth; blindman's buff was enough, stumbling around looking for someone, and always capturing a person other than the one you wanted.

And I should've stood up and gone out with the girls to see if the others would follow; I should've told Luis's wife to bring a napkin, or I could've made faces at her to see if the others would laugh, because if they didn't pretty soon we were going to have chaos, everybody, each one involved in his own game, all of them with a different strategy, but on the same playing field, one tossing baskets, another swimming, and over there a solitary figure playing soccer, goalie, center-forward, referee, Luis on his bicycle, there was still time, before Antonio peed his pants, or the gringo started crying like a baby and then managed to calm himself down, but I couldn't move, I was just like Juan, the only two who said absolutely nothing, while everybody else went slowly berserk, looking for a common ground, each one pulling and shoving everybody else into his circle, the imaginary tricycles bumping into each other, or throwing non-existent sand at each other, each one tearing down somebody else's house of cards.

La Negra left Pecosa singing to herself and said to Luciano: "Papa, one, two, three, five, ninety, forty-eight stars, Papa." I could have answered her, just to say something. But I said nothing. We wouldn't fit in the closet, I thought, watching Juan with a feeling of tenderness, as he stood there as serene as I was. And now, in a little while, there would only be he and I, in an identical position, not participating, just being witnesses, while the rest of them would move farther away, pushing each other, like cash register keys being pushed by an idiot. So, they didn't want their freedom, did they?

Elena came up to me.

"While the cat's away," she told me, and held out her hand. I didn't say anything; I just stared at it; her heart must have been beating faster; both of us inside one sponge; so you had come after all, and maybe there was a plan and Juan wasn't in perfect control of the situation. But I wasn't playing anymore, I could have told her; I'm sleeping or putting on my pants, or I'm sharpening my knife, or I could have taken that hand, the only thing that was real inside that demented flux into which we'd all fallen, I don't know how, but I kept quiet, just staring at her.

Antonio must have been drawing by now, on the wall, by now he was drawing an April sun with a happy face and one twisted eye, and then a back made of rays; he was about to mark the wall with a gigantic red pencil, who knows where he'd gotten that, his pockets were like his head, a bottomless bag of tricks, and Luis was not going to say anything to him, even though it was his wall, and Juan would not say anything either, even though it was his game, and it had been his idea. Juan was still there, very attentive, but withdrawn, or maybe with nothing on his mind, but with his eyes closed now, I don't know the exact moment when he shut them; he didn't budge, there in the middle of that oval space that all of us had formed, and everybody was dancing around, Juan and I being the only fixed poles, and now Elena too, forming an ellipse, superimposed and concentric almond trees like any three-year-old might draw; Juan and I were the eyes in the middle of that round, pancake face, and I don't know what Elena was; she was a hand that could get me out of there, and there he was with his finger still on the trigger, the jerk, a sweating, marble statue, an immobile, searching, blind-man's buff, but with no blindfold and nobody running away, everybody ready to be tagged; let him throw us in the pot once and for all, and then somebody else would be there in the middle and he'd throw Juan in the pot, but Juan would have no part of that, he wouldn't budge, just his jaw moved a little, as if he were praying, or chewing gum, but nothing came out of his mouth, not even a comic strip bubble, with little words that we could read when we were eight years old, a manual that would direct us and relieve us; there he was, as stiff as a statue, Juan, and me too, non-communicating glasses, neither of us sending out even a balloon, that would get bigger and redder and rounder, not even the satisfaction of bursting, not a bang, the race would never begin, and everybody else, even Elena, looking for the playing field, the pool, the big sale with bargain prices, Juan, I wanted to tell him, Juan, that's enough, let's get started, for God's sake, or tell us that it's all over, you choose the one that has the spirit of a child, but there was my own game coming to meet me, the hand of Elena, who was dying there in the darkness, so close but without touching me; but she was getting closer and I didn't want her to touch me or to find me; I made myself invisible; I was going to have to run away to keep her from catching me; I'd have to go with you, Elena, and I don't want to; I want to stay here with Karolina; I like being a kite, Elena; I don't love you at all, girl, leave me alone; while Juan's finger still didn't pull the trigger; he was never going

78

to give the signal to go; he'd stand there forever; and now the gringo was interrupting Antonio; the gringo was pretending he was a lion; Antonio was going to abandon that marvelous drawing, the blue sky with the blood-orange trees standing out against it, or maybe it was the sea that was blue, and I really felt bad that he wasn't going to go on drawing, the wall was going to be only half finished, it might fall down, I almost told the gringo, come on, I'll play with you, me, who never played with him, who really doesn't like him very much, even though I spend hours with him and we always go to the cinema together, but I didn't say anything to him, answer me, but I didn't say anything, you broke the flowerpot, and I don't even know if I broke it or not, and the best thing is just not to confess to anything, no words and no comments, head hanging down, or maybe I do like you, gringo, like all of you, just sometimes and with the enthusiasm of a distant bell tower, fevers that come and go, and I almost tell him, let's play, but now Antonio was Tarzan, or maybe it was the other way round, they would fight and I would watch them, from, well, how the hell do I know from where, from my window, I guess, they never invite me, right; Tomás, you're always afraid of losing, you always stayed there in the window, Mama, I'd rather read, Mama, and they really lit into each other, banging each other against the ground, until they'd really draw blood, the kind that stains, not even saying I'm sorry, with a good, healthy hatred. Crack!

"Come on," said Elena.

Nancy was watching us, from behind a half-opened door, just a crack of light and Nancy watching us.

Juan, on the other hand, was not watching us. His eyes were shut tight, his jaw now didn't move a bit, a drop of sweat hung on his neck, but didn't fall; I loved him with incredible intensity from some inexplicable part of my being; the night could have called itself Juan; I don't want to share you with anyone, Juan; and what about the others? What thoughts must be galloping through their minds? I didn't have the slightest idea what the others were thinking, and it made me furious; I should be playing along, and not be there with you in your damned solitude; dawn was going to break and you'd never know that I was the only one that was faithful, the only one who was still there, letters that are never mailed, here I was, like some idiotic pilgrim, who instead of going off to my own sanctuary, was playing the part of a road sign for another guy who only looked at me enough to take the direction indicated; I was the dictionary for the others, just as they were mine, just for the hell of it, that's all. And who knows how long that was going to go on? I hoped that at least Elena would keep on coming closer and then I'd have to decide whether I was going to go or to stay, because Liliana had fallen asleep at his feet, she had a crazy job, and the next day, Sunday, she'd go to a shanty-town to treat the sick; she was the only sensible one, a responsible kid, who gave herself over to adoration there on the floor at his feet; and tomorrow she would treat cases of diarrhea, and she was absolutely right; I started to feel a blaze of shame well up inside me; and Juan just stood there, he didn't even start again, whoever has the spirit of a child, the train's leaving; Karolina started to giggle from the tickling; he'd finally found her weak point.

Karolina, I tried to think, but I didn't think it; I said nothing.

Like so many other times, she didn't know I was there; there she was with her silent little deaf-mute screams, and I was going to be with her forever; I was still trying not to lose, trying to keep on being a copy, a second-class imitation, hoping they wouldn't notice her, so organized, efficient, elegant and perfect; they'd finally found her weak point, but she still didn't give in; I still didn't hear a sound come from her.

"Don't go to jail," Luciano whispered quickly, and I was amazed at how well he knew me among so many strangers there that night; maybe the night was going to take shape in Luciano.

She pulled her finger out of her mouth, pretty little mouth, and burst into convulsive laughter, shattering the head of a chicken against a shiny, bronze bell, a bloodbath of sound, shit, Juan, I'm going crazy, if you don't speak up, nobody can control this, if Juan didn't say something soon, nobody could predict what would happen.

Luis's wife came in, and walked straight up to me. "Don't get melodramatic on us," she said, and handed me a pile of little yellow and red cars, along with one blue one, while she held on to the napkin. She must have read something in my expression, even though she never read anything and never gave anything of herself to anyone - she was completely a lost cause, good to play dominoes with and nothing else, a good cook, but nothing else, a model mother, you might say. But she understood what was happening to me and she'd try to fix the situation, and of course would do a lousy job.

"Let's play blindman's buff," she said in a loud voice, like a fortyish old maid - she'd been an old maid ever since she was born - even in the middle of her marriage to Luis, she was still a squeamish and unbearable virgin.

So right then and there, with a "they lived happily ever after" attitude, I decided to play blindman's buff, then Elena said to me:

"What's the matter with you? Did you pee in your pants?" But she said it in a joking way, and I didn't respond.

Nancy heard it, she had to hear it from between the bars of her cradle, of course she was listening to our conversation, every little murmur. The only face I ever showed Elena suddenly went out like a light; I had nothing to give her; her hand would have to hang there, without mine.

"Who wants to be the blindman?" But nobody was paying any attention to her; they could all care less.

"Oh, sweetheart," shouted Karolina, always from far away, with me always climbing up her distant breasts, separated by whole continents of sweat. "I haven't had so much fun in years."

Luis smiled. He showed her the ant.

"The kids, the kids!" Luis's wife said, a note of urgency in her voice, because precisely at that moment Antonio was tumbling off the sofa, with a half-stifled cry, while the lion-gringo followed, growling and landing on his jugular.

"Kill him, kill him, gringo," said Pecosa, Antonio's wife. "Bite him, gringo."

"The kids!" But who was she talking about?

"Wake up, Liliana," said Luciano, who didn't want her to miss this for the world; but he just caressed her; he didn't wake her up.

Luis's wife crossed the room toward the gringo. "Look, Carlos, keep it down. It took me forever to get them to bed. Anybody that wakes them up. . . " and she made a gesture as if to spank them.

"Baby promises to be good," the gringo babbled.

Antonio was no longer shouting, and Luis's wife was tired of feeling ridiculous as usual. "And no dessert for you, do you understand?" And by then Luis's wife had forgotten all about blindman's buff; we all could have played; too bad she was a total flop as an organizer. She could make a chicken salad that would melt in your mouth, but she couldn't explain anything so that it made sense, and she had no idea how to draw everybody into one definitive game; once again we were alone, all of us.

"Oh, Tomás, Tomás," said Elena, as if she understood everything, or better yet, as if I had guessed what the hell was buzzing around her brain; but, of course, at that moment nobody knew anything, and me, less than anyone, and the master of ceremonies who had offered his services free of charge had forgotten his lines, while the audience was tearing the theater to pieces, Juan, so close in the distance of the center ring, maybe understanding everything and planning everything down to the last detail, even our present

82

rowdiness, like an orchestra director who does a lousy job, so they'll let him retire; and there we were, in the meantime, hanging on to who knows what, what the shit are we hanging on to? Why didn't we just dissolve, simply leave that house and walk serenely away, putting it all behind us and tomorrow's another smile and another game and once again, Elena, the time might come to go lie down with you, under the lemon tree, let's see if we can leave, let's see if you do come through, gringo, if you do wake up, Liliana, or what about you and I, Karolina, roads that are no more than automobiles, another opportunity would present itself soon.

"Tomás, Tomás," Elena said to me, and now she was no longer coming closer. Eeny meeny miny mo, catch a tiger by the toe, if he hollers, let him go, eeny meeny miny mo, I choose you, but nobody ever chose me, always the last one; I wanted to be one of her kids, but I just stayed there alone in the corner while the tidal wave of bodies washed over me, what would you like, your highness, while the ball passed over my head, just a reach away, but I couldn't possibly stretch and grasp it, Simple Simon, Simple Simon, Elena, don't go.

My dear friend Fermín:

Here goes the first report that you asked for, in this case, of *Interventions,* Manuel del Fierro's novel. You can see by the length of this letter (and, I suppose, by my thoroughness), that I'm taking literally the agreement we made back when you convinced me to accept a position as literary advisor at Editorial Aquí. You assured me that you were not interested in outlines, quick reads or pro forma reports, that what you wanted was for the reviewer to establish a clear and consistent orientation, and in that way to educate the company's executives, so they would know how to promote the new creative waves that would arise as Chile moved toward socialism. You also wanted us to serve as a guide to the new authors, so that the press could discover those talents that were on their way and whom it was our obligation to encourage with grants, workshops, loans, advice, etc. In spite of the amount of work I already had then and still have, I accepted, because I had always proclaimed the need for precisely what you were attempting. Besides, it's probable that by stimulating these young writers, by publishing their works, regardless of their length, theme or degree of experimentation, etc., in a word, *by taking risks,* we will achieve as a consequence an increase in the general interest in literature.

Such is the case of *Interventions,* with its weighty appearance and its venerable 800 pages, and I recommend its publication in any case, despite some reservations which I shall elaborate on at the end.

The novel's action, if it can be called that, takes place in a company which has just been nationalized, after a year and a half of struggle. The narrators are all those present at a party, which is being held to celebrate that event. And that includes not only the 250 workers themselves, but also some official and unofficial guests (for example, X, Tobías, a beggar who's famous in the neighborhood, who has come to help himself to a few drinks and a piece of meat). In the strictest alphabetical order, from Abarca, Antonio, to Zenteno, Clara, each one tells, in greater or lesser detail, about his or her work in the factory, his or her participation in the movement that led to the take-over and eventually, after months of mobilization put pressure on the government planning office and forced the nationalization of the company. In addition, there are passing references to life outside the factory itself, a few of them adding predictions about the immediate future.

As you can see, the first impression one receives is that it's just raw data, semi-journalistic interviews, as if an underground radio station had gotten inside the minds of its listeners and had decided to broadcast from there without any particular selective criteria. One's second impression is that the whole thing has to be as boring as you can get. When we get to Barahona, Lalo, and we notice the testimonial steppes that are stretching mercilessly ahead of us, no doubt the reader feels a shiver down his backbone. But, in spite of that, one keeps on reading, and gratefully realizes eventually that both impressions are erroneous.

Above all else, the result is an X-ray of vast sectors of the Chilean population, with special emphasis on the proletariat. Not only do you find members of most political parties (Communists, Socialists, members of MAPU and the extreme-left MIR, Christian Democrats, some right-wing Nationals and even one member of the CIA), but also representatives of the most diverse sectors in the nation, bearers of the richest and most varied of experiences, having occupied a multitude of political offices, and now living in the imaginable and unimaginable districts of Santiago. There's something for every taste. People with party support, independents, the angry and the disoriented, the drunk and the embittered, the generous and the tired, the honest, the energetic and the determined, the boot-lickers, the peace-lovers, the organizers and the organized, something for everybody. Each narrator is clearly differentiated by the variety of interests, motivations, projects and experiences. We move quickly from one point of view to another, from a white-collar to a blue-collar worker, to a secretary, a journalist, from a visiting executive to another blue-collar worker, and then to a foreman, etc. For example, there's Pérez, Alfredo, an illiterate packager, a passionate singer of boleros, as he demonstrates when he steps center-stage to do his act, a man who admires Sáez, Dagoberto, the activist MIRista; he speaks just before Pérez, Bernardo, an accountant with twenty years experience, chief of Finance, who suffers from nightmares, and sees all these procedures with a certain amount of resentment, because he fears the possibility of disorder that may follow; but he's disposed to keep on working, and thinks about his daughter who in another week is going to marry a young engineer, an active member of the National Party.

There's no uniformity among the invited guests either: two or three peasants who throughout the strike brought food to show their solidarity with their *compañeros*; two wives of workers who "slipped through" to bring their husbands back home so they wouldn't fall into the clutches of Gutiérrez, Estrella, famous for pinching male asses as they pass by, good for a quickie; some professionals from CORFO, where the affirmations of a bureaucrat, a man who thinks and plans technocratically, you have to look for ways to make the workers think they're really participating, when everything's really being decided upstairs, are answered 25 narrators down the line by the other professional, one who is a revolutionary, who doesn't want to manipulate anybody and understands how the process can suffer if the workers' control over production is frustrated.

One might presuppose that this is an attempt at individually incarnating broad sociological laws, each voice exemplifying a thesis that Del Fierro had thought up *a priori*, with a stack of polls and statistics at his fingertips. But that's not the way it is. If they are at all representative, it is because of the intense vibrancy with which they live out their own selfhood. Above all they are human beings, and they can, therefore, vaguely represent certain social roles, sometimes breaking through the stereotypes we tend to create about the category into which they would supposedly fit. We're not dealing here with a series of monotonous windows in the side of an infinite apartment building in a housing development over-looking the North Panamerican Highway, each window occupied by a solitary inhabitant who can never talk with his neighbor nor look up, down or to either side. Because, like feet under the tables in restaurants or legs and whole bodies under the sheets of hotels at night on San Pablo Street, kites rising from every hand inside a classroom bursting with wind, behind those windows there is constant movement, caressing, fighting, intertwining like the thousand arms of an octopus. The less they look at the person talking beside them, the better they provide their part in a whole structure, tying together and untying all the interaction that has lead them up to this day of celebration, the same interaction that will go on piloting them toward new rivers, formed by currents and against rapids, weaving a common history.

The author has rejected a procedure that would have been perfectly legitimate and would have given him a sure-fire bestseller: he might have chosen just ten, the ones who organized and directed, or their most tenacious opponents, and with them he could have unfolded a classic narrative on the workers' struggle. Although, as we shall see, he does tend to give one or two of them a treatment we might call preferential, in quality as well as in quantity, he refuses to distinguish some of them as main characters, avoiding entirely the kind of preselection that means using categories like "hero" and "anti-hero". Of course some of them constantly attract the attention of their comrades, their names are passed from mouth to mouth, like lighthouse beams that signal danger on a stormy night or islands that beacon us to rest on a calm day. But the groupings that form around certain focal points come from the workers themselves and not from any previous determination of the writer. "Why should I want a volcano," says one of the characters, referring to other wives as compared with his, "when I already have an earthquake."

A great deal of suspense can be generated by this technique. The narrators, after all, admit the truth about what they are and not the notion that others have formed of them, allowing us to witness a reconstruction of the past, like a puzzle invented by a blind man in a brightly lit room, one which simultaneously records the public and the private history of that strike, all the complications, hazards, mistakes, successes, guesses, and mix-ups that came together so that they could land so precisely on this shore of the future, with this company now in the hands of its workers. Only Olivares, Pablo knows that the take-over was on the verge of failure due to his own lack of courage; he had decided not to go that night with the key to the side door; only he knows that the providential arrival of Hernández, Daniela, had forced him to decide, I thought you'd be in the factory already, I came by to see your sister, if you want I'll go along with you, it's getting late. Olivares thinks that Daniela will probably reveal his cowardice someday, but when it was her turn to tell her story, she didn't even mention the incident, only indicating in passing how much she admires Pablo. Peralta, Guillermo, on the other hand, a taciturn man, not much given to words, has never given a detailed account of the beating they gave him at the police station by direct order of the judge who was drawing up the case against them for usurpation. No one ever mentions it; they don't consider him to be the same as Olivares, but the reader has the opportunity to rest in that man's slow, serene courage.

In all their movement, the characters gradually harvest echoes, opening up questions that will only be answered forty voices later, anticipating small mysteries that will either be clarified or lost, without our ever knowing for sure exactly what happened, calling each other on multiple telephone lines on an over-loaded switchboard, answering, denying, accusing, suspecting, making plans that will or will not produce results, going on the offensive, until piece by piece, like the intertwined branches of a single family spreading across the earth after the first day of creation, the story appears before us, incomplete but completing itself, never finished, always about to be finished, the story of their struggle. Like the slow fall of snow flakes during a storm, the soft breezes that stir up flies on a summer day, the twisted meanderings of tree roots in a May forest, the colors with which blankets and bedspreads greet the first day of spring sunshine after flooding, like the manufacturing of one of the objects this company produces, in which all the sections participate, in which so-and-so and so-and-so collaborate and leave their fingerprints, their blood, their strength, their solitude, imprinted on the heart of the object, just so do those voices weave the cloth of the novel, building once again, once again reconquering ground by the efforts of their own language, leaving no room for doubt, singing at the top of their lungs of their undeniable right to the factory.

The multiple networks of wills that influence each other and interact (José loves Hilda; later we find out that Hilda has already tired of him and is dreaming about Tomás; Tomás wants to take a tumble with her and then forget her), the secondary conflicts, the partings and the mutual support, barely exist in isolation, all of them submerged (personal rivalries and friendships, sports preferences, family connections, political parties, disciplinary problems at work) in the irresistible groundswell of the collective *We*, an enormous, underground wave of solidarity and struggle that comes together in its advances, its excesses, its boundless energy, and everything else, subordinating the individual actor-witnesses and carrying them along. What is fundamental and decisive is the experience they gained, the transformation that shook them, during all those months they fought for their industry.

That's the miracle. With all those problems, with the traitors, the doubters, the neutrals, the confused, with all the divisions within the left, all the manipulation by management, government bureaucracy, sabotage, misunderstandings, the soup kitchen getting emptier and emptier: how could they possibly have reached the point of staging this celebration? Looking at the whole affair in retrospect and from a different perspective, how is it possible that the workers actually won? The way in which that victory is narrated is an exact reflection of the way it was actually won:

89

it's a victory for the community, for that chaotic and overwhelming totality that we call the masses. There within it, each individual lived through his own small defeats, his great leap toward the dawn of a new day; each one became part of the machine of history and of industry. As those voices file before us and push and empty themselves, we have the undeniable feeling that that is precisely the way freedom, progress, and the future of humanity are shaped. Several of the narrators mention, some only in passing, others with greater detail, the case of one González, "it seems like he finally saw the light," "I don't believe it; once a Christian Democrat, always a Christian Democrat." Could González really have changed? "I don't like that jerk, he always moves to wherever the grass looks greener"; "fortunately González got the message, convinced his companions, told Frei and his mafia to go to hell"; and now we're ready to hear the truth from the lips of González, Jeremías, himself, and there, he details, simply and modestly, how he has changed, the problems he encountered in his shanty-town when he resigned from the Christian Democratic Party, his doubts with regard to Marxism, his decision to never again let himself be deceived and to move ahead, the companions who helped him most, and the ones who still don't trust him completely.

The author constantly uses this method which allows us to understand in all its profundity the miles and miles you have to run in order to advance just a few inches, but what a pleasure it is to be here, so far along. Take the case of the saboteur, for example. Everybody obsessively repeats the same concern: there's someone, probably more than one person, in the industry who has been sowing discord, creating problems, spying for management, and all that just increases suspicion and distrust and produces lots of guessing as to that person's identity. They know he'll go back into action, so they have to keep their eyes open. They run down lists, speculate on who it could possibly be, make guesses. This focal point of tension increases as we hear more and more voices, but the person responsible is not revealed. Can you imagine our surprise when we get to the S's, Salazar, Perico, whom no one had ever suspected. To the contrary, he is the most respected of comrades, one of the pillars of the movement. But Salazar, without so much as a blush, and with a snake's cold-bloodedness, admits to being the saboteur and furthermore to being an agent of a foreign organization. When later narrators reiterate their admiration for Salazar, and in fact Vargas (the current president of the union) thinks about entrusting him with certain high-security jobs, the reader realizes that the problems have only just begun.

The question of the company's future, what steps will be taken next, also contributes to the suspense of the story. Just as the workers have earlier overcome some major problems that afflict the revolutionary movement in Chile, they now foresee some with even greater ramifications. Out of that beehive of converging, contradictory and semi-coincidental opinions and directions, the reader is struck by a sense of an enormous force, but one whose projections are uncertain. The future is just around the corner, in fact it's already being shaped, at this party, and to the extent to which each one develops his thesis, his aspirations and his slogans, one senses that clashes of personality and of political ideas are inevitable in the factory, just as they were during the last year and a half.

We're going to create our power base here and now, we'll coordinate all the industries, and extend our influence to other factories in the area. We're going to have a little respite. The first thing we have to do is to prepare for more conflicts. Our priority has got to be to increase production. We have to get rid of those who hold us back. We're going to move ahead carefully, and without showing partiality. We'll change the name of the company. Initiate contacts with DINAC. And create our own commissary. We hope no one suggests forming a commissary; that'd be just one more evidence of paternalism. We're going to reorganize sections B and C. No time for rest, *compañeros.* This process won't be irreversible until all power's in the hands of the workers. When negotiations for new salaries come up, then we'll ask for aprons. We have to keep track of every cent, understand? Now's the time to put a little order into things. We'll have to go on with the old plans until a new kind of market opens up. And we've got to find a new chief engineer, this one's a real fascist. Fortunately section B is just fine the way it is. And that's the way the ideas and plans flow, all the tendencies and fluxes, all the passive, neutral and active forms, the Communists, the Christian Democrats, the technocratic recovery that the chief engineer will undertake, everything culminating in everything else. We know that Farías's plan to coordinate the factories at a communal level is going to fail; the atmosphere in the industry is not right for it. But he doesn't know that and he'll try it anyhow. He'll repeat the same mistakes he committed during the take-over: lack of realism, lack of intuition as regards their true state of mind. Yet Farías's hot-headedness always kept his comrades on their toes.

All of them make up the movement, the obscure, dirty and multiple voices of the chorus, the collective body. And we realize that they will repeat their mistakes and confront limitations and difficulties, but they'll come through it all right, just as they successfully brought off the transfer of the company to the public sector.

It's possible to make such an affirmation precisely because the author avoids any tendency to idealization, any saccharine note of sentimentality, as he presents the proletariat and its unstoppable push forward. It is not a thesis that the author imposes on the work. It is an irrefutable force that runs through and unifies every isolated effort.

The very first narrator, at the opening of the book, says it all. Antonio Abarca has the first word: "This is only the beginning." And Carla Zenteno, the cook, has the last word: "There's plenty of time. We'll see tomorrow. Pass me the bread."

That is the novel's meaning: to show all these forces, supposedly a cross-section of Chilean society, in conflict, yet coming together in a rich and complex action and inter-action, like branches moved by a single wind and shedding their blossoms at different moments of a single day, one current of air and all those branches, a single sound among so many scattered colors. And they move forward, not in spite of all their differences and contradictory opinions, but rather because of them. They are the cause and the shape of the movement, its very essence. It is a novel written at that shaky moment between "only the beginning" and the "tomorrow, pass me the bread," between Abarca and Zenteno, between the man who that very day saw the birth of his first child but who doesn't want to miss the chance to drink a toast with his comrades, and the woman, who has cooked for all of them, who has fed them, the great mother, that powerful, floating presence on which they've always been able to depend, a work written without previous explanation, and without a point of view to impose an order.

Our knowledge can come only through the perspectives offered by each narrator. Whatever they understand, mis-understand, misrepresent, are indifferent to, whatever they remember or forget, provides that irreplaceable route to reconstructing the take-over and to foretelling the future. Order lies in the social class, in the working people, in the forces which that class builds up in order to keep on advancing through the maze of obstacles, enemies and internal divisions. It is the general direction that the great majority will adopt; it is there (even though one of them may express it as the desire to be able at last to found a folk-singing group, while another sees it as the possibility of learning to read and write, and a third sees it as a way to organize their powers) where the ability of that class is frankly, I would even say brutally, revealed, there in that give and take, in the collective body that is greater than the sum of its parts; it is there that one sees the future and the revolution.

It is also there that we see the writer's "commitment". Not in any unbridled praise of the workers' qualities, not in pamphleteering or in the division of the world between good and evil, certainly not in any psychological simplification, nor in being blind to their weaknesses, their stumblings and their falls, but rather in the fact that the reader must, with his emotions, grasp the workers' spectacular leap and their energy, not isolating any particular factor within that advance as being essential (whether it was so-and-so's push, or this person's leadership, or that person's careful balancing of power, or somebody else's enthusiastic and contagious blasphemies, or stubbornness, or courage or sacrifice). We do not even know for sure at which exact moment they won that first battle in the struggle, nor what was the impact of the enemy's mistakes, their occasional vacillations: only their general, immense power.

Therefore, the author does not take sides with any one of them. He simply allows each voice to flow freely through the work, with the only limit being the presence of all the others. He allows any esthetic and moral sense of correctness to arise out of the magnificent multi-faceted order which the other orators impose in their fluctuating, but certain advance. It is they who provide any sense of sanction, any commentary or context and it is they who offer us a panoramic view of the movement, everything accommodated to the attitudes and objectives which the characters themselves propose.

Not even in the case of two notorious absences, two silences that weigh heavily upon the reader, does he work with either heroic or villainesque models. The great leader, the ex-president of the union, the one whom Jessica Palta

94

calls "our soul, our fist, and our skin", has been beaten to death by a band of thugs two months before. With his absence, his figure assumes legendary proportions, but at the same time it begins to become vaguer, to be more a name than an actual person. That homage which is injected by their voices is also a sign that the past can never be completely reconstituted and provides a certain tremor of nostalgia that mists the novel. The other person who is not present at the party, muzzled by his expulsion, is the company's ex-manager, and it is upon him that everyone's hatred is concentrated. Even though his spokesmen can express his point of view without being corralled either by the author or by the other characters, that most public representative of the exploiters is never given the chance to speak.

This does not mean that the author's hand cannot be detected. Just as the factory itself converts nature's raw material into consumer goods, so the novelist elaborates his human material in order to show its revolutionary potential.

Precisely these ambitions on the part of the author shape whatever reservations we might have to his creation. He so desires to present a total picture, more than reality itself, that everything ends up being a little too representative. It's not that he is trying to borrow novelistic techniques in order to present a conveniently pre-digested scientific study for the masses, like the one we find in *Here We Speak,* that testimonial book written by Jaime García about the coal miners. The sociological procedures he adopts lead to a different fictional reality. He doesn't pretend that this really happened in some factory, with such-and-such a name, and with such-and-such directors and such-and-such an executive from a particular bureaucracy, but rather as if this place stood for all factories, the entire country. This desire to include all the possible contradictions in their entirety weighs the novel down. Perhaps the author didn't notice that reality itself is always a partial construction, and that a perfect imitation of reality should copy that partiality, that marginal, oblique and sometimes dim way of acting and of existing, which never uses up nor juxtaposes every aspect in each isolated manifestation.

Another serious problem is the language. To be frank, here he has not known how to overcome the old problems of expression of the working class, the debates between colloquialism and stylistic order, between the use of Chileanisms and academic regularity, between what is idiomatic and what allows for universal comprehension. Besides vacillating between the poetic and the trivial, the novel seems to set itself up, but without much clarity, as a great linguistic experiment. From time to time, in the middle of a monotony that occasionally does not lose its plasticity and clarity, he throws a thunderbolt: someone who speaks in comic book language, or like a sports announcer, or in stream-of-consciousness, with all kinds of spelling errors, with frenetic eloquence, all of which do not necessarily correspond to the character nor to his expressive needs.

Doesn't this demonstrate some literary, rhetorical ballast, a generational marker, which the author has not been able to shed? It's as though Del Fierro had chosen this means, the language, to demonstrate his skill and ability and how in touch he was with the latest literary fads, as if in this way he were showing any possible critic or friend that he could really do it. In two cases he copies a sub-language, a semi-incomprehensible but interesting dialect. But why in those two cases and not in others? It's also evident that when he approaches especially conflictive characters, like Perico Salazar, Dagoberto Sáez, Walterio Montecinos (the negotiator who must now depart), Jeremías González, etc., their language is standardized and becomes nicely shaped. Almost all the linguistic experimentation is done with characters whose participation has not been crucial to the plot or the take-over, as if their insignificance somehow justifies their status as guinea pigs.

But this - besides not resolving the linguistic tensions let loose in a process of change - may basically be a problem that arises out of the author's concept of the masses and which sums up his disdain for the vanguards. He feels, perhaps, that he has not taken sufficiently into account (as a traditional novel would have done) the weight that would have been exercised by the party officials and their most outstanding representatives, and he has tried to compensate for this, to offset a certain glorious anarchy in the novel's development, by giving special treatment to the linguistic dimension. As a result he sometimes irritates the reader with certain inconsistencies and residues. Is this another way of reaffirming the novel's central thesis? Let's not stretch things too far, turning defects into much desired and sought-after marks of genius. In the process of interpretation you can justify almost anything, but something tells us, almost intuitively, that in these areas the novel does not really manage to get to the bottom of certain problems that our literature has been confronting for several decades.

Finally, Fermín, I suggest that you don't change the title, charged as it is with multiple meanings. On the one hand, there are the narrative *interventions,* what each individual declares. And the novel's action and its memory revolve around the way in which they brought about the *intervention* of the government and all its structures in the control of the industry. An *intervention* is also something that interferes so that a process cannot unfold in a normal fashion, and in that sense it means the obstacles, what intervenes to prevent a process from bearing fruit. Finally - an idea which surely never occurred to the author, but which has occurred to me; what can you do when you're so used to literary acrobatics? - the entire book is an *intervention inter,* the product of many minds trapping and supporting each other mutually, an interdefinition that tries to determine the other person's life from one's own viewpoint and vice versa (another good title for a book: *Vice versa*). It is the word's ambiguity which

97

attracts my attention: as in an operation, the patient can be cured or he can get a passport to the next world, the intervention may be skillful or inept, but in any case no one denies that it must occur.

As for the public to which the book is directed, those waters are too deep for me to wade into; a person could drown. The author will be applauded for having dared to produce a "collective novel", without cheap paternalism. He'll also be attacked for trying to direct the working class from his privileged petit-bourgeois position. He'll be told that no worker has either the time or the money to read a book that long and that, at bottom, it's just a bad substitute for *praxis*. And he'll be told that this is the way to open new possibilities to replace socialist realism. Confused, treacherous, revolutionary, brave, sterile. The opinions that arise from among the readers will be as varied as the words that intervene in the novel. Or the silence that arises from them. In any case, that is a sign in itself that it is worth the risk to publish it. We find unanimity only in graveyards.

With warmest regards,
Alberto Hinostroza

P.S. When I was about to send you these pages, Manuel del Fierro himself appeared at my house, along with *Reports,* a second manuscript. He had talked with you, he said, and you advised him to come and present his points of view to me, since to publish *Interventions* we would have to commit ourselves to *Reports,* a second complementary volume. I have just taken a quick look at it, after several hours of pleasant conversation with Del Fierro. We've discussed the possible plague of "collective novels" (Del Fierro disclaims that categorization: "I don't know if it's appropriate") that would take off after the publication of *Interventions.* We also discussed possible modifications (a less fluid point of view, unifying nuclei on which the narrative would focus, the creation of choruses with a floating "we" within which, tangentially, the individual terraces might appear), but more than anything else he has explained *Reports* to me.

It deals with the occupation of several soccer fields by homeless people and the ultimately successful attempts of the local neighborhood poor to regain those lands which they had set aside for sports and recreation; thus, it portrays a confrontation between different sectors of the people. Perhaps that is why he does not use the same procedures as in *Interventions.* Quite the contrary. It appears to be a collection of strange and distant looks which are "objective" and external, a collection of dispersed and disconnected materials in which you never hear a single one of the warm voices of the previous novel. First there are reports from newspapers (representing all political tendencies), where the reader is presented with different versions of the "facts". Then there are passages from letters from some of the citizens, as well as statements on the radio and declarations to the police, etc. After these, there is a transcription of the court case against a group accused of provoking a death. Then petitions presented to CORHABIT, the housing agency. The death certificate of one of the babies who died of pneumonia two months later. Weather reports (rain, rain, number of inches). A petition to some bureaucrat. A promise, six months later, from the Ministry of State for Sport to install bleachers there. A memorandum of the Social Services Department. A list of prices (official and unofficial) in the local department store on the day of these events.

It's exactly like a photographic negative of *Interventions.* In *Reports* we have at our disposal only the public view. There's absolutely nothing intimate, nothing that went through any individual's mind, nothing that indicates who took part during those desolate days. Of course there are reports written by members of political parties, there are official reports, resolutions from the Mothers' Center and the Sports Club, and even a speech by the second member of the communal council.

The overwhelming feeling that oppresses the reader is that beneath those frozen, bureaucratic reports, the people, as a protagonist of the events, are drowning. It is an autopsy, a statistical report that found nouns and verbs with which to express itself, an archive abandoned at the bottom of the sea. There is no way to penetrate the mystery, to enter the consciousness of those who lived or collected those declarations.

That's why bureaucrats can't solve problems, Del Fierro told me; they couldn't avoid disaster; they didn't know how to give practical answers, because they have no interest in listening to what the real protagonists have to say; they have no interest in the "interventions". The novel's stammering development seems to demand the inclusion of some human scream, some act of tenderness, something so close and so soft and sandy and musical that the underworld of human minds opens, and filters some light through those closed blinds.

It is the absence of that perspective which causes the confrontation in the first place. Everybody (police, doctors, lawyers, reporters, politicians, sociologists, university students, housing representatives and the residents themselves) asks what happened? Let's determine pre-cise-ly what are the facts. Instead of wondering what the real reasons are, that is, their own weakness, their distance from reality, their dehumanization.

That accumulation of reports does not bore the reader, because, as the facts are hidden, as they don't reveal themselves immediately, questioning mechanisms begin to operate and these generate interest. Curiously, the narrators, those presenting the reports, appear as those really responsible, *post facto,* for the events. They search everywhere, looking for the guilty parties, for someone to "pay the piper", anyone, that is, except themselves, as they present their dull, stiff prose, their codified language and sealed paper, their schematic interpretations and official views, their whatsoevers and wherefores.

Del Fierro himself did not know if it was good to include these criticisms within the novel itself, through one of the characters (who might be, he assured me, "a reporter, someone who comes from outside, or one of the local people who lived through the events, but who has despaired of the word as an efficient instrument for persuasion"), a kind of matrix-commentary that would collect all the passionate hatred against those robots who descend on the people without trying to understand them. I agreed – without having read the novel – with his rejection of such a possibility, since if he hadn't succeeded in making his point of view clear through each report and its absence of humanity, then the novel was a failure.

"They may think I'm attacking the government," he told me, and something in his face clouded over.

"But it's a second volume," I answered, "and in *Interventions* you've already clearly established your position as being one of support and enthusiasm. Besides, you're active in your party, you've been with them every step of the way."

"They won't understand me."

Nonetheless he assured me that *Reports* was just as important a part of what's happening in Chile as *Interventions,* and that between the two of them they would form a counterpoint that might lead toward a third novel which would synthesize both points of view. That won't happen for a few more years, I thought to myself, when we know what this is all about, when we begin to ask ourselves what it was and how it was, when we have the time for analysis.

"Tell me something. If *Interventions* is the story of a working class victory, and if *Reports* is the story of a set-back, is it essential that this victory be narrated from the point of view of the people, and the set-back, from outside?

Or are there other methods?"

He didn't answer me. He started to explain that within *Reports* the desire of many officials to help was clear. Maybe he had loaded the dice too much against those who had written the reports. In the text, in declarations by the residents, in passing references from the lawyer who is to defend them, in certain insinuations within the police reports, one glimpses the way in which one could discover the truth and keep on advancing. But they're light bulbs that are tested for a moment to prove that it really was dark and then are put away again. Entangled in a language that overwhelms them, caught in a means of communication that already existed and before which they have no access to any kind of flexibility, both the narrators and (supposedly) the protagonists about whose story they are writing, experience remoteness as the daily perception of reality.

It's a sickness, a short circuit in the sun itself: there is a prison of words that dominates and invades the protagonists. That reality cannot be corrected, because no one has managed to understand it; misunderstandings pile up, as if autumn's fallen leaves were to be confused with an indication of spring.

More than the story of a search, *Reports* is the narrative of a process of concealment. The more they investigate, the more opaque the world becomes, the more the fleshy fullness of what happened becomes obscured. The more reports are written, the less is understood, and as they sense that occurring, people write still more reports, to see if they can, but they can't, every word hides more instead of uncovering. Again there are the images of autumn (the time of year when the events occurred): dry, withered, combustible leaves from an ancient tree that never dies. Reality - is that something which moves farther away the more we try to control it? Del Fierro looked at me, as if he had just realized that I had been listening to him. "It's like when you're talking to the woman you love and she doesn't understand

102

anything you're saying, and the more you try to fix it, the worse it gets. Do you understand? Is it possible that one book is just as true as the other? How is it possible that interventions can exist and then reports on those interventions? And is it possible to write reports on an event that will be a victory and interventions that tell of failure? Or is reality made precisely of the struggle between both forms of humanity, now and forever more?"

I didn't say anything to him. Why pontificate on the sense of the absurd and the struggle, bureaucracy and advance, the two edges of power, the masses inside the bourgeois apparatus, cold disintegration and the totality that constructs itself as it flows along? Del Fierro evidently thinks that his two novels perhaps go beyond the process in Chile and have touched bottom against the mystery of what a human being is.

"Do you suppose there's anyone," he asked me, "who will understand that I had to write both novels?"

Aquí Publishing Company, was my somewhat muffled answer, not loud enough for him to hear. So I take this opportunity to recommend the novel *Reports* to you for publication. Without having read it.

After all, why not have a little faith. Don't you agree?

Once again,
Alberto

Elena didn't leave; it was as if she had heard me. She descended like a mantle of serenity, something like a convent of light, and I could contemplate her hand now with complete tranquillity. I imagined all of her, part by part, and no longer heard all the noise from the others, only that hand existed there, without moving, with holy patience, between

103

my legs, caressing my hair, in my ass, but also between Juan's legs, standing so firmly there only a few feet from my glance and from that hand that was no longer mine. Elena didn't pursue me; I moved that hand of hers all through the universe, opening a can of peaches, paying the taxi, carefully putting the change in her purse, fingering a pill, a letter, another letter, a key, those hands always full of objects, and you too, Elena, were gradually recovering that moment when we were about to come together, covering your mouth when you coughed, scratching your knee, grabbing the chair when you played musical chairs, just to be sure it was yours, all those things that hands are good for, pulling your zipper down so that Juan could make love to you, and a slap in the face, or pulling a trigger, closing a door, tying a blindfold, catching someone else; and now she really did know everything I was thinking about, now that I no longer had to decide whether I was leaving with her or not and it made no difference if that wasn't the way it was, because I felt like she and her hand were with me, being born to the world and learning why this was so and why that was so, and this is hot, and you don't touch that, this hurts, that's soft, all the nerves and the metatarsus and the nails and all the other crap, Elena, don't go away, but don't come closer, don't say another word, don't move, do what I tell you, I'm just fine now, and for God's sake don't get Juan started now, and it was wonderful to understand that I didn't have the slightest chance of controlling that hand of Elena's, that she was there because she wanted to be, not because I demanded it, she went wherever she wanted, however she wanted, and tomorrow she might be here in my arms or she might have disappeared from my life and from her own life as well, me, so alone and in such good company, no one understood me and nevertheless we were all so close, I didn't know where mine was either nor where tomorrow would be or whom it would be with, probably with Karolina, so I didn't take it, Elena, simply because I was afraid, as clear and simple as

104

that, and perhaps in two more minutes I won't be afraid any longer, Elena, Karolina, Luis, leave me alone now, stay with me here, on your marks, ready, and I'll deal with that signal to "go" when I have to.

So it seemed completely natural when Luis commanded: "Go!" And everyone stopped playing and sat down in a circle, Luis's voice imitating Juan's, which was itself, no doubt, an imitation of some crazy circus clown: "Ladies and gentlemen, your attention, please - Tonight's last flight is about to leave. Answer me."

And, who knows by what twisted paths and games, we had all reached this point at the same instant, so I wasn't as alone as I had thought; everybody except Juan, that is, who did not sit down, who was still standing there with his finger on the trigger, as if they had locked him in a room, while from outside the voices of the other children reached him.

"Doggy and the bone. Doggy and the bone, let's play doggy and the bone" - but it was almost as if I couldn't remember exactly how the game went, and Luis seemed to have forgotten too - who knows?

We all found ourselves once again at that precise moment just before Juan planted his big, clown hands on his hips, when anything might happen, back to that moment when the night had slipped from our grasp, and somebody wanted to record us on a magnetic tape that wasn't ours. But Luis's voice was indeed ours, each one of us was a radio turned on in a house all night, transmitting the same football game that was heard in the next house as well as all the others, my radio, my ears, my lips, but the broadcast and the reception were everybody's; I was able to forget myself at last. And he wants to know if you have the bone.

"Me, sir?" said Elena, without moving, not even her hand.

"Yes, sir," said Luis.

"No, sir," said Elena, like a rolling thunderbolt of rustling wings, that was more or less the game, we'd almost forgotten, but it was something like that.

"Well, who has it then?" asked Luis. And how many kids were probably asking that same question, although at that time of night it was unlikely that any of them were still up. How many were probably repeating that question in their sleep, so we were in all likelihood the only idiots on the face of the earth that were playing this game, even though tomorrow would be Sunday, and then Monday while we worked all day and Tuesday, and meanwhile we were wondering who had the bone a little more, while they slept, maybe the question never stopped being asked in some part of Latin America, so they'd be playing at finding that bone again forever, or they'd be eternal cops, or nasty robbers, befuddled dogs, and it made no difference after all that we didn't remember the game exactly, that we'd forgotten how to play, where's the bone, here's the bone, where is it, here it is, where's the doggy; from the very beginning we had learned how to play well, and I guess every age has its game, and now Elena was answering:

"Tomás has it," and, with total glee, I realized that it wasn't true; that I didn't have it, and so I answered her with the only truth of that night:

"Me, sir?"

"Yes, sir," said Elena.

"No, sir," said I.

"Well who does have it then?"

"Karolina," I said, but she didn't have it either.

"Me, sir?"

"Yes, sir," I declared.

"No, sir."

"Well who does have it then?" I asked, and Karolina, sure of herself, hurled her accusation:

"The gringo."

So we went all the way around the circle like that, loving each other, completely absorbed in it; the game had all the grandeur and nostalgia of a waltz; it was an eternal mouth, and Juan was reduced to a dead tongue in the middle of our perfectly circular prattle, our ring of voices that were very careful not to mention him, never to accuse him, excluding him completely; Juan in the house where there was no radio or if there was, then they hadn't turned it on that night because they really weren't interested in the game or maybe the radio was being repaired or maybe his parents were quarrelling or couldn't decide which program to turn on, or guests were coming or they had fallen asleep early, but none of those reasons was true; Juan howling out beyond the wharfs, on a train that we now knew was going nowhere, incapable of pulling the trigger, impotent, a failure, a fraud, and all the while, me sir yes sir no sir was being chorused all around him, but he was deaf to the chant, blind to the shape of that bone; he couldn't remember the game; there we were pressing him, inviting him, asking him to accept what we had discovered, around and around without stopping, again and again, the wind can't decide to breathe through the leaves and the leaves can't decide to fall and the ground can't decide to receive them, and the rain can't decide to rot them, or the stream to wash them away; we had reached this point without consulting him and without a doubt it was going to reach a conclusion one day; we had gone back to the moment when this was possible, and the night no longer called itself Juan, it had all our names and none of our names, and Juan refused to play, maybe because he couldn't forget himself, Juan, come on, we told him, who has it, who has it, spinning around his head like birds flying out of a fresh, cool well in summer; he was the nest we no longer needed; how we must have sounded to him in the middle of that monstrous wheel of voices, thinking that maybe he still dominated us, that maybe he was still the silent and twisted center of our circumference, because we never asked him to speak, thinking, I made all this possible, always me, me, me, Juan, he wouldn't give in for anything, you were afraid, Juan, he refused to talk, and it didn't even matter any more whether he fired that pistol; we were going to be on his trail until he gave in, we were going to force him to join us, the way he had forced us, we were going to drive him out of the center and make his voice one more among many, as if the voices came first and then us; we just occupied them; I took Liliana's, the gringo took mine, Karolina took the one that belonged to Antonio, each of us occupied somebody else's body and yet kept our own, only Juan stood apart, around and around, from mouth to mouth, Pecosa said yes and Loreto said no, and somebody else said no, and another, then who has it, who, who, who could possibly have it; the whole group intertwined, found new combinations, I accused Luis, Luis accused Luciano, even Liliana, in her usual dry, definitive voice, a single throat on this night that was so much ours, me sir, no sir, until I thought Juan was going to explode, this was really it, he was going to speak, I have it, me, me, me, I have it, and then, I don't know why, I felt so sorry for him, yet I was mad at the same time, and I heard my voice answering Karolina:

"I have it. I have the bone."

A chorus of voices and laughter; the circle broke. That damned Tomás had it all the time.

Somebody plugged in the record player. Immediately we heard Paul's voice, Boy, you're going to carry that weight, carry that weight, a long time, everybody now going back to his own thing, becoming water for his own plant. Juan and Elena and I stayed there; Luis's wife went out to make some sandwiches, and from outside a gust of cool, early autumn air rushed in. Karolina came up and kissed me on the neck; she wrapped me in those two arms that were so warm and so much my own.

"Juan," I said.

Elena patted me affectionately too, on the cheek, like someone saying good-bye, but nothing had changed, absolutely nothing had changed between us. Just a pat as if she were reshaping my face.

"Juan," I said a little louder.

We were like that for a good while, Karolina like a little bunny nibbling on my neck, Elena leaning over a little, Juan with his eyes shut.

He finally opened them. "A great game, huh?" he asked, innocently and spontaneously, a note of relief in his voice. "We had a great time, right, kid? Right, Tomás?" He was smiling, pulling us all in with that radiant, satisfied smile.

So you weren't admitting anything; you could look me in the eye without a sign of pity or sadness. As if nothing had happened. In three years, who was going to remember that night? Who would be able to pull it up out of so many other memories as we built a free Chile? We'd have to start again, in a little while, like newborn babies, with infinite care, and maybe some day - I hoped it wouldn't be too late - you'd come into the circle, you'd say me sir, yes sir, no sir.

I had to talk to you; I was the only one who could.

"Let's go, Juan," I told you. "Let's go and talk, brother."

Mr Carlos Reyes
Production Manager
Avance Film Company

Dear Mr Reyes,

My friend, the novelist César Roccafitto, knowing that for the last year I've been working in your company's Filmscript Workshop, has asked me to offer you his work *Westar* as the basis for a film. I would work with Roccafitto on a rough draft of the script, since he's never written one.

Although I haven't the slightest doubt that you have read my friend's earlier work, *The Hero's Nightmare,* and are aware of the controversy it stirred among our most outstanding politicians and intellectuals, you probably haven't had the opportunity to examine *Westar* yet. In any case, this work can be considered an in-depth continuation of the germ of an idea that appeared in the character Renato Fardo's fourth nightmare.

The novel begins violently. A man, howling in pain, is running down a street typical of the American West. Several shots are fired at him, he suddenly dances in the whiplash of that sound and falls to the ground, twisting in agony. A cowboy approaches, and, contemptuously pushes his body over with his foot. We'd better be sure, he says. The cold, silver barrel of his pistol sparkles in the air. I'm going to kneel, says the cowboy. He does. He puts his gun against the fallen man's temple; the man doesn't move. If you don't want to pray, I'll do it for you. No, no, a woman screams. The cowboy hesitates and looks in the direction of the Jesse

110

James Saloon. The fallen man takes advantage of his distraction to grab the gun out of his hand and rapidly fire at him. We'll see who's going to get on his knees and who's going to pray, he says in a loud voice. He fires again; the cowboy doesn't move again.

Applause.

The faces of spectators.

The whole scene was merely the first part of a performance on a late September afternoon in 1971, at the New West World Amusement Park (modeled on Far West Town, in our Santiago suburb, Las Condes, but Roccafitto preferred to change the name because he didn't want his readers to get confused, thinking that he was narrating something that had really happened), a sad and under-developed replica of a small, cardboard North American town, one of those that we see in films or on TV. The novel covers the same time period as the show, from 2 until 7 p.m., four or five short dramatizations, separated by intermissions, during which a group of actors (dressed in rather moth-eaten cowboy outfits) present several typical plot-lines, with all the clichés and situations of the Old West that have been repeated on the world's movie screens for decades. As the theatrical piece unfolds (and in the novel the initial non-ironic realism is gradually abandoned, and is replaced by the kind of stock characters, slap-stick humor, and exaggerated, patch-work plots that are usual in such fiction), elements of real episodes from the American West are interpolated, sometimes just a few words, out of the blue, or sometimes certain resonances or coincidences, but presented just as they happened with all their violent brutality. Then, just as quickly, we are returned to the contemporary show at the exact point where we left it. In brief flashes, lightening-fast interruptions, in dialogues that strike us as palpably real and then fade, in descriptions that are harsh and dry, in moments of desperate intensity, the entire forgotten history of the West invades us with everything that is missing in the

111

parallel farce that is being acted out in Chile: Black cowboys; massive lay-offs; premature, isolated old-age of workers with no social security; the plundering of the Indians' lands; rampant alcoholism; worn-out miners; uncontrolled speculation; betrayal; and the venality of the law. The description of a hanging, minutely presented with almost masochistic delight. A prostitute, who after the departure of her last client at dawn, cannot go to sleep, cannot quiet the screaming pain in her thighs. The brutalized mind of a professional gunfighter, and the same fierce and torturous words in the heart of a sheriff. These creatures who must have existed once upon a time but who no longer exist anywhere slip through the cracks of shows that do not really present them; yet there they are, sadistic, confined, dreaming about an elusive fortune. The rage of those characters is born out of their impotence and their alienation, their transformation into parasites attached to scholarly historians, their double deaths (that most definitive of all deaths, Mr Reyes, omission). The more they cry out, the less the actors who are their supposed ambassadors pay attention to them. It's as if in the reality of their very lives, in that daily, soul-crushing routine of life in Montana or Texas or Arizona, they had sensed that nothing was going to be left for the future to remember.

If the novel consisted only of this juxta-contra-interposition, it would be only one more of many books that demonstrate the separation between reality and the pop fiction which pretends to represent it, but it would certainly not be an argument worthy of the author of *The Hero's Nightmare*. Because it turns out that those phantoms that have been betrayed by myth and later deformations, the ones that are known via Hollywood and cable TV, have unsuspected allies nowadays; they are not as alone as one might have believed. That show is put on by actors who have a real body, and that body occupies a very concrete place in time and space, that is, Santiago, Chile, September, 1971.

112

And, as we will see in the novel (and I hope in the film), while those actors, in their daily lives, repeat many of the presuppositions and the models of domination that they acted out in the performance, their immediate world has little to do with the Far West that they are portraying.

As the show unfolds, life in the amusement park, a government enterprise, also goes on. The teeming, partly frustrated, partly hopeful, existence of the workers (actors, carpenters, gophers, ticket sellers, electricians, mechanics, cooks, candy and soft drink vendors, prop managers, special effects specialists, bartenders, etc.), becomes intermixed with the action, flowing through the cracks and the pauses in the presentation, and soon begins to establish itself as the novel's primary focus of interest and of irony - because these poor workers mired in tremendous problems are the ones who must now propagate the false legends that eradicate the true story of their exploited and defeated first cousins of long ago. These cowboys, saloon girls, prospectors, as soon as they have finished playing their parts as Old Billy or Suzanne are revealed as who they really always were - Pedro Segura and María Neculman, and any one of them may be living with nine brothers and sisters, a mother, a father and a grandmother in a shanty-town (called Che Guevara) which is no more than a mile from New West World. With their physique, their gestures, their everyday dilemmas, their peculiarities, they crack the Myth of the West wide open, step by step, revealing the truth of a Chile which is putting on the false face of the United States, the pain of a Chile being made up with the vague and falsetto cries of Billy el Muchacho, the underdevelopment of Chile parodied by the overdevelopment of a West that never existed. But at the same time, of course, we realize that the dreams of many of these Chileans are couched in terms similar to those of the show's invented characters, that their lives are also being scripted for them from some collective unconsciousness.

The irony of that situation is not left for the readers (or

113

spectators) to decipher on their own: they are given a perspective on it by the main actor (do we dare call him the protagonist?) of the novel, Gallardo Stewart, a journalist who is acting as the government's intervener now that the original owners have abandoned the enterprise - and the country. His university studies have shown him how perversely the minds of underdeveloped peoples have been shaped by the media and by myths imported from abroad, how entertainment reinforces a competitive, violent society. These theories make him feel that the New West World show he is organizing, and, in fact, helping to script, is reinforcing the political and cultural power of Chile's oligarchy.

His burning desire, therefore, is to put an end to these shows. The reader suspects that it may be his mind, which at times can be read easily, but at other times remains mysteriously closed, that is the source of all those real Western situations which comment upon the New West World with such bitterness. But Stewart has been put there by the Labor Ministry to pull the enterprise out of bankruptcy. He knows that any radical change in the content of the performances would reduce the public even more and destroy the company. His main task is to boost income and to demonstrate to multiple creditors that the workers can bring it off without the boss. Nor can he save that amusement park by firing workers: "If we sink, we'll all go down together."

The central tension of the novel derives from the clash between the need to continue the show and the guilt and discomfort he feels by doing so, betraying his convictions. A dilemma which is at the heart of the Chilean revolution: how to use old structures to build something new.

The struggle between these two interests, and his subordination of his desire for a real cultural revolution to the compelling, unavoidable need to keep this business afloat, is never fully resolved. He is overwhelmed by the idea that he is, in the long run, betraying the revolution, mortgaging the people's conscience (that of the actors as much as that of the audience), especially when it becomes known that many of the values and techniques that dominate the show are the same ones that the workers project on to their personal and family relations. Paternalistic formulas. Machismo. Sanctions based on capitalist ethics. Love as the single solution to all problems. Preachy, empty moralism. Competitive drive. It is clear that this ideological domination is not absolute and that the workers are something (a lot) more than the monkey-like imitations of middle-class cultural models. This often leads to a poor understanding of the company's problems and to subtle forms of exploitation, the traps that still lie ahead on the road to liberation.

But more than teaching, Gallardo is really learning the values of solidarity and of interdependence, and he is acquiring a certain discipline which he lacked, as well as a willingness for sacrifice without complaint; he is learning to measure each and every path because hunger and lay-offs may lie at the end of any one of them; he is learning to place his own dreams within the context of what is possible (what is possible and a little bit more, he has told his wife), and to appreciate how far his university training was from everyday practice.

Gallardo is a dynamo, a veritable whirlwind of initiatives and orders and suggestions, who tries to solve problems along with the members of the production committee. He turns up everywhere, a band-aid for every scratch: Did the ice cream order come through? What happened to the brown paint? Adela always replaces Lucy in the kitchen. Enough of this, both of you, you're fighting like kids. Fire your bullets in the show, but not here with your co-workers. This feverish activity, with brief respites for cautious and even ironic observations, as if he were suddenly seeing himself in action, photographing himself, along with a scattering of memories and doubts, have made him indispensable, with the result that he has assumed far too much power within the company. His efficiency, his dedication, his unlimited enthusiasm, are undeniable, but it is also how he goes on, day after day, affirming the values of paternalism that he would like to deny, the ones that he despises when he sees them portrayed in the show. He is, in fact, not allowing the workers to assimilate the process of liberation on their own; he is controlling them too much; he has imposed strict limitations on them; he is doling out freedom to them (unconsciously and for their own good).

Unlike other novels that begin or end with the crisis, this one manages only to give us a glimpse of it, to suggest that it lies ahead, like some long-expected outlaw in a peaceful Nevada town. The situation cannot go on that way. There are small signs scattered along the road to the future, beacons signalling rocks that will soon rise out of the sea, rocks that Stewart does not see, but which the readers already sense.

It's true that this insistence on monopolizing the power within the company responds to demands made by the workers themselves, to a vacuum left by the old management, but it is reinforced by character weaknesses in the journalist, who was always overly individualistic, arrogant and intransigent.

In the novel Gallardo is surrounded by a series of characters who both reflect and deepen his personal drama and provide the kind of multiple perspectives that we have come to expect from the creator of *The Hero's Nightmares*.

One of these is his boss at the Labor Ministry, a man with neatly programmatic criteria, a "businessman" within the revolution: "You've got this baby here," he told me. "Either you make it grow or it's going to go to hell, it'll be a mongoloid, a cretin, or a dwarf forever. There's no way in hell that we can subsidize it. Do you understand? You not only have to pull it out of this slump, but you've also got to begin to pay the debts left by the last damned fool manager.

That's why we're sending you, a journalist. Not just one of these fellows who can keep accounts and organize, write and think. But somebody who'll look for ways to draw a bigger audience. Ideas. Ideas. Ideas. . . How did the Ministry get involved with this mess? What would you like us to have done? Throw 50 top-notch workers out on the street, disillusioned and cast aside without severance pay? So you stop analyzing newspapers, publishing bulletins, organizing press conferences, arguing with other coordinators; you stop screwing around and you concentrate on saving that company. I don't care how you do it. You just do it." I don't care how you do it.

The first thing Gallardo did, to ease his conscience, was to mount a publicity campaign aimed at high-income people. But that can't be the solution; it will raise income on Saturdays and Sundays, but the real problem is what to do on those empty weekdays. He realized a long time ago that the only way to produce earnings is to make agreements with the trade unions, with the Education Ministry, with certain municipalities and with taxi drivers. But that really does mean to go on poisoning the minds of "innocent" spectators, and spreading the ideological message to a broader spectrum of the population. The one who is most opposed to this policy is a friend who works in the Cultural Department of the Tourism Development Agency and who has been bitterly criticizing him and refusing to collaborate.

"What you have to do is bear the economic losses, and transform that business into a constant denunciation of the Myth of the Old West . . .

"Sure it'll go badly at first, but once you can draw the public inside and take their problems and opinions into account, things will take off again. Because you'll offer an alternative, understand? Don't go in and play the game by the rules of the middle-class cultural marketplace. Of course there's risk involved, but you can't keep on with the same old policies, the same old scripts. That's what Roy Rogers

117

and the Saturday TV line-up are for."

"Good idea," he told his friend. "We can offer the set free for a Saturday program. Good advertisement for the place."

Nevertheless, I found myself using Jorge's words with Hernán, and pulling out Hernán's arguments to persuade Jorge. I was the pretext for them to carry on a dialogue without meeting once.

And while he is becoming a battle ground, coming up with a different kind of theatrical work in his head, balancing expenditures and income, educating the workers about the bloody conquest of Chile, definitively consolidating the business in his own hands while the audience shrinks, especially in "this disastrous, rainy spring", time slips by, and it is an afternoon in September when everything promises to explode at last, "when everything is postponed again until the next day or the next weekend."

The novel's other characters are rather secondary, but in a film, their importance should increase. Stewart's wife, for example. Ignorant, apprehensive, short-tempered, witnessing a change that she doesn't share in, she believes that Gallardo is wasting his time, that he was made for better things (like carrying on television research or helping form a centralized propaganda center for the Allende coalition).

"If this was a real revolution, maybe I could understand you. I'd even go with you in search of gold in California or to kill Indians on the frontier. But here you are sacrificing yourself and screwing up your children's lives, and we never see each other, and all for a process that's going nowhere. OK, if you want to go down the drain, fine, but you do it alone, because as far as I'm concerned. . . "

If we do make the film, we want to work on this character a lot more, maybe even give her a rival, perhaps one of the cashiers in the park, to whom he feels drawn, but who is also an easy and false temptation, because this admiration, almost adoration, doesn't really affect his existence, doesn't bring into question the true foundations of his life; it just reinforces the domineering traits of his personality.

Some of the other characters are Gallardo's children, a pair of devilish twins who came to the show that very afternoon. They're always playing cowboys, since they've already absorbed from the television screen the law of violence that reigns supreme in the world, and the journalist sadly notes that he hasn't been able to do anything, not even in his own household, to pull away from those old role models.

"Don't worry," Jorge tells me. "At least you're getting rid of all that extra money that's floating around. That's the main thing, the most patriotic thing you can do. You're taking money from a pocket that otherwise would be emptied on the black market. Look, little by little you can change the focus of the show, without people even realizing it; you extend it to such-and-such a labor union and ask their opinion; you get advice from the Maintenance Department, you open up picnic areas, install a toboggan, stick in some authentic Indian weavings that people can compare with Chilean cloth; that way, if you're just patient, you can make a go of it, OK, friend?" He winks his eye, I would swear he did. "You rely on middle-class consumerism, you sell balloons, bring in authentic cacti from Texas for sale, organize a costume day, show films at night, inaugurate a smorgasbord. You'll be a hit, man. You can't fail."

Live broadcasts, songfests, a drive-in, a strip-joint with a cowboy motif; the next thing you know, we'll all go out at night and paint a wall, announcing the joys of NEW WEST WORLD, instead of writing POWER TO THE PEOPLE.

Anyhow, a few changes should be made for the film. One that Roccafitto suggests, is to have two managers sent from the Ministry of Labor, representing the two points of view inside the head of Gallardo Stewart himself, which are two fundamentally different (almost strategic) lines within the

119

revolution we're living. This confrontation would provide greater coherence and more action in the conflict. The most serious problem we face in translating it to the film medium is, above all, the matter of unity, especially in those interferences from the real past of the Old West. We wanted to film those segments in color and the others in black and white, but that remains to be decided. We'd also broaden the view of the park workers' lives a little. It's clear that the phantasmagoric character they have in the novel should be changed. Roccafitto understands, to be sure, that his personal obsessions about "The echo in the mud", as he calls that part of the story, have no reason to dominate the filming.

I can't close, Mr Reyes, without first detailing some of the advantages of filming the story. Above all, cost. Except for the main character (characters), we can use the personnel of the Far West Town in Los Condes (that would solve a financial problem for them, a plan that certainly didn't occur to the real intervener "whom I haven't had the pleasure of meeting," Roccafitto told me). The same thing applies to the movie set. No doubt the most serious problems would arise in those scenes where the real characters of the Old West would shine through, but we think that two or three weeks in La Serena or Copiapó could solve that problem. We'd even have all our props at hand there. And the filmscript has the advantage of being based on a novel that will surely be as famous as *The Hero's Nightmares.*

With nothing further to add now, I look forward to hearing from you as to when we can meet to discuss deadlines, terms, and possibilities.

Sincerely,
Juan Menguant

120

Dear Mr Menguant,

Mr Carlos Reyes has carefully examined your letter with regard to the novel *Westar.* Unfortunately, he feels that Avance Film Company is not at present in a position to finance the film. Although he will write you himself within a few days, explaining the reasons that have led him to this conclusion, he asked me to send you two reports published in *El Mercurio,* on the sixteenth and the seventeenth of November 1972. You will find them attached as Appendix 1 and Appendix 2 to this letter.

Don Carlos has also asked me to communicate both to you and to Mr Roccafitto his sincere willingness to continue discussions and to hear any suggestions you may have that would lead to an agreement.

Sincerely,
Ruth Azócar
Administrative Secretary to the
Director of Production
Avance Film Company

APPENDIX I
EL MERCURIO, NOV. 16, 1972

FAR WEST TO BE SOLD AT AUCTION

"Far West Town" will become a ghost town today when all its equipment and installations are sold at public auction. Some time ago, the employees of this picturesque little town took over the administration of the business, but lack of capital has obliged them to shut down the entertainment enterprise.

A total of 250 items, among which are included harnesses, saddles, century-old carriages, imitation antique lamps, and cots, along with modern pick-ups, amplifiers, loudspeakers, dishwashers, etc., were appraised and placed on sale to the highest bidder.

Far West Town opened in December 1969, the brainchild of

eight creative associates who formed Tourist Company, Inc. Their intent was to imitate an American Old West town with actors who would simulate cowboys, Indians, gunfighters and all the other legendary characters from the period of westward expansion in the United States. At first the idea stirred up a lot of interest, but in a short time conflicts of a financial nature arose and payroll obligations were no longer being met.

The first intervener who was sent in was unable to salvage the business and after three months he left the country. At that point Carlos Carrión assumed the direction of the company. He explained that his first concern was to put wages and salaries on a firm footing, but the business was operating at an annual deficit of 350 million pesos.

"With what we were bringing in, we could pay salaries and overheads, but there was just no way to pay off the immense debt that had accumulated," Carrión pointed out. Added to all this was a pile of payment demands that were not accepted by the intervener and the conflict was resolved in a manner favorable to the workers. This situation led to the presence of the auctioneer charged with assessing the value of anything that could be sold to meet the payment demands.

Last Sunday the final show, replete with sheriffs, redskins, cowboys and gunfighters, took place. Afterward, they retired sadly to their dressing rooms. Osvaldo Sepúlveda, with sadness in his voice, stated that three years of labor in entertaining adults and children had just come to an end.

APPENDIX 2
EL MERCURIO, NOV. 17, 1972

FAR WEST TOWN SOLD AT AUCTION
(Dramatic End for the Picturesque Town)

Far West Town ceased being a fantasy village and confronted a dramatic reality when the auctioneer's hammer fell today to mark the beginning of the public sale of its equipment.

All those present were adults looking for a bargain among the 250 items up for bid. These included everything from the horses used by the Indians to the refrigerators from the nightclubs that operated inside the park.

The mood among the workers was tragic. Ernesto Gutiérrez,

one of the actors, publicly requested that they not sell the horses that were the tools of their trade. "We've worked here to entertain others," he said, with tears in his eyes, "so now I'm asking you this favor."

He has ten minutes before he turns in the film.

But I don't budge. It's better to remain silent, here in the shadows.

Before, he would have taken advantage of every second. When it was Juan's shift at the all-day movie house, I would run from cinema to cinema pressing that reel to me as if it were a motor that gave me the energy to get there on time, leaping over obstacles like a horse; I'd run up the stairs two at a time, throw the door open without slamming it and beg Juan to let me see the end of the film that was running at that moment, and also, please, the beginning of the one that I had just brought in so far ahead of time.

"I bet you don't know what happened to that cowboy," said Juan, while he lined up the second projector for the change of reel.

He really didn't know what . . .

Héctor Remate explained that the auction had to take place. "We had no other way out. This way we can take in about nine million pesos that will have to be used to pay overheads and salaries, with some left over for our creditors."

Meanwhile, the auctioneer moved from the Jesse James Saloon to the other buildings, taking bids for bookcases, knick-knacks, lamps, mirrors, chairs, dishwashers, saddles, wine, foodstuffs, etc.

The land on which Far West Town stands was rented by a Mr Yenkis, along with some of the buildings that were renovated to make them look like a western town. Everything else was done with stage props. Although the workers said they were more united than ever, they were all aware that this was the end of a three-year dream.

. . . had happened. He didn't have the remotest idea. He was a cowboy marooned at the top of a high mountain, in burning heat, besieged by his pursuers. It was his last refuge on the face of the earth. At that moment he had heard Juan's voice interrupting: "You have to go; you have to deliver the other reel." And in the trajectory between the other three theaters, delivering and receiving the films, his imagination formed questions and answers, alternatives, predictions, and an overall sense of despair about how that cowboy could have gotten away and where he might be now.

"Go on, go on," Juan nudged him. "Take a look at it."

The seats lay before him down below, full or empty, depending on the time, like a dead man, without so much as a whisper, and above the audience's dark and adoring silence was the screen. Its images, voices and colors sucked at him until he thought he would be pulled out of the projection booth, float down and land in one of the seats below him. Of course the scenes were always the same, the segments he caught fleetingly were repeated throughout the week. She approached him, her eyes soft and limpid, and then she drew him into a field of very high wheat. The camera would focus first on her dress, and then a man's hand on the buttons, and now a soft voice, it wasn't clear if it was a man's or a woman's. A bird flew overhead. Suddenly the man slapped her cheek.

"Traitor," he said in English, and on the screen below you could read the words, "me traicionaste."

At that moment, Juan always had the other reel of the film ready.

"Hurry, you're going to be late." And before he left: "And if you're late, they'll know that you're watching the film; they'll catch us."

"I could be late for some other reason."

"Whenever the one carrying the film is late, it's always because he's watching it," said Juan. "That's what rules are for."

A sign on the door: Entry prohibited to all theater personnel.

124

One day I asked him if the owner wouldn't punish him if he found out he was letting me watch, that we weren't giving a shit about the rules.

"Cereceda?" Juan laughed. "Look, kid, I may not be able to use my legs, but I'm a real man in my own way. I'm not afraid of anybody, and especially not of Cereceda." And then he added under his breath: "Besides, I've got influence."

I looked at him, astonished.

"Yeah, yeah. It's true. You'll see, one of these days. I'll do you a favor and you'll see. So hurry it up."

Today's Monday. They're showing a new one. He has only ten minutes. But it makes no sense to hurry. He's over there, in the entrance to that alley, in the shadow of that building. He's lying down, on top of the reel, pressing it into the sidewalk with the weight of his body, waiting for his watch to indicate there's only five minutes left.

He never used a watch before; he didn't need one.

"You're punctual," said the voice of Cereceda, behind the window of the ticket office. He could see only his hands putting rubber bands around the bundles of fresh, new, lettuce-green bills. It was that same morning. "The company can depend on you."

"I do what I can."

"False, false, false. Absolutely false," sings Cereceda's voice, his fingers nervously tapping on the money. "Completely false. You do more than you can. A lot more."

Wait for five minutes to go by. Leave just enough time. Just enough to get there on time, just enough time for the new projectionist, the one who replaced Juan, to get hysterical. There's nothing to do, sitting there like that, in the extending shadows: stare at the cement, watch the shadows grow, see the sour, lined faces passing by on the street without looking into the alley. Then, when there's only five minutes left, stand up and go in the side door, slowly climb the staircase, counting them one by one, count the faces that pass by, up to the third floor and see the face of that guy Diego, waiting, furious. He'll take the reel and close the door; the sign on the door says "Entry prohibited." Down below, in the auditorium, there is a rumble of voices speaking English. There's a shot; the music becomes more intense. He can feel the audience's tension, like goose-flesh.

But I don't know what's happening, what it is that's spilling across the screen. Inside, Diego can see the film as many times as he wants, changing the projector slowly while he glances at the action from time to time, but here I am outside, with the door closed, until he decides to open it again and hand me the reel he just showed, which I have just not seen, and he'll lay something heavy on me, something nasty, something about Juan.

"I bet you can't guess who the killer is," Juan used to say, kidding me. "I'm not going to tell you."

"Don't tell me. I'm going to guess." And I pressed my eye against the hole in the wall, like a peeping tom watching sex. I see a profile, it's white and fades now into the heavy London fog. "That's the one. It's him."

Juan looks too. "I don't see anything."

"You missed it."

"You show me the next time, and I'll tell you." He finishes changing the reel and gives me the old one. "Hurry. You'll be late."

And the next time, there'll be both of us watching that eclipsed moon face there in the fog. "No, man. No. Of course not. What an idea! He's not the one."

"He has to be the one."

"Keep on thinking, OK, and come back Sunday, like you always do, and I'll let you see the end. How's that?"

It's Sunday night. The last show of the week, when I handed Juan the last reel, soft, round, smooth as silk. The other movies had all ended and Juan was putting the last reel in place. "Now you're going to see who the killer is. You're not going to believe it, you know. And he sat back like a real big man to see the end of the film that he'd been carrying through the streets every day, Monday, Tuesday, Wednesday, Thursday, Friday, Saturday and today, Sunday, imagining sequences, piecing together gestures and words, because Juan never told him what happened in the parts he missed, when he was running back and forth between theaters.

It was all part of the game, that I never see the whole film. Just the end, and that only once.

Mondays were special days. A new film started. Besides, it was pay-day and Cereceda paid everyone early, in the morning, using the money taken in over the weekend.

"One by one. That way I get to know everybody. By name. Then everybody's happy. Just one big happy family."

And he was happy too, because the night before the film had turned out just the way he had been imagining it all week. The images corresponded to the ones he had invented, running from theater to theater, right down to the last detail.

"You're getting too smart," Juan told him. "You guess too well. We'll have to cut your time. Or show you a different sequence."

It was Monday. He had hurried more than usual; he went in without knocking on the door as he always did and didn't even greet Juan, who was usually lying down, smoking, his crutches leaning against the wall, his cigarette smoke mixing with the blue-gray haze that rose from the projector. He put the reel on the table and his eye to the hole in the wall. A pair of lips.

"I know you," he read the words being spoken by the face that dominated the screen. "You hid," he read, "but you squealed on the others. You're really responsible. . . " He

127

read on: "Finally. The last one." And the camera focused on a whip. Before it focused on the other person, the one responsible, he felt a sudden tremor. A heavy hand fell on his shoulder, and forced him to turn around, away from the action on the screen.

He shook me.

"What the hell do you think you're doing anyhow? Huh?" It wasn't Juan's voice either.

How am I going to forget that moment, when, for the first time, I saw Diego.

He couldn't find the words. That was his film, how could he explain it, he had defended it on the streets, against pedestrians, traffic lights and bicycles; he had protected it when he was sweating from the heat or when it was raining cats and dogs, and against all the pushing, shoving people, a solid wall of arms and bellies, slipping precisely and mathematically through the only opening in order to dance between cars with the red light howling at him, and the mother-fucking drivers yelling, do you want to die, ass-hole, the film pressed tenderly, gently and softly between his fingers, not letting go of it for even an instant, crossing the square, past the glassy-eyed terror of pigeons, taking advantage of that incredible moment when you can cross diagonally from corner to corner while the traffic is about to move or has just passed by, almost knocking down the peanut vendor on Ahumada y Compañía Street, taking the shortcut through the underpass, taking the Western railroad tunnels, just to get there on time, to get there a little early and see what secret things were happening there inside, inside the reel, inside the theater, inside the eyes of the public. He had been charged with a mission that was not especially difficult, but it was his, to hand the treasure over to the appropriate hands, and give up his life in the process if necessary.

"You do the work of two," said Cereceda.

Always at the exact moment, at the agreed time, without fail, he deposited the gold so many times each day, like a good stagecoach, or the king's messenger, a speeding bullet, an arrow shot straight to the apple's heart, a kiss on the lips, again and again, the same scene, but with other obstacles in the streets, other and different pedestrians blocking his passage, requiring new efforts, shortcuts, detours, decisions and ideas, so the images would go on one after the other like an eternal, infinite, rotating, joyous waterfall, a film that was shown continually in four theaters while he ran, back and forth, with four motionless projectionists, Juan and three others, waiting for him to arrive, so the show could go on for another forty minutes, a world of action, love, danger, that never ended.

How could he be made to understand? If I failed, the audience would start to stamp their feet and then they'd bang their chairs. They'd protest; they'd ask for their money back. Anyhow, that's how he'd heard they behaved, because no such thing had ever really happened in their theaters. Cereceda emphasized that in all his advertising. Mr Movie Viewer. You're the King in our theaters. You can enter with the utmost confidence. Here we never interrupt the dramatic illusion.

And all that depended on his feet, much more than on the technical skill of the projectionists. He couldn't find the words to describe how he had to run, Mr Cereceda's four theaters were scattered all over the downtown area; he really had to hurry, especially if he wanted to watch a few, short, delicious minutes, just enough, to see the fragments that Juan let him see, if he wanted to catch the film, bit by bit, always the same fragments, just so he could have some idea

129

of what he was carrying around so efficiently - he didn't know that word - from one projection booth to another, from one Kodak projector to another; he had a right to those strong, multicolored clips, those tiny fragments stolen with bated breath and open mouth; he had to keep running.

"Don't thank me," Juan used to say. "I do it out of self-interest too. I mean if you don't get to watch a little, you'll stop hurrying. I do it for the good of the company. You work better that way." And then he'd kid him. "You see, I'm the boss's son."

He wasn't greedy. He didn't try to see it several times. Not even from beginning to end. Just to submerge himself in those eternally repeated fragments, with Juan's hand resting peacefully on his shoulder telling him it was time to take the other reel, and the end, to know how all this mad rhythm had ended up, all those actions and reactions, all that mystery, just to see the clips, the pieces they owed him, even though he couldn't really explain precisely why; it was like a loan, part of his salary, against the rules but still part of his job and his pay; he was satisfied with that: later he could fill in the immense gaps that opened up from one episode to the other, every forty minutes, imagining them as he ran through the streets, almost caressing and talking to the reel, imagining motives, faces, all the unknown and hidden misfortunes and joys that he was carrying under his arm without ever being able to see them. Galloping through the streets, taking a shortcut through the Petrizzio Pharmacy to gain a couple of seconds, stepping off the curb with motorcycles almost grazing his rear-end and jumping back just in time to miss a Pila Cemetery bus, crossing the street to avoid the crowd inside the Café Haiti, getting to know every nook and cranny of the city, always afraid of some ambush, a surprise, a crowd flowing out of Falabella or some other movie house where they did cut the films or where it was no fun because it was opening exclusively there, and there were no copies to be rushed somewhere else, always

130

mixing up the scenes, guessing what was coming before and after, moving faster to try to catch a few more snatches of the film, so he could put together a better idea of what was happening in there as well as in the four theaters at the same time, repeating the basic melody again and again like a backdrop, muted trumpets when the scene is threatening, cellos, violins and sometimes flutes for love scenes, he never got the movies mixed up, even though they were always action films and had the same gringo actors, all alike, but he kept them strictly separated, from Monday to Sunday, filed in his memory so he could tell the neighborhood kids all about them late Sunday night, but that's not what he wanted to tell Diego. And he didn't want to tell him what could have happened to that cowboy either. Not even to ask if they were going to be able to get the message back to the fort before the Indians finished them off. Would the act of revenge take place? Every gesture, every inflection of voice, every rise in the tone of the music, was registered there inside, and he would project them again, the caresses, the brutal, male fights, a giving and receiving face, and at the end of the week, that blessed Sunday. That wasn't what he wanted to explain, and couldn't, to Diego.

Juan let me see the end.

Not the whole film. Just the end. That was the main bit. That night, with his friends, he would invent the rest, reconstructing it whole in his mind. "Tell us what you saw this week," they would say. And then with abundance of detail, where he could, smoothing over missing links, adding characters, leaving out or adding scenes he hadn't seen, cutting out characters, imitating American accents, playing the roles of all the characters, but especially of the hero, who was always tall, blond, handsome, a real expert on women and guns, translating for his small audience, he would gradually give birth to that week's outstanding film.

"What happened to Juan?"

"Juan who?"

That voice, so like his own, but somehow different, ought to go back to its normal tone.

"Juan. Juan, the one that works here."

"Nobody named Juan works here. I'm the one that works here."

"Where's Juan?"

"Diego. My name's Diego."

"Juan was here last night. What happened to him?"

"You must be the delivery boy."

How could he explain it to him?

Cereceda's fingers stopped tapping.

"The company's very pleased with your work."

He couldn't see the face, but in the middle of the black curtain in the ticket booth, there was a small hole and through it he could just glimpse an eye, only a bit of an eye that seemed to change color, that never stayed the same. Cereceda could see him as much as he wanted.

"You're much more than a delivery boy. You're bright and strong, and a quick learner. I'm not just trying to flatter you. I really mean it."

"Juan was here last night. Is he sick?"

"I don't know this Juan you're talking about. Give me the film."

Juan told me there's a new one, that I should get here as fast as possible because there's a new one. That's what he told me last night."

"Stop fooling around. That Juan of yours left, disappeared, died. Yeah, that's it, dead. How the hell should I know where he is. Got it? The end. Basta. Give it to me."

132

I didn't say anything to him. He was big, a lot bigger than Juan, and young, and both legs were healthy and whole and firm.

"I can't run, kid," Juan had told him. "They mashed my legs to a pulp. I'll tell you about it someday." He tapped one of his thighs. "You've got some real muscles there, kid. I'd like to see you run someday. You could run in the Olympics."

"Go on out. Wait for me."

I gave him the reel. I didn't want to move. The whole thing seemed like a nightmare. I was caught up in a bad film and I couldn't get out. There was no way out.

"Look, ass-hole, are you deaf or something? Wait outside. I'll give the other reel to you." And he gave me a shove, a big one. "After that you move out."

I walked toward the door and before going out, I said to him:

"Juan let me watch. We were friends."

He didn't answer. He didn't even look at me.

He heard a voice down below, screaming; it was blood-curdling, piercing; it shook the building. Some implacable act of revenge or maybe an injustice that would be rectified during the rest of the film, the beginning or the end, and there he was, motionless, nailed to the floor, like a damned paralytic, while down below the audience devoured the screen without budging from their seats, galloping across broad vistas and embracing beautiful bodies. He stood there, watching him get the machine ready to change the reel, waiting for a miracle, like the time they left Tony Curtis for dead in a cave filled with snakes and he turned up years later, or the one about the one-armed man, hoping that when Diego turned around he'd have a big smile on his face,

133

he'd give him a hug and it would be Juan, Juan without the paralysis, Juan, hale and hearty standing on both legs, as fresh as you please, like when he was in those barroom brawls in the West or in France; he hoped that Diego would really be Juan, look, kid, it's a miracle, look at my legs, they operated last night, what a surprise, huh?, and then a big hug, and come along, come along, see what's happening, this is a new one, today's Monday, and he wouldn't be able to look at him enough, licking the darkness with his eyes.

Again, that voice needs to get back to a more relaxed tone, more like itself. It's not good to get so overwrought.

Without turning around, Diego said:

"Shit. Look, for Christ's sake, I like to work alone."

He remembered the other three projectionists, in their little booths; they said things like that too; they were all the same. All except Juan. They were all the same.

"I'm not going to be anybody's baby-sitter, not for what they pay me. Do you get it? Or do you think this machine is an air conditioner." Still without looking at him, still placing the reel, skilfully, a lot more carefully than Juan, no rancor in his voice, just indifference. "But, you know, I like this job, and you know why I like it?"

I don't know why he likes it.

"Because I can be by myself and there's nobody to screw me up. That's what the rules are for. The rules protect me. So I don't want to see your face in here. You give me the film, you stay outside, I hand you the other one, and you scram and bring me back a new one. Got it . . . ? And if you don't like it, then you can quit. There's a thousand more where you came from who can do the job. People are lined up looking for jobs.

"You're not the boss," I told him, but he'd already slammed the door shut. From outside the door I said to him: "I'm going to tell Mr Cereceda."

134

At night, before falling asleep, with his feet swollen and his sneakers falling apart under his cot, his mind would go on spinning like a carousel, filled with faces, building bridges between one scene and another, a face would appear, fill the screen and the next time it appeared, it would be identical or different, or it would simply disappear forever, swallowed up mysteriously by the action during those minutes he had missed; and with all those pieces he would construct a great pictorial wall, one that was completely stationary, motionless and silent, like the theater itself, while he, who by now was sleeping, ran in circles around the room, looking for the door through which he had entered. When he would awake, he would have several different ideas and sequences representing the parts of the films he had missed, and he would take those ideas to Juan.

"That's not bad. You're improving. Your damned imagination's getting better. In a little while all you'll need is a glimpse to be able to tell me the whole story. You won't even need to watch the film anymore."

And he'd run faster to be able to enjoy a few more minutes of that celluloid tape that was imprisoned in the metal case underneath his arm, trotting from theater to theater, with that film within his grasp, yet needing a projector to reveal itself, grabbing a sandwich in one of those businesses on the Square as he passed by, a tall, silver-haired Texan, because that new film always awaited him on Mondays, and the end of the old one on Sundays, and those conversations with Juan and later with his friends; so he had to be the fastest guy in the city, suntanned, and always gazing into the trees, his hair blending with the sunset, moving along almost effortlessly, crossing himself in front of the Cathedral, and not stopping to hear what the fools in front of the Union Club had to say, pressing that film against skin that was soft and tenuous, hair blowing violently, almost passionately against his face, but not tickling his lips, no sweat dripping down his thighs, his breath coming easily, until he knew what was going to happen, until he could guess everything that was happening in those four theaters, without having to be there either as a spectator or projectionist; he ran on that way, through the streets, in the desert, on the decks of a pirate ship, running down Estado Street, like a submarine, until by nightfall, he had guessed what would take place, point by point, image by image, down to the last musical note; he saw a sheriff in every policeman, a cactus in every window dummy; he ran on, spinning around inside the projector lens, down Estado, to hand over the reel just in the nick of time and thus save the day; then it'd be back up Huérfanos, which was being repaired, so the whole street was his, no cars.

"That happens to some people," said Juan, at night, later. "But most people get bored. Like me. It'd be good if I didn't have to watch anymore; I've seen so many. I'd like to go somewhere else. But this is the only thing I'm good for."

Besides, they gave him a room to sleep in; he was a sort of night watchman. That was convenient; he never had to go out. He hated the city. There was no place to go.

When the door opened, he asked:
"Is Juan going to be sick long?"
Diego handed him the other reel. "I'll ask Cereceda."

And when I came back to bring him the next reel, he was waiting outside. He didn't even let me in. He whispered:
"I asked him. He says you're crazy. He says stop screwing around. They never hired anybody named Juan. You're crazy from watching so many movies."

And when I came back the next time, he was waiting by the stairway. Inside the booth I could see the way the moths fluttered around the projector light, like crazy people in an asylum. "That Juan of yours. I've been asking around. . . . It

136

looks like the police showed up last night and put him in jail. They got him for being a notorious fag. He went out at night corrupting minors, hung around waiting for them after the shows.

"He let you in, huh?"

"They paid you today," he told him, when he brought the other reel. "Why don't you buy a little gift for your friend the fag? What's his name? Juan? Yeah, for Juan. Just in case you didn't know it, he's in jail. I'm just letting you know. It seems that somebody turned him in."

And later: "They fired him because he was an invalid. They don't want invalids around here. A new rule."

"They say that somebody pushed him downstairs last night. Somebody who thought he was a real he-man. He shit all over the floor. They're looking for the killer."

The next reel.
"They're going to call you in to file a report. You're his little friend, right?"

"I was real old," Juan murmured. "They offered me this job. I was tired of what I'd been doing before. So I accepted. They pay me better and I have a place to sleep. We could be good friends, you and me. I'll show you how to work the machine."

Diego, always there in the door frame; and the reel that came and went; it always seemed like the same one, but it wasn't; and the same words; and always the same time to hand it over, and the same street; but there's no hurry now.

And Diego told him, while downstairs he could hear the crowd breathing, as he was climbing the stairs, while the film

137

rolled over and over, completely bewildered; it was a new one; and while he hurried around town with a different reel each time, it was hot and flies buzzed around faces, and he forced his way through the barrier of bodies and he had to stop for every light and Diego told him:

"They fired him because he broke the rules." Rule number one, and this Diego guy, this little Diego, knows it real well: No Entry into the Booth. "Can't you read? Come on over and read it, man, read what it says there. That's why they threw Juan out. No Entry into the Booth. And now you want them to fire me. You're a spy. You're here to tempt me."

"They say you're in real good with management, that you're a good worker."

Cereceda's fingers started drumming again.
"Look. I'm going to make you an offer."
"What kind of offer?"
"Listen to me. And listen real good. Then we'll talk. But first you listen."

And the next time, the afternoon was coming to an end. People would be leaving work; the streets would be full of backs; you had to really sweat to find avenues and open spaces, and out came Diego with another reel:

"Hurry it up, get going, you're going to be late. And they'll fire you if you're late." And then, like a dagger: "Little squealer. You little squealer. You told Cereceda that Juan let you watch the film. You told him."

"Look, kid. Don't pay any attention to me. Sometimes I like to joke around. Friends?"

Or he doesn't say anything to me. Nothing at all.

138

Diego takes the film and closes the door; in the darkness you can hear the click, the lightning flash that marks the change of reels, and down below they haven't even realized that it's another reel, that there's a perfect synchronization, that somebody ran around outside all day so they could see the film in such comfort, without any switching on of lights, without interruptions. Diego hands him the other reel:

"We're strange birds; you'll have to forgive us. Up here, all this heat affects our brains, you know. We start doodling, or reading, or thinking, and we imagine things."

He hears the voice of Cereceda saying:
"Do you like to see films, kid?"

So he doesn't have to hurry any more. No matter how fast you are, you always end up in the same place: sitting here, in this alley, counting the ants and the shadows, with only five minutes left and time to deliver this reel. Everything repeats itself, always the same, each time, while inside it's all technicolor and wide screen. Open the service door one more time. Climb the stairs, pretending it's fun to count each one, feeling the bated breath of the audience down there. The projectionist's face appearing starless on the plain, blocking the entrance.

What will he say this time? "You're doing great, man," Diego will tell him. "A real example for everybody. I asked around. I'm real sorry. I didn't know you were so important. Cereceda says your conduct is exemplary. Of course I didn't tell him you wanted to come in and watch the film. With workers like you this business can't lose. Not bad. We all get our cut, our piece of the pie."

Or he'll say: "Congratulations, my man. My heartfelt congratulations. Do you want a medal? Well, we'll see that you get that too. A real hero on the job. That's the way I like it. Give me the reel. We'll keep on talking later. . . Don't leave, OK?"

Or maybe he won't say anything. Maybe Diego won't open his mouth.

All you can see are his hands, still, and a little bit of eye, green or red or yellow, just a corner of the eye, floating inside the hole. Cereceda says:

"Movies are great. And I've seen a lot of them."

Stand up, open the service door. In the light that filters through from the alley, he can see the incinerator. I'd never noticed it before. The two of us got along so well up there in the booth, as if we'd taken over a place and the cops would never get there. I hopped up the stairs like a rabbit, like a bomb out of a DC-4, and Juan was waiting for me. He would have waited like that the rest of my life.

"I'm going to show you how to run this machine, kid. But you've got to promise me that you'll keep on with your work. I mean you're real important. You're our legs."

And when he answered that he wasn't interested, Juan said: "When you're older, you'll thank me. When your legs give out, it's good to know how to run one of these machines."

Sundays, after the last show.

He said he didn't have any interest in learning anything about the projector, that he'd rather see a little bit more of the movie, a little more of that meadow of faces and sunsets, to travel like a machine gun or a bird without touching those dirty sidewalks, that burning concrete, the frost it was so easy to slip on, volcanic lava, snow on German battlefields; he wanted to astonish the whole city with his flight. That was the fun part, and also telling his friends all about it, the ones who worked, poor bastards, standing in some factory or selling pasta behind some counter, not able to move all day.

I'm free as a bird. Why should I want more?

"You'll have time to see all the movies you want. Let me give you some friendly advice, OK? Sundays after the show. How's that?"

The service door closes behind me. There's the stairway, leading to the second and third floor, to the projection booth on the third floor. Through the walls the sound of shots can be heard from the auditorium. But I don't have X-ray vision; I haven't gone through a time machine; I'm not a creature from outer space. I can't see anything. This darkness won't allow me to see what I brought over by express, Her Majesty's Navy, safe-and-sound without interference from thieves. I can put my ear against the wall, listen to the voices speaking English, or sometimes Italian, but I don't understand what they're saying.

By this route the only place you get to is the projection booth and Diego.

"It's no small thing, being the legs of the organization. Everybody has his function, you know. We're one big, beautiful body, hands, head and legs."

As if he were someone else, as if someone were guiding his fingers from afar, a voice giving orders to his hand, watching an actor performing his big scene, he opens the door of the incinerator, he can hear the roar from inside, can see the red glare, can smell the suffocating, scorched odor, the smell of ashes, and the fire down below. He puts the film inside; it fits perfectly.

It's like a baby, he rocks it a little, back and forth, trying to get it to sleep, don't cry baby. Ssshh, sshh, sshh. Don't make any noise.

My hand is sweating.

His hand is sweating.

"I'm no good for any other job," said Juan. "With these legs, I'm useless. I'm not mad, kid; I'm not out for revenge. Sure, sometimes I start to think about it, but I'm OK...

141

Maybe I'll tell you about it some day.

He lets go the door of the incinerator.

I don't open it any more to see the gaping hole, to imagine the reel falling down a thousand feet, the perfect crime.

When I walk out of the alley, my two hands empty, I find myself in front of the theater entrance.

The woman doesn't look at me.

"How many?"

"One."

I pay with one of the bills Cereceda gave me this morning. Will he count it again tonight?

They tear my ticket in half at the door, I go in, pushing aside the curtains at the entrance; nobody recognizes me. It's dark there inside, and there it is, up there, on the wide screen, a fierce sun, like a temple in the middle of the night, up there, the great white god. The usher lights my way with that flashlight that peers through the darkness.

From up in the booth, up there where Diego is, falls an avalanche of colors, a sparkling white dust that tears through the darkness.

"Where would you like to sit, sir?" the usher asks. His voice seems slightly familiar, like all the others.

"The first row."

There the screen seems even bigger, overwhelming. A single face fills it from top to bottom and from left to right. The seats are soft, deep and comfortable.

Up there, above me, immense, is the vast, lonely desert, battered by a merciless sun.

Only three minutes to go. Keep one corner of your eye on the clock, the one glowing beside the exit.

They've got the hero stretched out on the ground and four of them are kicking him. He knows what's going to happen now, after this scene, he knows it all. An expert, we all go through that, you get used to it. Now he's going to try

142

to get up, one of them strikes him with the whip, and now they're going to attack him again. The camera moves down the wound left by the whip and then focuses on a drop of blood that soaks into the sand. Then one of the horses stomps on him; one leg breaks, then the other. They say in English "That's for being an insolent rebel." At the bottom of the screen he reads: "Por rebelde, por insolente." Somebody spits. Then he says something: "OK, kid, now try to run; let's see if you can follow us now." They mount up and ride off. The man on the ground doesn't move.

Only one minute left; only thirty seconds.

The camera focuses on the face. He has no water, no horse; he's abandoned; his eyes demand revenge, justice, if there is any justice in this world. There's something familiar about that face there drying in the sun. He lifts his head, his eyes closed, the sun hits him like a chill and he starts to drag himself away. He pulls himself along with his arms, moving off toward the horizon. His face, for just an instant, and then the blood stains on the sand and on the rocks. He swears he won't die, that they haven't beaten him yet, that he'll find everyone of them, one by one, even if he can't walk, somebody will avenge him, his son, his nephew, someone, so they'd better not be boasting in the saloons or the streets about how they got rid of him; he'll find somebody to tell his story to before he dies and they'll search out the four of them. But he'll tell whoever it is to look for the other one especially, the one who hired them; that's the one.

A rider appears, just a dot on the horizon.

"I started out just like you, working the streets," says Juan. "One day Cereceda offered me this job. I accepted. What else could I do? Hell, kid, life's tough. Believe me, life's real tough."

Then it happens, what only I know is happening up there in the booth. Diego is staring at the empty doorway; my footsteps aren't on the stairs; the reel on the projector is

143

running out.

The machine coughs; the darkness becomes denser and denser and the lights begin to flicker.

"I need somebody I can trust," says Cereceda. "If it's not you, it'll be somebody else. That's the thing."

A real scandal. The audience is getting restless. A general wave of indignation. A light comes on. The screen is empty. A murmur of voices. It's the first time such a thing has ever happened in one of Cereceda's theaters. A serious blot on the company's reputation. Unheard of. We guarantee the dramatic illusion. Crooks.

They're going to be going off in other theaters too, like the lights in a house with a lot of children.

People in the audience look at each other disconcerted; this has never happened before; let's hope they fix whatever's wrong. Have a little patience. We can wait. But as the delay becomes more prolonged, as whatever is interrupting the film looks as though it will stretch out eternally; the first signs of anger begin to appear.

Now's the time to act. Before some voice can explain that it's just a momentary delay, please pardon the interruption, the film will start again in a moment; before Cereceda's voice directed at the "distinguished ladies and gentlemen" can soothe their nerves; he makes himself more comfortable in his front row seat, and then shouts, like a vulture flying back to its nest, its beak held high; his words take flight in the air above them and everybody can hear them:

"Crooks! Crooks!"

"OK," says that voice, so different from his own, "what do you say? What do you think of our offer?"

"What about Juan?"

"Don't worry about Juan. Just give me an answer." The voice takes on the tone of an accomplice; the face is about to come out from behind the cashier's curtain. "So tell me. What's it going to be? Do you want to run the projector, Diego?"

144

First in isolated outbursts, then in groups, the roar increases. OK, hit it now. It's time for the rest of the crowd to roar like a lion, without me having to say anything. Let the others shout, howl, green and red and yellow, like traffic lights in a crazy house, a masked ball where nobody has a face, without me having to join my voice to the chorus of protests that is rising and flooding the room. Money back, money back, you bastards. They're starting to kick the seats and tear the upholstery. They're knocking the ushers down and storming the ticket booth. In all four theaters a flood of tigers and rivers flows out; the dikes can't hold them back; the glass shatters.

It's time to go. Time to look for another job. In a factory or behind a shop counter.

"I accepted," says Juan. "I had to do it. I was really screwed. You'll do the same thing when your turn comes. You'll see."

Behind me the screen is empty. A piece of metal ripped from a seat makes a hole in the white window of its face, a black and eternal rip in the middle of that blinded moon face.

"No," says Diego.

"Think it over good, kid. I'll give you a few hours to think it over."

"I've already thought it over, Mr Cereceda."

"OK. Fine. So what do you say?"

"No, Mr Cereceda. No thanks." Diego turns half way around. "Oh, one more thing, Mr Cereceda, one more thing I wanted to tell you. It's about the projector, Mr Cereceda. You can shove it up your ass."

145

Prologue to *Birds and Worms*

When the Quimantú Publishing Company agreed to publish *The First Forty Measures*, it could not foresee that it had stumbled inadvertently into a full-scale literary battle. In that book, well-known writers who support President Allende's program each offered a story to demonstrate how far we had come in the forty basic measures promised.

Since the opposition had few, if any, writers, they decided to answer with a series of testimonials. Declaring their name, surname and profession, officials, citizens, union leaders, etc., denounced the government's failure to fulfill its promises and spoke of their disillusionment and anger. Reporters from the Agricultural Radio network, collaborating with Radio Balmaceda, and under the direction of Rafael Otero, compiled and recorded all those statements under the headline: "We still have a tongue to nag, citizens." When he presented them publicly, impresario Benjamin Matte stated: "Let them write fiction. We tell the hard facts."

The response by the Allendistas is *Birds and Worms* (a far better title than *That Spot on Your Back Where No One Can Scratch Himself*, which had been proposed by Hernán Lavín Cerda), the anthology for which we are now providing the prologue, and which shows that fiction can also be full of hard, rock-hard, facts.

We are introduced to the first of our *gusanos*, or worms, in "Under the Shower" by Poli Délano. The versatile author of *Barter* alternates a monologue by a rightwinger who's in the shower (justifying his imminent departure from the country) with several episodes from that individual's past life wherein we fully grasp what a fool he is and always has been. No matter how much soap he uses, he can't wash away the causes for his deep personal crisis.

146

Cesar Roccaffitto offers us another expression ("Improvisations") of his ability to combine irony with apocalypse as he confronts two policemen with a rich, young Nazi enthusiast whom they've just arrested breaking a store window during a rightwing riot. En route to the police station, he speaks endlessly to the guardians of the law, trying to convince them to let him go. The policemen haven't been trained to deal with people of a higher social class. Although ultimately they don't let him go, demonstrating a determination and a strength of character that seem to surprise the fascist (and the reader), doubts slip through our minds: when the crisis comes, which side will the armed forces take?

Several stories could be drawn from *Free Fire* by Antonio Skármeta. The one chosen was "The Cigarette", where the narrator explores the ruthless ambition and guilt which plague the protagonist, an unemployed adolescent from the slums who works as a thug for rightwing squads. A disturbing story that asks how many such people exist, people who are ready to betray the working class into which they were born?

We see a similar, although perhaps inverse, ambiguity in "Broadcasting" by Gonzalo Farías (taken from his book *There's Still Wood in the Tree of Faith*), in which a young female activist in a leftist party listens on the radio to the statements of her rightwing father, during one of the marches in opposition to democracy. Her response to her father, for whom she has a profound love, is to sleep with her boyfriend right in her parents' bed. It's not clear whether or not she will be able to survive her love-hate relationship with her old man, whether or not she'll end up leaving home, whether or not she will end up self-destructing in this transition; and, even more worrying, whether she will be able to go on using this man with whom she makes love to sublimate her need for rebellion.

Another bird caught among the worms is found in

"Please, Traveller", where Gerardo Inibata once again offers us the Hemingway-like style that he already gave us in his novel *JAP*. In this current story he moves us toward a dangerous, collective madness in which some worms, exiled in Mendoza many years after Allende's rise to power, circulate, and in which the ritual recall of a splendid but false past indicates the kind of country Chile was when they were in power. Any *pájaro,* or bird, who falls into that verbal net is not going to fare well.

A *pájaro* with a more optimistic message is a female worker in a textile factory who, although she is suspicious of the Allende government, gradually realizes where her real interests lie, in the story "Ask María", by Cristina Báez, which won the literary prize offered by the Cultural Center, La Cisterna.

But actually the *gusanos* outnumber the *pájaros* in this collection of stories because it was hard to find writers who were dedicated to looking at the heroic *pájaros* of that process. It's worth noting that established writers in Chile are more interested in attaching themselves to middle-class consciences than to the world of the workers, which, though more prone to sloganeering, is also more important. Furthermore, when *pájaros* do appear they tend to come from the petit-bourgeoisie: their transformation into angels, even though vacillating and hesitant, takes place under tremendous external and internal pressure. An exception might be "C is for Comrade", an excellent collaboration by Manuel del Fierro (*Interventions/Reports*) with Gonzalo Millán. In this story an illiterate worker helps a comrade paint a poster he will carry in a march: "I don't know how to read, but now I'd really like to learn."

That explosion into national life, and also into the narrative, of those who previously had been at the sidelines, is what led us to include the story "The Assembly", sent to us by a woman who is a professor at the PRESCLA and who has asked to remain anonymous. We decided to publish it, despite the fact that it is cliché-ridden and the prose and the presentation of character and motivation are flat. Basically it deals with an assembly of workers who decide to offer the government some stocks which the owners had donated to them with the idea of converting their employees into co-owners and therefore into supposed defenders of non-intervention. Although the workers' generosity is moving, the story's poverty of style impairs its impact.

The defects of "Assembly" are not found in a story by another proletarian writer, "Ciao" by Raul Aldañas (a worker from Mademsa), dealing with a conversation between a group of workers and their former bosses, along with their lawyers, at the entrance of a recently expropriated factory. The workers start off defensively, but gradually expressions of insolence and vituperation and a sprinkling of insults are heard. Their tone becomes more and more surrealistic as they make fun of the stockholders, the Manufacturers' Association, the Supreme Court, the College of Engineers, The Confederation of Professionals of Chile, Nixon, and the B-52 bomber. Every threat is received with a burst of laughter and another joke.

From Elihce, Esteban Monreal's second book, the story "Love Is a Many Splendored Thing" was chosen. It is the monologue of a doctor who can't decide whether to leave the country or not. He would like to stay, among other reasons, because he is in love with a fiery dermatologist, but in order to carry on his research for a treatment for skin cancer, he needs laboratories, electronic equipment, and research assistants that exist only in the U.S. Although neither this character nor any of the others created by Monreal in this volume, can be considered a *pájaro* or a *gusano,* we feel it necessary to include him here. Perhaps a sizeable segment of the country is involved in the debate in that strange intermediate ground that trembles between the two types - the one that soars and resists, and the one that crawls away and burrows.

We see a tenderness for understanding those trapped in a process they can't explain that is similar to that of Monreal in "When They Persecute the Paranoid", by Juan Menguant, in which the author emphasizes an all too real case of sectarianism against a lower-echelon and irrelevant Christian Democratic bureaucrat. He shows how the bureaucrat tries to maintain his dignity in the midst of unfair attacks.

The reader must have understood by now, then, that it was not always the most "committed", or the most activist stories that were chosen. No one can doubt, for example, Jorge Caballero Muñoz's commitment to social change. And, nevertheless, what interests him is the person caught in a straightjacket of doubt, that is, in the process of taking possession, through art, of the true forces in conflict at a time of transition. "Whitewashing" deals precisely with this search. A supporter of Unidad Popular watches from his window as a friend across the street for the third consecutive day erases a mural that is insulting to Allende. He knows it's a useless gesture, since it's not going to stop the rightwing people who painted those words, and that it's really a waste of energy that could be put to better use for more important tasks. Only as the man across the street moves ahead with his big brush do we realize that the one watching him also has a fascist emblem painted on the wall of his own building and that what's really at stake here is that he's afraid the rest of the neighborhood will find out what his true political sentiments are. We leave him just at the moment when he has to decide whether to buy some white paint and take up the brush himself – or whether it's better to wait and not reveal his true identity. Undoubtedly his confusion corresponds to the tremendous insecurity which, ever since the "Empty Pots" Demonstration and the threats by Patria y Libertad fascists, is beginning to eat away at many people.

As a response to this climate of uncertainty, we chose to close the anthology with "The Phoenix Bird, I and II" by Arístides Ulloa, who may certainly be considered one of our own writers, despite the fact that he happened to be born in Venezuela.

Part I is narrated by a South American dictator, who knows that he cannot die, that he will rise up like the phoenix from the ashes in the hearts of anyone who would overthrow him, that he'll be reborn in the spirit of competition and envy, that his wings will take flight yet again in the "little man with his little business", and he will never die, that he will live on in empty legalism or in the driving ambition to earn more than anyone else; they think that by burning my body they can kill me, but I'm the past and the future, I rise again in every deviation, every mistake, every egotism; they think they can kill me, but I'll be back.

Part II is told from the point of view of a victorious guerrilla fighter who wakes up in his lover's bed, at dawn on the day of victory, while the people are dancing in the streets: I have bread in my hands, the children are filing by, one by one, and I give my piece of bread to the smallest of them, he bites it and smiles at me, and then goes away dancing, the sun comes up, my lover is sleeping, while I'm awake, I wait, I know how to be born too.

Mama was waiting for me outside the theater and for a moment erased Victor from my mind. Enough for me to bring things off as usual, describing the film I had seen down to the last detail for her. That was the only reason she always gave me permission to go, and walked me down to the theater herself, in spite of my bad record. Describing it for her, when the only thing I had really seen, sprawled there in the seat with Victor entangled between my thighs and stretching my panties, was the light cast by the projector. Out of that brilliant but neutral flood of light, I had to reconstruct what was happening on the screen, which I had not even graced with a glance. All so that Mama would let me go the next time, movies are so lovely, it's such a shame my poor eyes have given out, the old lady didn't realize it wasn't her eyes that had failed her, what she really needed was to see that low, searing flight of butterflies of light over her head, and a man like Victor beside her; all you really need to get a good grade are some crib notes of the novels.

FINAL TERM PAPER

To create a new humanity now, immediately.

All you need is the will. "Look, you move into an old mansion, you invite all those friends, men and women, who doubt the petty individualism into which their lives have sunk, the yours and mine of material possessions, everyone who's ready to do away with schedules, isolation, and routine, and to form one family, to reach into the impenetrable depths of other human beings and to leap toward him or her, even at the risk of having to invent your own ground as you go, or even invent your own feet to move on, to rescue this adventure which is my skin reaching out to you like a leopard, this final opportunity to change, before it's too late, before someone blots out the Spring and Summer and Fall from this calendar, and I end up being the cage cleaner in a zoo where all the animals died long ago."

High-sounding objectives, poetic language, beautiful people, a cosmic dance, allowing the universe to flow through your body.

And yet early on in the novel *Games* by Esteban Monreal we sense that this attempt at communal living is going to be a failure: dreams of love and brotherhood are impractical unless they take into account the real, concrete, social world that is Chile in 1971-72. The author has an axe (and a thesis) to grind from the start; in that sense, the cards are stacked against the success of the experiment from the beginning.

The cracks are already visible in the sunlight

even before dawn, so the slow dismemberment of the tribe can come as no surprise to anyone; all the disagreements, breakdowns in communication, misunderstandings, conflicts, fights and contradictions arise from the "outside" that they have installed "inside", the cacophony of voices that can agree only on increasingly general objectives. It's all a logical, almost unavoidable, result of the fact that the men and women who in April of 1971 occupy a house just inherited by Carlos are not ready for the collective liberation that they support in theory, nor can they actually manage to channel their energies and desires in new directions.

Nevertheless, this is not the story of a process of frustration. There's no reason why the magic of an experiment should show only the errors of a particular thesis. It may also put to the test both the quality of the material being examined and the capacity for correctness and flexibility of the scientist who is examining it through a microscope. Each one of the "ingredients" (both actor and witness at the same time) must be living through a radical experience that will force him to confront what he really is, has been, and will be, will place him before the outer limits of his own illusions, of what he thought were the defenses of his personality, the prejudices and the blindfolds which have always nourished him. When, finally, a year and a half later, the friends separate, they have, for better or worse, become different people. That's why by having the laboratory explode, thus making it explicit that it was a laboratory, the experiment has been a qualified success. What each one takes from his stay in that house is like what we take from life itself: what we give, paraphrasing the Beatles, who are quoted in each chapter, is equal to what

154

we put into it.

The narrative method allows the reader to grasp precisely the authenticity or inauthenticity of each character, since all thirteen characters have the chance to speak twice in rotation (with the exception of the one who begins and ends the book, Tomás, who speaks three times, once more than the others, with his third intervention coming at the exact center of the 27 chapters, in chapter 14). The author takes the "inside" of what the characters are or think they are, and the "outside" of how others continuously define them , which they also are, of course, and interweaves them, in that way anticipating the context within which their plans will unfold or will collapse, as well as what they will have to learn from themselves and what they will teach others.

Thus, in reality, they don't escape inwardly, but rather run toward the outside world. However much they wanted to, they cannot hurry along a process that has not yet matured; they cannot deny the contradictions that they themselves bear engraved on their personalities. How will work be distributed? How will specialization be avoided? How will an elemental system of justice be established to solve the minimal, daily problems for which any clear and definitive norms are lacking? How will children be educated? Will they continue to depend on products that come from society? How will they deal with the question of the position of women, liberation vs. domination? What freedom will there be in male-female relations? How will they deal with the particular psychological limitations of each individual, when people inevitably compete or lie or deceive each other? What will happen to private property? How much should they be willing to surrender and to accommodate themselves to others? Even though Monreal starts from a clear position (these men and women have committed a serious historical mistake), he is not interested in condemning or judging his characters. For him, according to an interview in *Ultima Hora*, the only way to understand what is going on in Chile (or anywhere else) is to use the "indirect or reflective method", where what is happening on the screen is hardly detectable from the reactions of the spectators, "as if we had to reconstruct the murder by scratching out and bringing to life the last image frozen in the victim's retina." The immense social chain which they have not taken sufficiently into account is present at every moment in the novel, forcing them to confront their dreams with reality, the tremendous capacity they sense inside themselves against the real possibilities of using that enthusiasm. At the end, we are left wondering if Karolina or Elena will not lose faith, presuming that one failure indicates that one should stop trying; whether Luciano or Juan can carry on with the experiment, being more cautious and less isolated this time; whether it will be la Negra or Nancy who will finally assume the full complexity of the world, channelling her energies into the same search but within the framework of society as a whole. At any rate, when he finishes the novel, the reader does realize the distances each character has had to cover, how far they've all come from that first night and that first chapter, narrated by Tomás, which serves as a kind of prologue, just before Carlos inherits a house they all can settle in.

The main question they must answer as they hitch-hike to maturity is about innocence: can they learn about the world and grow up without losing a certain child-like joy?

Perhaps that's why the novel is called *Games*.

Each chapter, in fact, is constructed around some game that is being played by the characters, whether chess, Monopoly, soccer, or cards. It's as if they are incapable of telling their stories except on a board or a court, with specific rules, the presence of referees, an attempt to find allies, define adversaries, form teams, imagine difficulties, let loose creative juices. They use the games in order to get closer to themselves, gradually to reveal more and risk more in order to live together and to share.

By successfully dealing with the world as a game, or as a dream or illusion that is projected upon others, by accepting the fact of withdrawing from the game, the characters leave the house as mature and liberated people, ready at last to confront their duties as adults in an adult world.

LORETO APABLAZA
Third Year, Spanish Major
Catholic University of Valparaíso

It is clear that the student has not thought the novel through very clearly. She's offering us her own problems and not those that arise out of Monreal's work. For example, she fails to relate *Games* to the theory on "communicative imagery" which that novelist had developed earlier. She has made no reference to the fact that the imitation of others is the primary form of domination in that chaotic and bewildering world, and that this has deep roots in the Spanish American phenomenon of the abuse of foreign models, a primary theme in 1970-71.

She ignores the innovative linguistic dimension. She

should at least explain the strange sensation the reader has that each narrator is living out his experience with a tremendous outpouring of joy, which nevertheless is inserted into a general tone of distrust on the part of the author himself, an extreme use of imagery that, confusing and over-lyrical, enables us to see how each character falsifies him or herself. Nor does she seem to understand that love is the work's basic theme, human beings in search of otherness. Tenderness finds a way of expressing itself at the most difficult moments, understanding and selflessness are offered in almost every chapter, offering a backdrop of transcendence and solidarity which indicate that, far from failing in their experiment (although superficially it could be interpreted that way), they have managed to anticipate conditions for solidarity which are needed in order to be able to live out a process of social change. Ms Apablaza fails to see that now they (all of them) can go on to destroy their own egotism, because they have found their foundation in others, because they are no longer alone.

And this is the major weakness I find in this part of the paper and almost all the papers this young woman offers. She always seems to place the novel, and all literature, into a false genre, to which it does not belong. It is not social realism; it does not seek to reflect the contradictions in the process. She has completely misunderstood Monreal's "indirect method". What we really have here is an allegory about authority, how human beings try to create totalitarian states at every moment of their lives, because each person has the chance to be king for a day, as happens in fairy tales, and he wants to be sure he doesn't miss his chance. Nowhere does Monreal state that his characters were mistaken. Nor does he give any indication of who has come through the experience in a better or worse state. He is only interested in emphasizing a fact that this student might well have taken into account before reducing it to inappropriate terms: the only way to guarantee that some people won't impose their will on others is by previously changing the soul of every human being. You can't build socialism with corrupt hearts. That is Monreal's message, and it is in complete accord with his entire previous work. Whoever fails to see this reality, cannot possibly construct the world of free relationships that Monreal proposes, in which art will be equal to labor, and in which life will be a game without losers.

Or if not, our student will be like someone who "hesitates in front of the ticket office, unable to decide whether to buy a ticket or not, without realizing that the ticket office is already on the train that has pulled out with you, and everything else, long before you decided whether it was important to stay behind waving from the platform" (from *Pools*; just in case the passage isn't recognized).

She should rewrite the essay.

Immediately.

Double-spaced pages.

The literary-artistic exhibition SHIT has just completed its third successful week in the Carmen Waugh Gallery. Its central theme seems to be life as a process of perpetual deprivation. Although we will later detail the material dimensions of this first "novel-object", we should clarify, at the beginning, that it consists of a long narrative written on a roll of toilet paper and should be read continuously as it is unrolled.

The story being told is basically the story of the roll of paper on which it is written. Although the roll does include some reflections, dialogues, memories, short poems, etc., that do not refer to the paper itself, most of the text is made up of the paper's own reflections on its strange destiny, of having fallen into the hands of an eccentric novelist, rather than serving the usual functions that would have been assigned to it, and for which it was better prepared. Its individual and melancholy voice pursues the collective experience of its fellows, if they can be so called, and it goes along dreaming of the wooden rod on which other toilet papers were unrolled and put to different use. The bathroom, the kitchen, parties, wounds, spills, dirty spots, all the uses that were denied it.

As the paper considers other possible existences, the author himself intervenes with thoughts of his own, ecstatic at witnessing so much cornered vitality, burning itself out uselessly. He analyzes decomposition, the way in which human beings fail to communicate, the oblivion that awaits all of us, etc. One critic with a surrealistic bent has noted an internal order to such wanderings, a parallel between the sterile and lyrical life of the writer and that of the toilet paper roll, as it becomes thinner and thinner, as it drains the experiences of others and seems to be realizing - too late - that its own development and use will have no meaningful

160

culmination. It never complains, never confronts the writer nor contradicts him, not even when it comes to its last, by now very weak, words, not even when it is certain that its situation is extremely and disproportionately unfair. It is never permitted the dignity of an act of rebellion against the voice that has torn it from its normal destiny. The reader, to use the words of the journal *The Spare Tire,* ends up desiring that the author understand "one uncomfortable night of diarrhea, when the storekeeper has stashed away the toilet paper, expecting an imminent price increase, that there are better uses for it than to be the victim of someone else's words."

Our weekly, *Tiempo indefinido e infinito* agrees: it's dangerous, indeed symptomatic, that some crazy artist would conceive of a roll of toilet paper as Minerva, his inspiration and his Muse, an instrument of spiritual expression, simply because the economy is being sabotaged from inside and outside our stores and writing paper is getting scarcer. But this author, who just flutters around the surface of the phenomenon, the problems that arise from the struggle of our consumers to satisfy their everyday needs, touch him only to the extent that they allow him to pose a roll of toilet paper as a subject of and at the same time an instrument of art, a mixture of the abstract and the concrete.

Let us keep in mind that the form of one's reading depends on when you get to the exhibit. If you arrive when no one else is there (rather difficult at that kind of miniature State Fair, that intellectuals' CHILEXPO), you can sit down comfortably in the chair that is in front of a mirror and surrounded by tiles making it resemble a bathroom, and unroll the paper backward over an ingenious pulley mechanism, as you read it. If you get there late, you'll have to sit down in the second seat, or third, etc., all the way up to ten, and wait in line to read. According to Carmen Waugh, there was only one seat the first day, in accordance with the wishes of the anonymous author. But people poured in like "noodles crazed by the sight of tomato sauce or like tooth paste squeezed out all over the place by a troop of kindergarten kids," to use the same imagery the roll of toilet paper uses to express its faith that there'll be some happy future for it too.

The exhibition had to be closed and reopened two days later with a larger seating capacity, although only on that first magical throne, surrounded by the ambience of a bathroom, can we presume that the author's true spirit is captured. "He refused to put more than ten," the boy who cleans the area at night told me, confidentially. "He stood there, as stubborn as a mule. They're going to ruin my art, that's what he said."

So the reading takes place on a cyclical continuum, like a real pulley, although we must remember that such was probably not the original intention of the creator, who conceived of it as an individual experience on a solitary seat, like so many moments we spend in the world's great toilet, a metaphor that, perhaps because it is so obvious, he does not employ. The exhibition has a guard on duty at all times, and there's also a man with his hand on a control stick, in case a slow reader tries to hoard too many feet of the narrative at one time. Whenever anyone finishes the novel, he is immediately replaced by the next person in the line of ten, who can read the entire work from beginning to end, and then make way for the next person, etc. The constant change of readers does not mean, however, that the paper wears thin, for it is treated by the public religiously, as if it were the canvas on which the Mona Lisa is painted, or better said, as if it were the skin of Mona Lisa herself. The face, breasts and buttocks of La Giaconda, Leonardo's buttocks.

Nevertheless, it is difficult to dislodge the suspicion that every night they replace its well-worn face with another, even though, I suppose that would actually be in defiance of the expressed orders of the author who, either did not anticipate the triumph of his story-machine, or did anticipate it and desired such an eventuality, so that the roll and its creation would devoutly expire at the same time, disappearing in shreds, between the fingers of unknown esthetes, thus symbolizing that extinction that has so fascinated him. That is, the meaning of his art consisted not only in the hope that the reader would wear out the work, but actually in the insistence on such a process. The work ends only when the object upon which it is written itself ceases to exist physically, thus attempting to transcend the merely ideological consumption of the book-object. It is even said out there that the local Noh Tribe is planning to create a poem made of chocolate and to put it out to melt in the sun or that Aurelio Sirquis thought that the magical words of our salvation lay in the letters in a gigantic bowl of alphabet soup in which all of us would swim and write as we dove, sinking, floating, eating, using the letters like innertubes or floating balls, and forming a message that only someone in a helicopter could decipher.

But these efforts cannot have the deep, nihilistic meaning that the present exhibit displays, because instead of using food, which is a rival, a happy adversary, a nourisher of blood and movement, he presents us with a roll of toilet paper, which is consumed precisely to smother that glorious ejaculation of the jaws, and because, besides, the author finds it significant that both literature and defecation involve paper . . . and oblivion.

Perhaps for that reason, there is a constantly repeated theme written on the roll: an eternal song for a woman, a departed female body. But she is not compared to withered lilies or disappearing clouds. All imagery is taken from the sewer, from whatever is fallen and violently torn apart, love expressed through decay and loss or forever silent. It isn't because he hates her; it's just that there's no other way to express what separation from her means. It's the same searing tone with which the roll of toilet paper expresses its own lack of meaning, its distance from its "roles" (a collective merging of male/female where there are no longer any distinctions), the fullness of a world which can be touched only by our imaginations. Yet another way of synthesizing toilet paper and poet, it also involves a deep opposition. What is hope for one ("the sewer where 'we' meet once again like cotton bandages after a case of gangrene"), is bitterness for the loss of someone else ("the black ditch of your love-mouth, your throat of dark love", "remembering here the anesthetic of your fingers"). The only thing the roll of toilet paper wants is to become something departed and broken away, something torn and stinking that is as miserable as the narrator's lover, because in that way he would perform the function for which he was created. The author's spider-mind is flooded with nostalgia for the purity and freshness of someone like the roll of paper, like the woman before her departure, a sparkling glance, the atmosphere on the first day of creation, devotion and simplicity, absence of anguish, the desire to be used, the joy of being continuous and round, in a word, to be a roll of paper and never words. It is the poet, rolled up, twisted, gnawed by guilt, who imposes his own pain, inverts the roles, and who must destroy the paper; he needs to destroy it in some way other than the usual joyful climax with which it would ordinarily meet its end at the hands of other human beings. The paper's humiliation and enslavement, its deviation from its usual simple and innocent life, its alienation from freedom, the dark envy the novelist feels for the white lady on whose skin he has "spit out his childless black sperm", at the same time allow us to understand that the author's punishment is his own captured and wounded expressiveness, and that the hell he imposes on the toilet paper is his own journey toward something that is too mediocre to be called demonic.

Only one problem remains to be addressed.

How do we explain the extraordinary resonance of this exhibition? The critic Gonzalo Farías has offered his opinion: it is its passages of heightened erotic tone, its boldness of expression, its almost pornographic sensuality, its petit-bourgeois masochism.

Nevertheless, I would like to venture a kinder hypothesis. Its readers experience something that goes beyond a mere curiosity, which could, after all, have been satisfied by reading Henry Miller. Sitting there, holding on to that roll of toilet paper that winds and unwinds, back and forth, passing before their eyes again and again, endlessly, reading together and successively, perhaps they achieve that sense of communion and certainty of eternity which the work they are reading tries to negate. No doubt it would have been quite another matter if we read it alone, if it piled up at our feet, like a pet dog that died a long time ago but has no master to bury him.

That's why we can imagine the author's desolation when he realized there would be ten readers, ten faithful people, collaborating and forming a sense of solidarity despite the toilet paper's dark and vexing content.

Someone was going to arrive by chance on the first day. He would sit down and start to read, unrolling the paper; then he'd finish reading, let the paper fall, shake his foot to disentangle it ("Chaplin steps in a pile of shit, but without batting an eye or asking for help from a passer-by, he simply shakes it off"), and he'd stand up, and the next person would come, and seeing the useless pile on the tiles, would toss it in the nearest garbage can and smile, and upon seeing that in this picture entitled SHIT there was no toilet paper, just another example of pop-art, he would yawn and leave.

Maybe that's the way the novelist conceived it, as a unique experience for that single reader, any reader. If that is true, he was cheated by the roll of paper itself, which preferred to go on singing its world of sorrow without end amen.

Having read all too patiently up to this point, allow me as a reader to make the following comments, without attempting (yet) to discuss the matter fully, not on toilet paper but on a clean sheet white as can be:

1. A chapter is needed that will delve into the literature, whether of the highest or lowest quality, which has been produced directly by different sectors of the poorest people themselves, as they have been stimulated by the revolution. This could mean attempts (I insist: with all the variations of good and bad taste, with all the ideological denominations and the new values of solidarity) both in the area of what we could call the traditional genres, and in more recent developments (poster slogans, dramatic works in the nationalized industries where the public participates, and songs created in centers of popular culture).

2. Along with this, no one seems to be looking at "popular" forms, such as folklore, legends and tales, which have taken on tremendous importance, especially in the countryside.

3. There is a literature - a series of reprints of old novels - which, even though it has been repudiated by some intellectual circles, is somewhat in vogue nowadays: it is Socialist Realism, which was born under the pressure of building the socialist order in the USSR under extremely arduous conditions. Even taking such conditions into account, it is clear that it was the product of a profound misconception regarding the relationship between art and society, and of a superficial reading of Marx. It becomes even more deformed when transferred to a dependent and underdeveloped country which has a completely different experience as well as other kinds of problems. At the same time, we must rise above the contempt with which such forms of expression have been treated, since often, in reality,

we have no other way to disseminate information on the life and aspirations of the working class than to go to those novels from the past. I see very little about the Chilean workers, not to mention peasants, in the pages of this book so far.

4. As a corollary, I would recommend a serious critique of the attempt by so many contemporary writers to use the people in a parasitic way, more as inspiration than anything else, to endorse a creation which instead of representing them, in reality, wants to replace them. These authors present the people as a backdrop upon which other problems are projected. Just as in earlier periods of our literature those living on the fringes of society served as a stimulus to the sheltered middle-class artist, or just as the sexual fantasies of the upper classes focused on the forbidden pleasures of relationships with members of lower and menial castes, now there are those who would like to use the proletariat as material, only to lock them yet again inside books that would be bought and understood . . . only by elite readers. The fact is, the entry of the working class into novels must be preceded by their entry into the spheres of political, economic and cultural power, understanding that therein lies the possibility for workers to buy, read and reject what is being written about them.

5. Thence, the refusal of one of the writers who has been or will be mentioned in this work to go on producing literature for the elites. He feels compelled to go out and gather collective testimonials of the magnificent experiences of the working class, placing his technical expertise at the disposition of a group of voices who want to express themselves but who still have neither the ability nor the means.

6. The attack upon the aforementioned position as being too "proletarian", as having completely lost its direction. It is fine to carry out those eminently political tasks. But can't the writer become a political activist on whatever front he

chooses without simultaneously ending his problems, doubts, ambiguities. He should not run away from the fact that he is the product and depository of a tradition right up to the moment when the majority decides to use him or to cast him aside. The worst thing he can do is to falsify his voice: that would be a true betrayal of himself and the working class.

7. From here there's only a step to the position which defends the rights of the artist as a judge of the revolution, as the voice of a silent majority that finds its faithful interpreter in him, as the incorruptible foundation and guardian of purity. (But what a step that is!)

8. If we go just a tiny step farther we find those who say right up front that it is the duty of art to probe the deep problems of the epoch, in all their magnitude, and that if we write for the unlettered of today we will be repudiated by their great-grandchildren tomorrow.

9. But of course there are those - and many - who prefer to write peacefully for the educated of the present day. The position of those authors, and of those among them who are not of the left, but in fact could be considered political adversaries of the social process itself and especially as esthetic critics of the type of narrative perpetrated by Ulloa, Del Fierro, De León, Farías, Roccafitto, Menguant, and Nicomedes Guzmán, has not had and will never have a place in this novel. It is as if they had disappeared from the literary map of Chile after 1970. And that is false, not to mention wilful. In his resentment of them, the author goes so far as to have the only representative of the group we have seen up to now (Iriarte) burn his manuscript and experience a conversion, like some hysterical Roman emperor facing the Holy Cross in a Cecil B. de Mille spectacle. In the long run, as the Cuban Revolution has shown, these authors may become the defenders and allies of those included in numbers 7 and 8 above. "We shouldn't get answers, but rather ever deeper questions; let's be the agents of an insurrection of the spirit; freedom to create, to say

168

what we feel. Literature is not politics." It is possible that some of the decade's finest writers are among this group.

10. By not taking the work of this last group into account, it would seem that art itself, and the examination of its methods, do not occupy a significant place in the book. The author may despise anything that is not political; may be unable to accept the fact that everything does not focus on ideology; and yet feels the need to justify the time he devotes to the pages he is filling. He would do well to remember that the writer is always the real protagonist of his work, and that the difficulties he confronts in the creation and construction of his fiction are inevitably reflected in the way in which the central character will live or will destroy his own passage through life. To put it another way: one must not ignore that ineffable factor which is form, style, narrative method, sensory order, words, because these are the author's weapons, the means by which he accompanies and reinforces his vision.

11. We will have more to say about this later. What I do request is a blank page for another reader to use. I would like to avoid the sin of assuming that mine is the only valid voice, that the book you buy has already been unalterably written.

12. To be filled by other readers:

JAP-ENING

Gerardo Inibata, *JAP* (a novel),
Editorial Proceso, 1972.
Reviewed by Juan Menguant

Another work which portrays the moral and
psychological evolution of a character who
confronts progressive politicization and transformation as he becomes more and more committed to
the revolutionary process. In this case the character
is Julio Fuentes, a bank employee, who for various
reasons (the quest for justice, the need to deal with
food shortages in his neighborhood, Nuñoa, a
certain sense of tedium, the certainty that he will
succeed where others have failed), becomes in
1971 an honorary inspector of a JAP, Junta of
Alimentation and Prices, that grassroots organization trying to control distribution problems at the
local level.

The central thread of the story is provided by the
suspense accompanying Fuentes' almost
detective-like efforts to search for a mafia of
retailers, wholesalers and middlemen, who are
speculating, cornering the food market and creating
an enormous black market. But in order to do this,
the protagonist must live through new experiences,
which means in effect presenting an X-ray of certain
contemporary social events here in Chile. At the
same time, as he progresses, and learns more,
acquires deeper understanding and clarifies the
situation, he himself changes; he is, in fact, in
search of himself. Nevertheless, somewhat as a

policeman is destroyed by the gangsters he pursues, Fuentes also suffers an avalanche of disasters, which cannot be attributed to any human hand: his son dies in a traffic accident, his wife leaves him, his workmates begin to resent him as an opportunistic johnny-come-lately to the Allende cause, some neighborhood people pressure him, he misplaces his driver's licence, and his gas heater bursts. It is as if someone or something were punishing him for having broken with the normal functioning of the universe. In spite of these catastrophes, our Job or Hercules goes on stubbornly ready to leave behind his middle-class destiny.

This apprenticeship in pain ("there are two kinds of pain: the one that comes to you because you do not see reality [inauthentic] and the one that comes to you because you'll be damned if you're not seeing it [authentic]") does not end, nevertheless, until the moment when he recognizes his inability to get rid of those dimensions alone, and he is grateful for the help and solidarity of the other members of the JAP. Only at the moment when he stops imagining himself as the lonely hero (one of those incorruptible, Glenn Ford fighters for justice who struggle for their ideals under miserable conditions on some moral plateau) can he trap and defeat his adversaries. It is the necessary step to crossing over to other problems, ones which arise after he is fully committed, when he has earned the right to criticize, when he is no longer struggling to decide, but rather to know to what concrete results his decision will lead.

Dear Gerardo:

As you can see, I could not write extensively about your novel in *Tiempo indefinido e infinito,* although I liked it very much. It was not for lack of space. Actually, I wanted to say more. You will no doubt note a certain formality and distance of tone, a monotonous buzzing that is not habitual in me, even in my briefest reviews. I'm going to explain why.

The same Thursday that I sat down to write the review (the deadline was Friday), I by chance came upon one of those inexpensive paperbacks that are sold in news stands, a kind of sub-literature, you know the kind I mean. The title is *Heroes Are Everywhere* by one Henry Santana, a gentleman I've never come across at all. I say it was by chance, because it's a well-known fact that people who read good literature rarely indulge in the kind of trash that circulates out there in cheap, popular editions.

So, what has any of this to do with your novel? A lot. Or nothing. Since it turns out that the plot is almost identical to JAP: a man by the name of Julio Fuentes gets involved in a Junta of Alimentation and Prices (yes, Henry Santana is Chilean and is writing here in our country about our problems) and discovers a mafia, and ends up destroying them. That, on the anecdotal level. Action after action, both repeat certain investigations and steps. Are we dealing with the same novel, then? Not at all. In this unprepossessing work, the multiple inner divisions and conflicts of the character have completely disappeared, along with all his hesitation, all the back and forth of his political movements. The catastrophes are not the result of some greater tragic Promethean destiny, but rather are the acts of directly implicated killers. His wife does not leave him. She is kidnapped. He doesn't need to look to anyone else for support. He's a real he-man with pistol and fists. That doesn't mean he's not an ardent supporter of socialism. He is immovable. But all the difficulties have been removed

172

from the process, as well as all the criticisms of it. All the complexity of the elite novel *JAP* has been reduced to a simple struggle between good and evil; all its powerful imagery has been simplified into easily digestible patterns.

So, now I want to know the truth, Gerardo. Is this a case of plagiarism? Did you read Santana's work and decide that this was a necessary theme which a semi-literate, cliché-ridden mind had been incapable of giving real form to? Or, on the contrary, did Mr Henry read your work and take from it an essential core, what in effect would be picked up by the people and would inspire them to keep on working? Mr Henry understood that a Julio Fuentes worthy of Sophocles was useless, while, on the other hand, what was fundamental was a Julio Fuentes worthy of Julio Martínez, our beloved sports commentator.

And which of the two works best fulfils its function? Which is more political? Which is more truthful? The one that simplifies in order to be able to influence a vaster and more accessible audience; or the one that complicates in order to be able to present the hidden structure of our time in all its contradictory colors?

You know that I have extensively studied the problems deriving from the difference between literature and subliterature. You know that I think that both of them are complementary faces of the division between the elite and the masses, between selectivity and popular consumption, and that they have always influenced each other across the centuries.

That's why it was so difficult for me to review the pure novel *JAP*, when the context within which that life of Fuentes was inscribed was so much richer and more expressive. Furthermore, I have the sense that from now on, whenever I confront any literary text, I'm going to be thinking about the version that Henry Santana must be writing somewhere, somehow.

In any case, it occurs to me that the specific key to the

two works is precisely in their coming together in that great collective mind which is the public and which was temporarily located in my poor particular head. That must be the author's truth, his displacement between two needs and two challenges, trying to satisfy two demands, attempting to live for two publics, right, Henry or Gerardo or whatever I should call you, you literary bigamist?

Phantasmagorically yours,
Juan Menguant

PROLOGUE

Reader: hear my curse.

You will read this the way a deaf mute watches a ballet, intently absorbing form and color, image and movement, with the secret hope of some day recovering your hearing, liberating your voice, and in that moment being able to associate all that pantomime - that one, and so many others - with an eminently meaningful text, something that will unify and give order to all the division, sonorous syllables without chaos (yessss, thissss isss alliteration, you knew it). That, dear reader, is the way we store up supplies for the savings and loan of winter, while the vampire horizon sucks the blood of the sun, that's the way you build a country, get ready. But you wake up and there's nothing to see; there's no longer anyone on stage; it's true you can hear something now, and you thought you were deaf; it's true that whatever it is that is rumbling wings way off there in mouldy ears seems to be music, but where are the dancers, why did they go home, or why didn't they go home instead of waiting there behind the curtain for the audience to get more and more restless (and the fact is it's always too late, we always have to catch the train that already left and there we are with just a useless ticket-stub in our hand); and the world is peopled with emptiness or maybe it's this fog, something settling like a sunset on my eyelids, and you start to hear pretty well, actually, you're super-ears, you might end up on TV with your own series that'll last longer than *My Three Sons*; you have X-rays on your ear lobes; fear also makes a sound, eyes that don't chew; you can pick up the footsteps of an ant walking tippy-toe to keep from waking up his aunt; you can hear the dancers counting the people in the audience; you can hear how the curtain rises, and the theater

175

is filled with voices and applause, whispers and violins, the vast space of your sonority, and yes, the ballet begins again like the ringing of a bell; it must be the same as before, and there you'll be, it's always late, survivor, Mr Anybody, or just you yourself, a blind man, yes, a blind man, a blind man giving preferential attention to every note and to its harmony, to the entire scaffold of linguistic signs, with the desire not so much to find images that must correspond to the message and to the music, form and color, movement; and are we really ever anywhere?

"May I help you?"

"I'd like a love story, if you have something you'd recommend."

"One of this season's bestsellers. Sexual life in an orphanage, *Nephews and Little Nieces*. It's been on the bestseller list for several . . . "

"No, thank you. Not that one."

"Well, in that case, perhaps you'd like *Debts*. The main character discovers at the end of his life that someone (a woman millionaire that he helped across a street when he was a child) has been looking out for him, surrounding him with good fortune, creating conditions for his success, paying teachers to promote him, paying off women to make him feel like a Don Juan."

"What about the love part? Where does that come in?"

"When he finally inherits that money (remember, he never knew that all this was being arranged behind his back), he has to review accounts, reports, cancelled checks, he must see his entire life from another point of view. He looks for some love of his own, something that belongs to him, that wasn't bought for him. . . "

"Didn't I tell you I don't want anything political. What about *The Ancestors*?"

"Narrated by an individual's ancestors, who inhabit his body and control him without his knowing it. Meanwhile that man can't free himself from a woman who has always controlled him, who pulled him away from what was his real destiny."

"Very *déjà vu*."

"What about *Games*? It got good reviews."

"I read it. Didn't like it. Complicated, too lyrical."

"But what is it that you want exactly? Trying to second-guess you like this, we're never going to get anywhere."

"Something different, a love epic, a modern version of one of those old medieval chronicles. A coming together of the lovers in spite of evil dukes and assorted shipwrecks. Or better still, let's eliminate the various and sundry difficulties and refuse to introduce the ogre in the story. A love that blooms like a chrysanthemum."

"Impossible. We're in the twentieth century and this is a university bookstore. Go look at the soaps."

"You misunderstand me. Look, if you will, to be realistic, around the island of characters, with their absolutely complementary personalities, you can observe the sense of desolation: I mean, you know, divorce, adultery, absurd deaths, misunderstandings, lies, tiny disagreements that when put together bring on a double attack of hysteria, dissatisfaction in the sexual labyrinth, weak answers, anticipation of everything your mate will say, laying on the guilt trip, the sickening feeling you get when you realize what a farce the whole courtship routine was, whatever you want. Let's fill it up with every degradation the contemporary novel can stir up. But as far as they're concerned, we won't even touch them with a feather. There they are in their life-jacket, while the continents drift away, not even asking whether they're in the ocean or in a swimming pool, or why they keep on swimming."

"Well, there is a new fashion leading works in that direction, sir. Literature that goes back to simple things, you know."

"But tell me, is it so hard to believe that two human beings have the right and the possibility to find happiness together?"

"That's precisely the case in *A Crown for Georgina,* a book I was just about to recommend to you. It's number 2 on the bestseller list. It's about a man who lives by inventing a reality, full of hope, plagued with mistakes, and along with him is his wife, Georgina, who criticizes him, won't let him live in peace, a woman who wears away at both his hopes and his mistakes. She deserves the crown of a princess, for helping him, and another, a funeral wreath, for destroying him. But it has a happy ending."

"No, I want a novel called *Love*. Nothing more."

"*Love Story*?"

"No, not that piece of trash. Of course not. I want a novel where everything will go well, go too well for the characters. But the reader has no right to judge them. That's where the author has to use all his talent. We need also to fall in love with those soft, healthy little beasts, with the spontaneity with which they confront any suspicion of cheap sentimentality."

"Nobody can have it that good."

"But it'll go well for these people. There's no need to dig around for childhood traumas here. They don't even feel guilty for being happy."

"But of course they have to suffer to reach that kind of love. Why should they get free what the rest of us never get, no matter how much we search for it?"

"They're the only clean monastery in a country without hospitals and with the bubonic plague raging outside. I don't care. That's the novel I want."

"Impossible. He'll fall in love with somebody else. Or they'll fire him from his job. Or she'll get tired of family life and will turn to outside activities for satisfaction, and the crisis will begin . . . "

"Not at all. And even if it did happen, it wouldn't really matter. What happens in the outside world is not going to affect the relationship they have between them. It's as though all the innocence, purity, lust, sensuality, and harmony had been poured into that ideal complement that is the couple, leaving the rest of the world empty."

"A really perverse novel. If you really think about it, that pair of angels are witches who have inverted and isolated the world."

"Not true. They're like the sand inside an hourglass. They've excluded everybody else. They're right. They're happy and spontaneous."

"And how should it end?"

"He dies at age 67. After all, that's statistically normal and probable. She calmly waits a few more years."

"OK, now we really collect on our bets. She won't be able to stand the solitude. She'll commit suicide; she'll confess something horrible just before she dies. Now we get to the misery."

"Not at all. She dies; the novel ends. That game of Russian roulette you proposed was played with water pistols."

"All right. So tell me, what does the author have in mind writing a novel like that?"

Now I'm taking it off. Even before I start pushing people, elbowing this lady out of my way, shoving that fellow who's standing on tip-toe to see better, they turn around to protest, but then don't say anything, just move away, when they see that I'm taking off my shirt; the crowd opens up, clearing a path for me.

I can stand in front of him. He must be dead, that's not just blood, that yellow stuff that's coming out of his belly. In the hot silence, no one moves; there's not even a murmur anymore.

The driver has skilfully parked his truck near the corner. For the ambulance, he explains to us, as if he were worried about having removed the evidence, of having made a serious mistake. He's very pale. His hands hang down on his thighs, sweating like two useless hams; look how I'm sweating innocently; it wasn't my fault; you can tell them that; he just stepped in front of me all of a sudden, right in the middle of the block; yeah, sweating, of course, but it doesn't occur to him to take off his shirt.

Nobody, not a single solitary soul on the entire planet, not one person standing by, offers that body as much as a handkerchief.

Here's the last rebellious button, demanding all my attention and special care not to break it, trying not to think about the bleeding; I'd better not think about my face, as I rub my hand through my hair, as I push back the lock of hair that's falling over my forehead, just the way I always do when I'm nervous and somebody is staring too fixedly at my movements. In the distance, up the street - more like an avenue, it makes me dizzy it's so wide and long, and it's like those flowers over there are going to explode in the mid-summer heat - I can hear an ambulance. To hell with this shirt! I'm crazy to be worrying about it so much; I'm never going to wear it again. The button pops off.

I finally get the shirt off. The sun's heat totally engulfs my bare back, like a dry wave from the sea, and when I stumble, just for an instant, I look up at the impenetrable fog of faces in a circle around me staring indifferently and then a little lower, the clearer shadow of their shirts, as if someone were filming them with two cameras, from two different distances, exhibiting their faces and their clothing in two different and distant neighborhood movie houses. Not a word issues from this sunset of mouths. They were talking, making comments and diagrams, holding up fingers, gesturing, only a moment ago. It's not the driver's fault, he tried to avoid hitting him, he put on his brakes, just look how long his skid marks are, but I was there too, he did everything he could, life is a bitch. But now, they're silent.

I cover him with the shirt, so now they won't be able to see him, they no longer look. But there's no way out; now, against their own wills, their attention is drawn to my shirt , waiting for the blood to soak through the cloth, a signal that they can start their conversations again.

It's a beautiful shirt. My girlfriend gave it to me. She worked hard, saved money, by-passed the smiling sales-girls who tried to sell her another shirt, clapped her hands together gleefully when I was trying it on, now you can't get away, lover, I'm your second skin, lover, I'm going to take it off you myself now and then I'm going to put it on. Where is it? she'll ask me, and they can't help their eyes being captivated by the redness seeping through and covering it, still not aggressive, it's true, a little sheepish, perplexed more than anything else, you lost it, and their eyes also scrape across the shine with which my back hardens in the violent, summer light.

Up on the left side, it has only one small pocket, that's where you can put my heart, lover, that's where I'll always be, watching out for you, so you really have to behave yourself, there's a tiny bluish ink stain there and every-body watches how the seeping blood surrounds it, engulfs it, and it's losing the certainty of its own blueness, becoming an indefinable purple. I don't want to stand up, I place one knee on the cement, I wouldn't know what to do next, one more person among so many, caught in the community of their stares, although my shins hurt and a slight hint of a cramp creeps up my leg, I don't move. A stirring of rage growls at me because I am bothered by this knee that's now burning. I don't want to stand up.

"A friend?" says the soft voice of the policeman.

He's not going to understand if I tell him "no", that I don't even know him. But that's really the only thing I can say. No, because the fact is he's not my friend, after all, I'd never seen this man before today.

"It depends on the author. If it's his first novel, there's no place to get a real grip on it; you just have to move with the flow. Now, if it had been Roccafitto, the whole structure would have been put together to criticize the couple's conduct. The analysis begins to take place when you close the book. On the other hand, in the case of Monreal - whom I don't like, personally - you can rest assured that he's writing it so we'll worry about the simplest things, every nook and cranny of life. Farías would have done it like a bolero, but with the rhythm of a novel. In the case of Inibata it would be like an ironic commentary on *Nocturn,* one which only he would understand. If Teresa de León were alive, and in a way she is, remember, I suppose she'd say this is the only thing we have, love, this brief territory is the only place where the eternity you're going to spend with me actually happens. Don't rationalize so much, Gonzalo Millán would say. All he means is that a man loves a woman and wrote a book for her. It's not written in code, he says what he means and that's that."

"And what if Father Hasbún wrote it?"

"Then we have to destroy the novel, hack it to pieces with an axe. Say it's an incomplete love story. Just there in potential, backstage, in the wings, always about to come on, never really allowed to by that priest."

"I insist you should buy *Love Story.*"

"Hollywood would never accept the plot of the novel I want to buy. It's for a Chilean Andy Warhol. Romeo and Juliet without family rivalries, Pyramus and Thisbe without a wall between them, Helen of Troy with a happy husband whom she's left, and no cancer out there anywhere. There are no witches, no angry gods, no dragons, no moral blackmail, no little Lolitas driving men into a second adolescence. There's no ejaculatio praecox, no conniving mothers-in-law, no frazzled nerves, unjustified accusations, equally unjustified revenge, sudden revelations in the middle of an alcoholic stupor, no festering resentment over stacks of dirty dishes or piles of soiled diapers that nobody wants to wash, no insane brutality in the middle of love-making just to prove you're really a man, no frigidity or excuses to show there's no reason for jealousy."

"I don't like your novel. There's not much suspense or

narrative flare."

"You're wrong. Whenever something's missing, whenever we're expecting something and it doesn't happen, interest grows."

"All right. I'm going to tell you the truth. If I were reading that book, I'd want something to happen to the couple. I'd want some handsome stranger to burst implacably into their lives, or a war to be declared and he'd end up spitting blood and curses on some distant battlefield without ever remembering her, or they'd be divided by political differences, or she'd be horrified by his sexual excesses and the experiments he wants to try out, or they'd have a mongoloid child, or he'd turn out to be a wife-beater, or they'd have money problems and get thrown out of their apartment, or some irresistible woman would pass through, or their propane tank would be empty and he'd disconnect it in a rage, but the company's a long way off, and he can't take the tank on the bus, or he'd lose the shirt she gave . . . "

"But you act like it's some Hollywood idyll. Not at all. Rock Hudson and Doris Day would be miserable in that world. No petty mistakes or complications. Not even a pretence that anything could go wrong. It's not a saccharine novel. It's absolutely realistic. Why shouldn't there be at least one couple, among billions, whose story is worthy of being told in *Love*? Not even just one?"

"Not one. That novel's not representative of anything. And the proof is plain to see. Nobody ever wrote it."

"OK. Let's not argue. So you don't have *Love*?"

"I don't have that novel."

"So I'll take *Nephews and Little Nieces*. What else can I do? Gift wrap it please. Maybe my wife'll like it at least."

184

That was before Jane arrived. In spite of the rustling vastness of the trees beneath that incessant rainfall, everything was intimate. Small I might be, but I already sensed the difference between what was mine, this tiny house at the top of a vine-covered tree where he left me every time he went out to save the blacks or the elephants and where he would find me faithfully waiting on his return, and the external world, that jungle, hesitant as a hushed drum with no hope of hands to beat it with the green thunder of birds, that deafness in which thousands of insects scratch and copulate in the tropics. I stayed there watching, Tarzan,

It may come as a surprise to no one that the first work of fiction offered up by Ariel Dorfman, the co-author of *How to Read Donald Duck*, is an incursion behind those very

how you became a dot, a stain, a crazed eye traced in the air on the horizon, hoping that your white muscular mass would soon return through this same hole on the horizon. I was very young and small, just a baby really, who had no way of knowing that people say one thing and mean another, that the love they pledge today is gone tomorrow, that things change. I had no way of knowing it. Now, after Jane fries the potatoes and washes the pan, after she puts the oil away and sticks the left-overs in the refrigerator of the bungalow that now seems so immense, I realize I should have guessed it back then when for the first time I was alarmed to notice that Tarzan came back another way, he left that hole in the jungle open and didn't close it behind him like a curtain so they wouldn't see us.

enemy lines that have been his obsession, a message sent from the deformed inner platform of fictional heroes which the mass media have created as habitual companions of every inhabitant of this planet.

Everything started with that constant coming and going. That whistling in the air cut our peace like a knife and allowed strange forces to invade our home. Never leave a door open for the wind or the wife of a stranger to come through.

The narrator, at times intense, at times ironic, confronts the most familiar

Never let another woman enter your house. Of course back then he didn't mention Jane to me, he didn't explain about the public, and the producers and the Metro Goldwyn Mayer lion. But I sensed something was wrong. Later I managed to overcome my fear, when I started to accompany my hero. "Now you'll see, my sweet," he told me one day, responding to some mute urgency in my eyes, "when you go out with me," all of which he said in my own language, the one we always use, the one Jane doesn't understand, the one you speak with a scream and with fire and as if we were hurrying the end of the world along, "now you'll see that everything in the outside world is peaceful and simple. There are rules, my tiny-eyed sweetheart, my silly little worry-wart monkey, rules for living that protect us, clearly defined forces that threaten us, and not the ones you think. There's nothing to fear, my dark-skinned, rose-fingered little beauty."

characters from comic books, television, and radio, mixed with others, who are apparently more real (the story "The Memoirs of Onofre Jarpa", and "Jaime Guzmán's Mattress"), subject to the same everyday limitations that all other human beings suffer. There they are, reproduced by spying recorders, the real lives of our idols: Robin, the Boy Wonder, trying to explain to his psychiatrist...

186

It was true. I found that out the day we went out for the first time, flying against the sun and with him, crossing shadows, above waterfalls, slipping among vines and leopards. But that's not what I feared. In fact the only thing I really wanted was to become part of that life, which was his life, but was also mine by nature and instinct. The jungle wasn't the real danger. The real danger was Jane.

> his disturbing dreams, bad grades, his shyness with
> adolescent girls with their budding breasts, his cold terror
> at the thought of death, his horror of bats; the sexual life
> of Tubby and Little Lulu, now adults, in a

Not just for me, a mere nobody after all, a poor little abandoned primate, transformed into a maid, an errand girl, a clown of babbling sounds and foolish somersaults; no, she was a danger to the whole jungle, to Tarzan himself. Don't you see that we could accept anything from him, in spite of the fact that he was white, the same as all those others who hunted us down with the dark moons of their rifles and their asthmatic nets, in spite of the fact that he was finally going to learn the language of the ones who carried in their pockets the keys to zoos, slave markets and diamond mines, in spite of the fact that he was more intelligent, don't you see, because he made himself one of us, he became king by following our rules. He didn't use his hands to build helicopters nor his voice to telegraph orders. It was after Jane arrived that we realized our mistake. But by then it was too late. And love isn't something you can just erase and start over from one day to the next.

> town that keeps on repressing them; the black character
> in *Mission Impossible*, married to a woman who belongs
> to the Black Panthers; Cheetah, the monkey, furious with
> Jane, first of all, because she's an agent of civilization,

Because it's time you made up your mind, Tarzan. Which

world do you belong to? The world of the lightning flash or of General Electric? As for me, I want to get out of here, oh great white god; I want to go back to those days when summer was a never-ending warm hammock.

> only later to realize that Tarzan was always tied to that human female; Woody Woodpecker as a scab, crossing the picket line at a studio; the pitiless cruelty with which Superman glosses over the starkest problems of the human beings he says he's defending; the menopause of a soap opera heroine who never managed to get in bed with anybody, because the script systematically skirted that experience; all the characters who are a collective (CONTINUES OVERLEAF)

Today I discovered the love letters that Tarzan exchanged with Jane, all typewritten, with stamps and envelopes and postmarks and airplanes. They were written before I was born. They're proof that it wasn't Jane who brought the curse to this jungle, which is now falling apart, losing its foliage, melting like butter under a blue hourglass; yes, they prove that Jane's not responsible.

> lie imposed on us day after day. That material and emotional poverty that buds in those dry, truncated lives is the result of the invasion of the reader as a marginal and underdeveloped group; it is the revenge of the reader who has been displaced as a real participant. The subversion of a normal and routine

"The readers ask me for it," you explained, "they're letters from my admirers, my fans," and behind the heavy, multifaceted wall of bushes I imagined the glare of those spectators, who were watching us, who refused to let us live in peace. Why did they have to show up? I forgave you everything, Tarzan, even those jokes you slipped into your letters to Jane, everything, but not that submission to the taste of people who had nothing to do with us. We were

It is necessary to anticipate that before the *Final Project,* which is explained at the end of the book, all the writers mentioned in the previous sections had gotten together. But, by chance, one night, (it may have been the fifteenth day of the strike, when the right, financed by the United States, tried to paralyze Chile in October, 1972), they all turned up at César's house. We were all drawn there as if by a magnet, and we were so absorbed in conversation that before we knew it, we were caught by the curfew. Maybe that's why we'd gone there, pretending we didn't know that at midnight military patrols would prevent us from returning home, so we'd be there together, improvising plays, telling anecdotes, making predictions, measuring the strength of the competing sectors in conflict, relaxing just a little, and wondering how we'd get out of this one, God help us, and somebody just happened to say that if he weren't so busy with politics, what great stories he'd be writing.

Sure, why not, but a lot of good it'd do us to have a literary renaissance if we ended up without a country; it was the same old vicious circle. We had believed the government was eternal, giving us time to work out the future peacefully, and now the fascists wanted to cut out our tongues; they were getting their public back, talking about the highest patriotic values, and as for us, well, we would be screwed. What sense did it make to write at times like these?

"Why not?" Who was it who said those words? We no longer remember. All times are like this. We're always in a state of permanent crisis. Power has been up for grabs every minute since 1970. The only difference is that right now things are at such a fever pitch we can no longer avoid facing reality. Your conscience won't permit it. A month ago, for example, I was writing another novel. Now I've said to hell with it.

He said it without any sense of sacrifice, almost happily, the nostalgia would come later. Nobody was taking notes; nobody needed to worry about leaving words behind. That first sentence that leads irrevocably to the rest of the story was unravelling in our different heads, and we were saying good-bye to it without even a see you later. There were other things to be done. Of course there was still the unconfessable trust that some intimate blackboard might be registering some of these experiences, like the blinking of an eye. The important thing was to survive.

Everyone was bursting with ideas, and had been waiting for an occasion like this to discuss them, to remember the nurse they called La Rata, or a sergeant one of us had known in a regiment in Chillán who hated "low-class" people like him, but ended up admiring the good-for-nothing recruits - and now together they had to stand up to an aristocratic landowner who was sabotaging the wheat crop.

So each one gets caught up in the general enthusiasm, joins the conversations of everybody else, positions are polarized, until, with everybody giving the wheel a spin and trying to talk just a little louder than everyone else, and the others trying to be heard, they reach the island of the magical final project. They are a collective entity, a society of artists that will be able to drain every last drop of what the country is going through, every story, nothing will get away from them. When it's all over, the main thing is not to let what happened to each person get lost, with a whole flotilla of secretaries, typewriters that never break down, and a special supplementary item for paper. They get more and more excited about the idea, with the whole country collaborating, and after that there won't be any need for any other project, it's the last of them all, the Straits of Magellan of all the literature of all times. Like it or not, objections arise, putting a dent in the over-all carefree mood; different styles begin to appear: how much longer are we going to waste our time with these useless, impossible efforts?

Fools that we were! We thought it was just a matter of entering the forbidden world of the workers, a world we knew only as informed tourists, and then publish a travelogue when we got back. Fools! Go ahead, stay there a while, just see if you can get back, see if you can hold up against the typhus, see if you think the veneer of quick visits is enough. I really mean it, plunge in there. Maybe you'll never write the same way again, maybe writing won't even be important to you anymore.

Conversation had drifted off. Nobody remembered that final project any longer. They thought that after living through the October crisis they'd be so changed, it was better not to make any plans for the future. No one could predict what would happen.

"Instead of a good novel," said Inibata, the sceptic, "maybe you'll decide on a good life." We detected in his voice evidence of some sort of transcendental decision, one that in fact did materialize a few weeks later.

Monreal added, I mean, it had to be him. Just look at the image: "Any writer who looks for experiences that are too radical may become like the smuggler who ends up married to a customs agent."

By now they've forgotten the *Final Project*. Now everybody's searching for the image that best demonstrates the fact that often the sea turns the diver into a fish on a platter. I'd been working overtime the last few days as a volunteer in a milk processing plant. After that, I didn't want to hear about cheeks like cream! Just let somebody wax poetic about how we're all empty bottles, waiting for the milkman to fill us!

"Like an impotent genius," said Farías. "All he needs is a woman, that's all, and he'll write the definitive chapter, just one experience, but he hasn't taken into account that his initiation into sex will effectively remove any desire to keep on writing and transform him into somebody else."

On and on they went. Somebody would like to do a thesis on Michaelangelo and all he needs is to see the Sistine Chapel to round out his ideas and when he leaves the chapel, he's the one on the judgement seat, the one being created anew by God's lewd finger, so he burns his notes and the university as well.

It was time for apocalyptic theses about literature to flourish.

We fell asleep. All the brothers went to sleep.

They've already forgotten that project. The sun rises over Santiago. We have to walk home. They say the bus drivers have joined the strike. They say the real confrontation will be today.

Their story was going to be told in the *Final Project* too. Theirs too.

Mr Carlos Reyes
Production Manager
AVANCE Film Co.

Dear Mr Reyes,

It has come to my attention that you were considering
filming Josefina de León's epic *Story of a Potato,* and that
you later abandoned that idea due to technical difficulties.
Later, it seems, you examined my story "Measure No.19",
where I presented the protests of the luxury cars of high
government functionaries which have been destined to serve
elsewhere (in health, civil service, etc.), and how a strike
attempt by those high-toned vehicles was frustrated. Unfortunately, you decided that my story was also inappropriate
for film. Since it's clear that you're looking for a story that is
pregnant with the point of view of objects (a characteristic
both aforementioned works have in common), I would like
to bring to your attention an idea I have for a film dealing
with the phenomenon of dependency, precisely from the
point of view of the objects themselves, from the crux or the
crust or from that point that lurks inside everything,
exploring in the very heart of the thing that profound
domination they all endure much more than the human
beings who use them.

The film would be divided into two parts: everything to
do with the inner life of the object would be portrayed
through animation, but these segments would be interspersed with others filmed (with cameras, I suppose, and
actors, preferably in black and white) inside a factory. I'll say
more about this second sequence later.

In my view, imperialism is encrusted in the essence of
every object, deep inside every material thing in America.

We don't have to show a Yankee marine or a dollar bill or a bottle of Pepsi, because they represent only the surface of the phenomenon of terrible subjugation against which we all are struggling. It's what goes on in the soul, as Poe said; that's where the true distortion is expressed, there in that monstrous, black gut into which we've all been transmogrified. It occurred to me that the only way of communicating this, beyond slogans, posters and propaganda, and beyond action, which is, of course, a form of expression, was to recreate a dictatorship in the heart of every object, a secret, hierarchical network wherein obedience is absolutely compulsory. To open up before the eyes of the spectator the fantasy of a world beneath the shadow of terror.

Deep within each Object, at the end of its darkest alley, behind closed shutters, lying in a bed on the top floor is the Representative. You never see the Representative in the animation, only his shadow on the wall, like mould, just a splash of a solitary shadow on a wall. Every Object that exists must have its Representative and his every desire must be gratified.

It is the dark world that lies beneath and within the smile with which Objects present themselves to human beings. In corners, behind the scissors, reclining on broken bottles, like cockroaches, the Representatives exercise their command. They seem to be sleeping, but their thousand eyes are scattered through the air, scarcely breathing in the humped backs of old people, or in the cancer of decaying bread.

The Representatives have fur like a cat's, enabling them to communicate with each other, and to unite against any Object that dares to rebel. In addition, they have advanced technology at their disposition. Rays that penetrate every pore and are transformed into stomachless mouths, which bite and chew the insides of an Object without ever having to digest it and without ever tiring. Tiny bees that whisper dark messages at the center of the Object's brain. The Refrigerator, which erases all previous experience, freezing memories. The Containment Glove, which blocks any communication between the Object and the outside world and prevents it from being fed, or from growing or reproducing. The Executioners, a substance like the hide of a crushed Bambi, a gelatinous material that isolates the Object's geography, and which progressively subdivides, cutting all telephone lines if ever there is an assault. The Collectors of old clothing and bottles, who, under the pretext of their profession, patrol houses and yards, setting up a system of buying allies. The Laughs, a musical group which combines melody and rhythm with sounds recorded in an insane asylum, great guffaws of laughter that deafen the hearer, mortify him and force him to flee. The Heels, armies of shoes that tap out their steps with all the rigor of Cartesian logic, and that walk over the Object's ears until it recites exactly what it has been told.

In this nightmare world, its body invaded by a thousand disguises, where everything is an enemy, a pulsating electronic music, it would appear that the Object can do nothing. Worse still, Objects cannot even speak. A creature called The Ventriloquist, formed out of pestilential airs and long, greasy hairs, has taken control of their mouths. In order to help The Heels, a Wall has been constructed in the Object's ears; it rises, falls and rises again, in an unceasing, undulating movement, rising like a god, then tumbling down, and between its bricks there are at times snatches, the merest gurgles, of messages, a smattering of words that, like a candle's flame in the middle of a storm, manage to transmit the distant splendor of something green and whispering. The Representative has also succeeded in transforming the Object's eyes into two bulbs which, when lighted, illuminate a vast Screen on which are projected films, TV series, and colors, all of which communicate directly to the skin of the Representative's dreams, as he dreams in a bed he never abandons in the next to the last house on the alley.

In this universe, the Object has, nevertheless, two bridges to link it to the outside world, and these are closely watched by the Representative who can control or even close them, but which he ultimately cannot destroy. They are conditions essential to the very existence of the Object, and therefore, they are also fundamental to the Representative: every Object must go on being engendered (it has a "before", something or someone that produced it, and an "after", a similar Object that will go on existing when it is gone), and it must be useful for something, it must have a Function. These are the Object's two Hands, against which the Representative can bring certain pressures, in cases of disobedience. He can allow the Object to rot, to be hidden, to be hoarded, to become so expensive it will never be used; he can punish the Object, like a naughty child kept in school during summer vacation. He can castrate the Object, leave it only half made, prevent its maker from getting spare parts, fresh kisses; he can paralyze it, forbid it to dream of its offspring, stop it from accelerating, or he can screw up its distribution.

Rebellion against Tyranny is possible for the Object thanks to its Hands, at the ends of its two bridges. Because the Object is in love with its Hands. That's why the ultimate goal of the Representative is to take over that Lover, invade each bridge and move toward the Hand and toward that vast body that extends beyond it, the center of the human constellation. And it succeeds. It crosses the border every time the Hand and the Object brush against each other, like a blood-red poison without a lung. The Representative knows that if he ever gains total control over the Hand he will be the master of the world; he will never again have to worry about bridges; and he'll be able to close himself off with the two of them, Hand and Object, in his miserable room, and enjoy them, transformed into a mirror of himself into which he can fall infinitely. From there his mouth will grow, devouring everything, even the Representative himself,

198

who is searching for Nothingness and loves it as much as the Object loves the Hand.

But the operation isn't that simple either. At the same time the Representative invades the Hand, the hand also penetrates the Representative's territory, disputing his control over the Object. It sets up bases, energy sources, power centers, joy, conscience, and it stirs up rebellions with the purpose of murdering that greasy stain in its bed. There are rumors of vast meadows of liberated Objects, lands where Hand and Object live in peace, where there are no Representatives. The Representative's hatred of the Birds who bring this kind of song is unlimited. He orders them to be hanged with vines, their bodies left to feed the Ventriloquist.

This endless, devastating battle is the theme of the animated sequence.

Parallel to this, you film a very simple story about a group of workers in a factory, confronted with a broken-down machine that refuses to go on working. They must repair it in order to continue production. But there are no spare parts. And there's no money. They call a parts distributor. Nothing. Requests for help go out. No response. All the technicians are already working on other machines which are also broken down. For one moment, we have the impression that production in every factory in Chile has come to a grinding halt. Destruction is tightening its squeeze on the country. They have 24 hours to repair that machine, with nothing more than what they have at hand and a spirit of brotherhood; there's no time for sleep, they must take advantage of the time to clean and paint and to improve distribution. They work hard; they test this piece and take that one apart; they argue; they try again. We soon realize that every action in the outside world, in that Chile blockaded and beleaguered by a foreign Empire, assaulted and dependent, has its effect inside the Object, in the Hand's struggle to overcome and be free. The worker does not completely understand that terrible world lurking in the heart of every Object, but he senses something, how fleeting connections link one action with another.

At the end of 24 hours, they manage to come up with a substitute for the imported Object and thence to defeat Imperialism. The Representative is stabbed in his bed. THE END.

The film should be called "Yankee, Go to Hell."

If you are interested, let me know.

Pablo Retamales

Dear Mr Retamales,

Mr Carlos Reyes has asked me to advise you, on his behalf, that unfortunately, there is no machine in Chile by which we could produce the kind of animation you suggest. Due to the balance of trade problem, the Central Bank has notified us that it will be impossible to import that kind of equipment. Due to a lack of external funding, we could not have the sequences produced abroad either.

We appreciate your kindness and hope that you will keep us informed of other projects you might have in mind in the future. We would like very much to collaborate with you in a significant film project.

Sincerely,
Ruth Azócar
Secretary to the Production Manager
AVANCE Film Company

200

In the mirror, on the other side of these mountains which are not even brown, vertebrate mountains, snowless and eagleless, on the other side of the mirror, just a little farther over there, lies Chile.

"I'm not saying it was Paradise. No. But it was a noble country. It had its dignity. You could live there, back then they let you live."

The bartender says nothing. He goes on arranging the glasses, polishing each one with a cloth.

"It had its defects, like any place, small imperfections, sure. But if you're talking about injustice, I mean real injustice, hell, I don't agree with you. Look, would you turn on the radio, please, on 89?"

"It's still not time," says the bartender.

"It's not time? What time is it?"

"No, not yet. It's not quite five."

"Five? You're right, not quite five. Time sure goes slow in this damn country. Back there, remember, time really went fast. We were busy all the time. Of course, when you live in a foreign country, I mean, I always said you can't sleep in a foreign country. I used to say it during my radio shows, back in Chile."

"Your program starts at five-thirty," says the bartender. "You've still got half an hour. More than half an hour."

"It'll be on early today. Fifteen minutes early. I taped it this morning, just this morning." The bartender moves away. "OK, bring me another one. Just like this one." The cashier walks by, one gin, straight up, and moves toward the other end of the bar, taking the bottle down.

Silently, somebody sits down beside him. A tie, a shirt,

201

still impeccably clean, neatly trimmed moustache, immaculate. Young. "Since you're fixing me one, bring one for my friend here too. Whatever he wants . . . that is, if you don't mind, sir."

"Not at all. Thanks a lot." The new arrival raises his voice a little. "Make mine a Tom Collins."

The bartender serves their drinks. For a few moments they stare fixedly at each other in the mirror on the other side of the bar, never looking directly at each other. Finally the first man says: "You're not from around here. I've never seen you in this bar before."

"I'm just passing through."

"A tourist, eh?"

"Not exactly. I'm on my way to Chile. The train leaves tomorrow."

"So, you're going to Chile? Really?"

"They're clearing the tracks. That's why I have to spend the night here."

"Well, what a coincidence! I'm from Chile."

"Yeah, I thought so." He downs the rest of the Tom Collins, and sets the glass carefully on the bar.

"You did?"

"Though by your accent I could have guessed you were from Mendoza."

"Well, the accents are similar. Besides, I've spent quite a while in Argentina."

"Sure. The accent's contagious."

"No doubt about that."

Each one toys with his glass. The newcomer signals to the bartender. "Another round," he says. "A Tom Collins and. . ."

"Gin, straight. They know me here and know what I like. I come in every day of the week. One gin, straight. I've been a regular customer for years. I like to listen to my program here." And to the bartender: "I've never missed a single one, right?"

202

"Never," says the bartender.

"Whenever there's a broadcast, here I am, right?"

"Yeah," says the bartender. "Every day of the week." He places their respective drinks in front of each man.

"Let me explain. You're not going to believe me, but the first day I recorded the program here in Mendoza, I happened to drop by here in the Condor Bar, just by chance. I liked the name; it reminded me of home, national bird and all that, you know. And when I came in, somebody, I don't remember his name now, turned on my program. Maybe I'm superstitious or something. Ever since then I haven't missed an afternoon. I have a few drinks, hear the program and go home."

The younger man asked: "Don't you have a radio at home?"

"Don't I have a radio? Of course I do. After all I make my living in radio. I've been doing it all my life. My wife listens, there at home. But I like it here, in the Condor Bar."

"I'm married too," the other man says. "My wife's from Chile."

"But you're Argentine."

"Yes. Of course."

"And you married a woman from Chile."

"I'm a doctor. I came back for my things here in Argentina. That's why I'm returning on the train."

"So you're going back to Chile, then."

"Tomorrow." He stares at the bottom of his glass. "When they get the tracks cleared."

"I'm never going back."

For a while now the bar has been filling up. But everybody is talking in low voices, in relaxed tones. Evening is falling. The bartender looks at his watch, but says nothing.

"You were saying something about your programs."

"My programs?"

"That you liked listening to them here."

"Oh, yeah. I don't know why, it's just one of those things.

203

I have this feeling that if I don't show up here, the program won't go well. So I keep up the habit. It's like soccer. Take a goalie, for example. Nobody's gotten a goal past him for ten games. By one of those coincidences, the day his team plays its first game, he forgot to brush his teeth. You think he's ever going to brush his teeth on a game day again? He'd have to be crazy . . . hey, Joselito, another round."

"Not for me, thanks."

"Come on, man, nobody's counting. Another round."

"It's just that I have to leave soon."

"Another drink's not going to hurt you. . . . Look, I'm telling you, this business about the goalie and not brushing his teeth. That's really true. I mean I was a sports announcer, so I know."

"Are you still working in that area?"

"Area?"

"I mean sports."

"Well, a few little jobs. But right now I'm mostly working on my program. It doesn't leave me much time for other things." The bartender brings the two drinks and places one in front of each man. "Thanks, . . . hey, why don't we go over and sit at a table?"

"Your program's about to start."

"Oh, I know it backwards and forwards. I'd rather talk a while. Besides, you were probably in Chile recently, right?"

"The hospital gave me a two-week leave. That's all. I'm a day late. That's what happens when you travel by train."

"Look, you're on your way to Chile. Come on, let's sit down. I have something to say." He stands up brusquely. He feels for his drink with his left hand and looks toward the street, at the houses on the other side, and beyond them the mountains that aren't really mountains, back there on the other side of the mirror. "Look, I'm going to be frank. I'm going to tell it to you like it is."

"I really have to go," says the younger man. "Some friends are waiting for me, some fellows from Mendoza that

204

I met years ago."

"You've got to hear me out. Come on. Just a little while. Besides, I really don't understand it. I don't know why you're going to Chile. Look, I mean I love my country, and I'm out here, far away. You're going back there. You're married to a girl from Chile. Maybe I even know her. What's her name?"

The other man hasn't budged from his stool, but he turns slightly. He pronounces his wife's name.

"No, I don't know her. . . I have a daughter in Chile. My only daughter. She's in Chile. I haven't seen her for years. Too many years."

The younger man stands up. "OK, let's sit down. But just for a while. I have things to do."

The other man stares at him fixedly now, looking directly into his eyes, and he puts a hand on his shoulder. "But I'm going to have to talk to you frankly. You don't mind, right? You're young, I mean, I could be your father."

"Let's sit down."

They don't say anything for a while. They stare at the tablecloth, tracing the flowers in its design with their eyes.

"Waiter!"

Silently, they bring over two more drinks. Along with some peanuts, olives, cheese.

"We haven't written to each other in years."

"You mean your daughter and you?"

"Yeah, my daughter. Not since we left. I only get news about her once in a while. From her uncles, my brothers. They stayed. I left, but almost everybody else stayed. And now you're going back there too."

"It looks like we're not going to agree on politics."

"I don't know anything about politics. I never got involved in that kind of thing. But back then you could work. It was a really nice country."

"I've got to go."

"I know, I know. You don't want to argue with me. You don't want to fight. You're going to Chile, and I left it. We

205

have nothing in common. You think I sold out, that I'm a *gusano*, just a piece of shit. You're Argentine and you're going to my country, and I'm Chilean, and I'm staying here in yours. But there's a difference. One difference. Know what it is? . . . You're free to stay or to go. But I have to stay here."

The other man, the young one, breathes deeply. "You must have made that decision yourself."

"Well, I'm going to tell you. Look, you don't want to argue, right?"

"Right. I don't want to argue."

"And especially with me, am I right? I mean, with a refugee, somebody that left. A lot of us left, but you don't want to talk to me."

"All right. If you really want to know the truth, mister, when I found out you did radio programs, I wanted to end the conversation right there, just as quickly as possible."

"You know my programs?"

"We get them in Chile."

"So they hear my programs in Chile?"

"Some people do."

"Just like my daughter. You sound just like her. My God, what's going on with you young people?"

His glance falls on the rest of the people in the bar, first the ones at the next table, who are drinking in silence; then shifts from customer to customer, until it comes back to the man who is sitting in front of him. "The young people are the ones who never wanted to engage in a dialogue. She never used real arguments, nothing but slogans, parroted slogans. . . But I'm going to tell you, in your case it's different. If it weren't, I wouldn't even bother to talk to you. Because that's the way it is. Neither one of us wants to argue. Fine. Just exchange some ideas, opinions. Talk a while. That's what we need to do over there in my country."

The Argentine doctor stands up abruptly. "OK, it was good to meet you. My friends are waiting for me, so please excuse me, I really have to go."

"Wait a minute. Don't get hot under the collar. I was actually praising you. I mean, you're really different from my daughter. And you know why?"

The other man raises his voice. "Waiter!" The waiter walks by him.

"Just a minute, sir. I'll be right with you."

"Waiter," he calls to the boy's back. "Bring me the bill."

"You know why you're different?" He looks directly into the young man's face, trying to reel him in, hoping he will look back. "You know why?"

Finally, still looking for the waiter with his eyes, the Argentine doctor says: "I don't have the foggiest idea."

"Please, sit down, while you're waiting for the bill. Don't just stand there. I mean I'm not going to bite you."

The young man shifts his weight slowly, pushing the chair back from the table.

"My daughter had some notion of what Chile was like before. She had the chance of knowing the world we used to live in. They brainwashed her just the same, but you, you weren't there back then. You must have come a lot later, after things changed so drastically, I mean really drastically."

"That's right. I did. That's exactly why I went to Chile. That's why I came back now to get my things."

"So you like Chile?"

The Argentine doctor again signals to the waiter, who yet again passes him, murmuring an excuse.

"Hey, listen, I'm in a hurry." And adds: "Yeah, I like it a lot."

"Fine. I'm not surprised. You didn't see what it was like before. You're not from Chile. That's why you can leave Argentina. That's why an educated man like you, a doctor, can leave your country and set yourself up in a foreign country. A really admirable thing, youth. A little bit blind, you'll see. Doesn't really see what's going on all around it."

"Look, sir. I'm going to be frank too. I see exactly what's

207

going on around me. And right now the only thing I want to do is pay the bill and meet my friends."

"That's why I call my show 'Remembering'. Re-member-ing. I bet you've never listened to it, back there in Chile."

"I don't have time."

"Exactly what I was saying. You don't have time. Well, that's what vacations are for. It's as if God Himself had blocked those tracks, maybe so you could be saved, so you could find out the truth. Now you're sitting over here and you have the good fortune to be able to meet the real Chile. Not this circus that's going on now, what the official propaganda machine cranks out every day. That's the way human beings are. They soon forget. You settle in. But you should never lose the best traditions your country has."

The doctor glances toward the bar. The waiter has disappeared. Only the bartender is there and he calmly returns the doctor's gaze.

"Look. It was the time of the Alliance for Progress. I mean it had just started. The late and much admired President John Fitzgerald Kennedy announced the Alliance, and a sense of jubilation swept over all Latin America. That's the time I'm talking about, and those happy years that immediately followed it."

From the counter, the bartender interrupts him. "It's time," he says, in a loud voice, so everyone can hear him.

"Oh, right. What time is it?"

"Twenty after five."

A frown darkens the speaker's face. "Didn't I tell you, didn't I? How irresponsible can you get! But I warned you they'd probably broadcast the program early today. Fifteen minutes early." The bartender makes no response. "Here we have this young man whose only purpose is to listen and form his own, independent opinion, and you make us miss five minutes."

The bartender turns on the radio.

"So many lies about the past. About so many glorious

208

chapters from our nation's history. Our heroic deeds. The price experiment, for example. We defeated inflation. Reduced it to zero. Banished it from the country. Everybody had plenty to eat back then. There was no need for all those feared and hated Food and Price Committees. There was no rationing of consumer goods. Businesses were not pressured. There were no runs on the banks. And do you know how all that was accomplished? Do you know how?"

"Where the hell is the waiter? I asked him for the bill an hour ago."

"No, no. You're not going. No, sir. You can't leave now. This is precisely when you have to stay."

The Argentine doctor says nothing.

"We've had ample opportunity to talk about the painful present afflicting our beloved country and no doubt we'll have time to continue with that theme later. Now it's remembering time. When times are hard, like these, the best thing is to hold on to the past and learn from it. A lot of Chileans have forgotten the words our President used to respond to President Kennedy's speech. You don't know about those things. They've hidden the truth from you. They've erased those words that were of such historical transcendence. But as long as one man remembers, they'll never disappear entirely. 'Progress is *ad portas*', the President said, 'But that doesn't give us the right to sit back and rest on our laurels.' And he added: 'Poverty will be eliminated; violence will disappear. There'll be no more beggars on the streets of Santiago.' And do you know what the President said after that?"

Suddenly silence descends on the bar. Private conversations, even the clattering of bottles and glasses, the clinking of ice and the scraping of chairs, cease. A few rays of sunlight shine indirectly through the door and window of the bar. It is an autumn sun, weak, hesitant, and sickly. In the mirror can be seen the mountains behind which the sun will soon sink. Then it will look for the ocean, which can never be seen from here.

"His Excellency asked: 'What good is progress, if people aren't happy? . . .Why emerge from the claws of unequal development, if we don't know what to do with our lives, with our leisure time, our freedom?' All the material problems in Chile were solved, but it was the spiritual ones that our highest executive authority was talking about. 'What good is welfare for everybody, if there is no clarity of vision as far as humanity is concerned?' "

From one of the tables, a man murmurs softly: "We're a single drop in the cosmic ocean of time, and we ought to think on what we'll do with these moments we've been given to live."

"Exactly! It was a philosophy of life and not of death. Not death. 'This is a problem,' the President insisted, 'that even the world's most advanced republics confront, and finding a definitive solution to it could be our specific contribution to humanity.' "

Now, glass in hand, the speaker stands up. He slowly examines the other customers, the ones at all the tables and at the bar, one by one, all of them now silent. He looks at the bartender and the cashier. And finally, at long last, he looks at the young man, seated below him, on the other side of the table, just a little beyond. The speaker's lips begin to tremble.

"The President called for a national campaign of meditation. And do you know what happened, dear listeners, friends? Projects and offers started arriving at the National Planning Office, as well as at the regional offices. First it was just a trickle, then a steady stream and finally rivers and oceans of proposals and ideas. My daughter never knew that. My grandchildren will never know it. Unless I remember it every afternoon, unless I preserve this tradition into the future. Your wife won't know it. They were very young, it was a long time ago. And later they had the nerve to say that there was no national culture, that the educational system had failed. They spouted off about illiteracy. But let them talk, that's what I say. Because those projects, those possibilities, bore the stamp of the people's creative energy and originality, the people's determined response to the crossroads into which leisure and abundance had hurled contemporary humanity, and after observing that the proposals covered every topic, every profession and every talent, it was decided that our country should be the first to put those plans into practice on a massive scale, so that it would become a showcase for the rest of the world, so that other, more prosperous but less happy nations would learn from us, down here in this corner of the world, what a population like ours could do when it set out to defeat the endemic evils of over-abundance, and the illnesses of advanced post-technological society. The problem, my friends, was not production, as was demagogically proclaimed years later. The problem was superfluous consumption, post-industrial society. Our projects solved those problems."

He raises both fists in the air, his head erect, his eyes closed. Without moving his feet, he rocks back and forth gently. Then he sits down. He looks directly at the Argentine doctor.

"And the projects were carried out. Every one of them. And do you know what happened then? Political promises, hatred, petty rivalries and passions."

The waiter deposits two drinks in front of them, a Tom Collins and a gin.

"Here you are, gents."

"But I was asking you for the bill. I've been asking for it for a hundred years."

"The bill?"

"And I'm going to tell you something else. There was real participation back then. People taking control of their lives and their futures. Funds were appropriated for every initiative, every project, without regard to race, religion or political complexion. We experienced total cooperation and

211

solidarity."

The waiter shrugs. "Sorry. I thought you said two more. If you want, I'll take them back."

"No, that's all right. Just leave them. But bring me the bill. And make it fast."

"We'd almost eliminated poverty. Why should we go on competing for more and more material goods, when the soul, the nation, was what counted? I'm not going to tell you there were no problems, a few neighborhoods where they didn't have televisions in every house, in some backward areas in the mountains. There were some. I admit that. But back then everybody was free. Look, I mean, even I had a place back then, and I'm totally apolitical. For example, you might ask, what did announcers do under those circumstances? Well, I can only speak for myself, because, after all, charity begins at home. I won't tell you there weren't other plans, for example, the price plan, but ours was the best, in long range terms. And like lots of other things in this life, it had very simple beginnings."

"Just a moment. One moment." The voice that erupts is almost a bark. A man has stood up at the nearest table. Tall, heavy-set, with enormous hands, he stands before them. "In my opinion, the price control plan was more important."

"Ah, Don Agustín. I hadn't seen you. . . Don Agustín, I'd like to introduce the doctor here. Doctor . . . Don Agustín. This young man's off to Chile. I was telling him something about the past."

"Pleased to meet you, young man. I'm a military man, a retired colonel, so we're colleagues. With your permission. . ." He sits down.

The doctor shakes his head. "I don't understand. What plan? What are you talking about?"

The radio announcer smiles. "You see? You're getting interested, right? Now you'll have something to tell your little Chilean lady when you get back."

"If he goes back," says the retired colonel.

"Of course. If he wants to go back. . . Since you ask, and since I got a letter inquiring about prices during previous administrations, I'm going to answer your concerns.

"But before that, I'd like to say a few words about the suggestions we made for the adequate use of radio. . . The National Anthem should be played. On every station. That was the plan. Simple, in appearance. But with unsuspected consequences. Singing out like a real Chilean. On every station. First, as a kind of warm-up. Singing the song just the way it was, about a thousand times, valiantly, then would come the basses and the tenors combined, and then the sopranos, any combination of voices. Naturally, we got the support of several bodies. The municipality of Santiago, the Mozarteum, the Society for National Dignity, and the professors of music. On and on, infinitely, with full employment, until everybody had the chance to sing. I mean, the Department of Elections, the Department of Statistics, taxi drivers, everybody offered their personal and technical cooperation. And it was a patriotic measure."

"For not by bread alone," says a blond teenager, standing in the doorway of the bar.

"For man does not live by bread alone. It provided incentive for other projects; it became a kind of backdrop for what followed. To fire the popular imagination with enthusiasm. So that everybody would understand that defeating idleness, carrying out some small project (and you had to offer at least one, or else you were fired, understand?) was a true patriotic duty." For an instant everything is quiet again. "I mean, back then we all devoted ourselves to what was basic, to solving humanity's biggest problems."

A third man approaches. He doesn't sit down at the table, but instead stands directly behind the Argentine doctor, leaning forward a little so he can hear better.

Farther away, from the radio, a voice goes on speaking.

"It also allowed for cultural exchange, and friendship

213

among all the world's people. There was no discrimination. Our song had to be translated and foreign choruses had to be imported. Or it had to be taught in the School of Translators, as an approximation to other cultural practices from our particular perspective. It would even be sung in Russian and Chinese."

"We didn't discriminate," the newcomer whispered in his ear, his breath grazing the doctor's shoulder. "Now that was real international solidarity!"

The radio announcer bangs on the table.

"No doubt about it. That was the most important proposal. And I'm not saying that just because *we* put it forward."

"Just a minute. Just one minute. Price control was more important. Don't you remember, friends? Somebody had managed somehow, who knows how, to lock all the prices inside a big trunk, which filled the central courtyard of the Supreme Court."

From the doorway, the blond teenager says: "My father was a judge. He remembers it. He says that seeing that exemplary punishment of prices helped him impart justice."

The Argentine doctor looks at him. For the first time he raises his voice. "Are you a Chilean too?" he asks.

"Everybody here in the Condor Bar is from Chile," says the blond youth.

The doctor doesn't ask again. In the mirror, the sun can be seen, far away, about to meet the mountains, and the final waves of light strike the bottles above the mirror.

"Everybody participated," said the voice from the radio. "It wasn't just one little group. Nobody tried to take credit that wasn't his. Every Chilean citizen provided an honor guard, so the imprisoned prices couldn't escape. We could count on the total support of public opinion. After all, it was a battle that affected us all."

"Back then," said the retired colonel, "everybody had a job. I remember it well. We, for example, were sitting on one corner of the trunk. Inside we could hear the cries of all those poor prices."

"The squeals of pigs cutting their own throats," says the radio.

"The cries of terrified children during long nights."

"The screams of traitors," says the retired colonel. "Then we all stood up together, and the prices, I mean they were really stupid, although they thought they were smart; well, the prices thought we must have gone away. They thought the prison services must have been on strike. So the prices stretched out a hand, then an arm, and at that moment, one, two, three, crack, we lowered the lid of the trunk. Crack. Later the people from the interrogation project showed up."

"My older brother was working on that project," says the blond youth, coming closer.

" 'Confess, damn it,' the people who interrogated warned him. They took down all the reactions and fed them into a special computer. Stick it to the price of meat, and they gave it a little electric shock, so it would learn to be a man and would drop any anti-Chilean attitudes."

"So they wouldn't proliferate anymore or have any kids. That's the way the people carried out justice, finishing off everybody that had tormented them for years. So, dear public, we did away with the torment of inflation."

"But the basic plan had to do with radio. You have to recognize that it was the only one that opened up unsuspected vistas for national and popular participation. When we dramatized the song, put it in a setting with characters and period costumes, and then broadcast radio dramas and TV series."

"There was no television back then."

"You're right, Don Agustín. I'd forgotten. But that came later. Progress had been announced, and progress came. And I curse the hour we built stations and imported equipment. All for them to control now."

"We won't make that mistake again, you'll see, man.

215

Don't worry about that."

Other customers are arriving. The bar is almost full. They go to the counter, order a drink and approach the only table where people are talking and listening. They wander over just to see what's going on.

"It was a job that demanded everybody's cooperation. It was possible to poll the public to see what verses they preferred, to hold marathons and races, offer tickets to Miami for the winners, or houses in the ritzy part of town, or yachts. But that was just the beginning. To defeat an over-supply of time, to confront the problems generated by idleness, the fundamental thing was to use science as an aid. Take a group of children, chosen by modern methods (for that, there were other projects that fed into this one), to see what effect having no contact with the national anthem had on them, that is, isolate them and not let them get near the goal post. And compare the results with the control group of young people who had cut their eyeteeth on patriotic milk, and then, in a rigorously precise, scientifically reliable, final report, denounce the insidious effects of keeping youth away from that fountain of music that nourished everyone, without regard for class. If it turned out to show what we expected, we could punish the parents of those children, depriving them of their right to vote and to work and refusing to finance their projects."

"Show them what it means to be patriotic," said the retired colonel.

"Because," the radio announcer continued, "they were the ones responsible for that state of poverty and ignorance."

"And like all the other projects," says the man breathing down the neck of the Argentine doctor, "the cost was minimal."

In the prolonged silence, the sun hurls one final ray, a red bolt that fades in the mirror, a dawn that becomes night once again, and the Argentine doctor, in a loud voice, says:

216

"I have to go. I mean it this time."

But he doesn't move. He looks for his drink and begins to shake it, hearing each piece of ice as it strikes against another or against the side of the glass.

"I insist," says the voice of the retired colonel, "that the price control plan had greater repercussions. I mean, look, I grabbed the price of meat with these hands and beat it to a pulp. You should have seen it. It turned to putty in my hands, as docile as a pussy cat. Confessed that the peaches really were very expensive, not to mention subversive. No sir, I said, you're the one that's expensive, damn it. Out with the truth, imbecile. No more talking out of the wrong side of your mouth. Who's really responsible? Who's to blame? Confess right now. And when he told me that the price increases were the result of the workers' unreasonable and exaggerated demands, I smiled right back at him. OK. Then the Director of Price Control put him and his crowd back in the trunk. That's why everybody could eat beef back then, roasts, steaks. And let's just see anybody try to speculate."

"Yeah," says a new voice, from a distant table. "I was sitting on the price of bread, holding it down. It wanted to rise, but I kept on biting it. Now who do you think came to its aid?"

"The price of wheat," says the voice from behind the Argentine doctor.

"The price of wheat!" says the new voice from the distant table. "What a scuffle there was! The only one who didn't get involved was the price of milk, a real coward and a fag! The rest of the prices gave it a real trouncing. Called it a yellow-bellied scab and a traitor. For not playing the game."

"So, dear friends out there in radio land, that's how we managed to control inflation, the scourge of the needy. Our country became a major tourist attraction. And now, who crosses our borders? Who sleeps in the shelter at Farellones now? But let's talk about those happy days. They came to see us. And the first thing our illustrious guests had to do was make the pilgrimage to that trunk, with all us Chileans sitting on top of it."

"They were visibly impressed."

"Some even felt obliged to sit on the trunk themselves. And the people from the photography project took a picture of them."

The bartender turns up the radio a little.

"And if the visitor was from the IMF project or had a friend on the Civil Registry, in those few cases, and also for de Gaulle, when he came, an exception was made. Some poor price was pulled out through the keyhole, so they could put their foot on its neck, like a lion hunter, while the price squirmed feebly."

"Until it realized it was better not to rebel, and lay quiet."

"With threats."

"And a few blows. . . "

"Threats and blows, both, and sometimes the price would even smile for the camera, thinking, perhaps, that in some official office or a less official bedroom its image would float sadly, caught, like it, in a frame, but with a higher degree of freedom and a broader horizon to view. Later, back into the trunk it would go, because if it got away, we were really pissed!"

"One day," says the retired colonel, "there was an attempted rebellion. Do you remember?"

"What I remember," says the radio announcer, "is the cost of toothpaste. The cadaver of that price, floating, decayed and rotten. That's where doctors were needed. We had to hunt them down one by one along white corridors."

"And that's all for today, fellow citizens. This has been the program *Remembering.* Another broadcast service of the Free Voice of Mendoza for all of Chile. Tomorrow, at this same time, we will go on remembering, reminiscing about that time that can still return. We must depart, but not without first reminding you that tonight, at 9:30, this program will be re-broadcast. Keep the faith. The sun always comes up tomorrow. Let's believe liberation will come to our country. Good night to all."

For a couple of seconds no one speaks. The bartender turns off the radio. All the customers stare into the bottoms of their glasses, avoiding their neighbors. From outside, the light from the street suddenly illuminates the semi-darkness.

"The same time tomorrow," says the radio announcer. "Because if that had been all there was to the project, then it would have been just one more among many, like the geranium project, or the massive campaign to provide aid for mentally retarded children. The national anthem proposal was really just a glimpse, what could be called a mere approximation and a first step toward what we really wanted to do, and that was (and here's the real stroke of genius!) to broadcast basketball and soccer games, automobile races, and gymnastics on the radio. That was our fondest desire. The business of the national anthem was OK, but it was really just a step, a pretext."

The radio announcer's voice went on resonating in the bar, drawing the other customers, who were at other tables, and who were now gathering around his words, tomorrow at this same time, in this same bar. Everybody came over and began forming a tight circle of bodies and breath, leaving just a little opening through which a little bit of the mirror could be seen.

"OK, I'm leaving." This time he stood up, shoving his chair back into the man who was standing so close behind him. He stood there like that, between the chair and the table, his knees slightly bent. No one moved. The bartender and the cashier were there, on the fringes of the group, looking at the announcer. "I really think they're waiting for me. . . They'll worry if I'm late."

"Don't be silly," says the colonel, without looking at him, "you have to stay."

"Sure," says the announcer. "I mean, you won't be able

to hear the continuation of the program tomorrow."

"I'll be on the train tomorrow."

"Exactly. That's why you'll miss the program. There aren't any radios on the train, right?"

"There aren't any radios on the train," says the bartender. "When I came, I couldn't use my radio."

"You see? And don't tell me that you're not interested in hearing about the end of the plan, how it all turned out."

"I'm interested, sure, but it's getting late. Really late."

"Fine. I'll summarize it for you. So you can at least carry a message back. You can look up my daughter and tell her everything. Because she doesn't listen to the program either. I give you her address, she opens the door and you tell her the whole thing."

"Go on with it," says the retired colonel.

"We were saying that the national anthem had been the first step. Because it so happened that one day, between one verse and the next, one of the basses interrupted the song, unconsciously and to keep up his flagging spirits, with a long and emotional description of a goal. The fact is it was a fantastic goal, beautifully executed. Picture-perfect. I happened to be beside him and I grabbed the microphone from him to describe what was going on in the middle of play and how the other players had prepared the way for that goal. But the one who was a real genius and understood the full meaning of what we had been doing, was a guy who shouted, give it to him with a right to the chin, and he's against the ropes again, the champ's staggering, he hits him with the left, then with both fists, the champ's helpless, he's falling, one, two, he's on the canvas, ladies and gentlemen, four, five, six, seven, the crowd's going wild, nine, ten, and Chile's won the title, Chile's shown the world, and he said it all with such aplomb that we all realized how important it really was (and remember that the whole thing was broadcast nationwide and live on every station) that we go on with the sports broadcast and have the national anthem during the intermissions, but now it would just be part of the background. You wouldn't believe the phone calls we got, the number of people who wanted to participate; everybody encouraged us to go on talking about the whole game, and not just the end. Not just the end."

"How much?" the doctor asks the cashier, as well as the bartender, who is farther back, with the other customers. "How much do I owe you?"

"We're all friends here," says the cashier. "We're all from Chile."

"My friends are waiting for me. . . Besides, they know I'm here. I told them I'd be in the Condor Bar."

"Great," says the cashier. "If they know, then they won't worry. They can wait a while longer."

"I'd rather pay you right now."

"Sit down," says the retired colonel. "Don't be rude. It looks like they don't teach good manners in Chile any more. Sit down and at least hear the end of the story."

"Sit down," says the blond youth. "We all want to hear about tomorrow's program."

"Well, it's not exactly tomorrow's. You know the programs have to be written ahead of time, to give them a bit of tone, then I can spend the rest of the day gathering material. News about the current situation. Research on past events. It's not easy."

"We know that," says the retired colonel. "That's why we demand a little respect from this guy."

"Thanks. But since we're in a hurry, and the doctor here's shown so much interest, I'm going to give a quick summary. I don't want to disappoint him. Besides, he's married to a Chilean girl."

"That's right," says the Argentine doctor, sitting down abruptly. "We're expecting our first child in another month."

"Your first kid! Well, allow me to congratulate you! Let's see. What do you want? A boy or a girl?"

The Argentine doctor takes hold of the edges of the chair

221

and moves it closer to the table. "We don't care," he answers.

"OK. Enough interviews. We can find out more later. Now let's get back to the radio project. Those broadcasts built up a large following. Now at last the fans could hear about all the games they wanted to see, but couldn't be there. Our teams beat the English, sometimes by the skin of their teeth, other times by a tremendous margin. We could even broadcast from Madison Square Garden, and the heavyweight title went to one of our own, at last a man from long-suffering Latin America got the championship, and we all wanted to turn out at the airport to welcome the champ home. Those were real crowds. Not like the ones now that take to the streets under pressure from the bureaucrats currently in power. Not like now where they have to put in an appearance at every parade. The Davis Cup belonged to our players. And Brazil fell at last, and in Maracaná Stadium, no less."

"Of course, sometimes, all those victories had to be seasoned with a little defeat. We didn't want to bore the fans after all."

"But even then we could talk about something really exciting. A bad referee, a last-minute injury, the superior height of the gringos on the basketball team, the pique the organizers had against us, the lack of facilities, an adverse climate, the other team's foul play, our national sportsmanship. And best of all: the half-time commentaries. And the public was thrilled; they made predictions, described their favorite teams, dedicated the Olympic Games to Rosa Esther and to Doña Sarah. And we held firm to our course."

The sun has already gone down, and outside, the streetlights are beginning to flicker on. The headlights of an automobile are reflected in the mirror and then disappear. Later, the sound of its motor is lost too.

"The government gave us its full support. It took advantage of intervals between plays to broadcast other kinds of news, not just sports. Commentators also included more daring and provocative topics. We were the masters of the country, whatever we thought was gospel and represented the common man, the oft-forgotten man in the street: weather, taxes, the plight of the handicapped, good and evil, religious education, reconstruction. Bach. The fact is we hadn't been bitten by the political bug. And what inspired us to go further was that within a short time the economic, scientific, and international news began to follow our example. Nothing but good news. The whole country was euphoric, for example, when they found out that prices were definitely outlaws now, they'd been removed from the trunk, declared criminals, and some of them would be shot by firing squad, an act which would be witnessed by representatives of the press, national authorities and special envoys from the Interamerican Development Bank, which had financed the entire project, along with the Ford Foundation. We sports announcers broadcast the event in its totality, interviewing the prices to find out if they were repentant. We also interviewed a well-known Dutch criminologist, asking him for his appraisal of our police corps. One priest, when interviewed, refused to say whether the prices had repented. But I'm going on too long."

"Go on, go on," says the voice from behind the Argentine doctor.

In the mirror the sky is slightly bloody behind those mountains; red clouds lie over Chile.

"What a time that was, dear citizens! What news! That project enabled us to keep everyone informed about the results of all the others. It was the natural culmination of and the model for all other projects. Through our project, every citizen who had participated in the campaign to eradicate idleness, that grand campaign of meditation and activity, had a free voice and could communicate his good wishes and purposes to everyone else. Do you remember? Do you?"

"Yes," says the retired colonel. "I remember."

"Yeah," says the bartender.

"My father told me about it," says the blond youth. "That way, I can remember too."

Like a chorus, yes, yes, I remember, sure, you remember, of course, in the still darkness, shadows moved, lips moved, yes, they remembered, everybody remembered that time.

"The housing problem solved! Another oil reserve discovered in the Bay of Reloncaví. Purchased by the United States for millions of dollars. Unemployment ended. We'd won a war against a neighboring country, with a lightning thrust, and all those territories and resources which pusillanimous officials from the previous century had given up under the pretext of convenience or brotherhood, were restored to the nation. Our first nuclear reactor was inaugurated in the capital."

"One day," breathed the voice behind the Argentine doctor, "child malnutrition disappeared; it just drifted off and no one even noticed it. Nobody even attended its funeral or pronounced any farewell speeches.

"That's the way things were done in our country!

"The candidate of the Marxist opposition had declined his nomination, recognizing that the government had fulfilled the public's worthiest demands. Our scientists discovered an anti-cancer vaccine.

"One of our countrymen broke the world swimming record for the three-hundred-meter butterfly.

"Our wine was the best, featured in a bulletin from the FAO.

"In an international contest of national anthems, we tied with the *Marseillaise*. We could follow the semi-finals, because by now the entire population was bilingual. Berlitz himself came to study the phenomenon. The mystery of Easter Island was solved. The tax on liquid gas was reduced. We had discovered a cheap method of desalinization of sea water and our desert was blooming with bellflowers. The national flower could be found all the way to Atacama. We eliminated the entrance examination for our universities.

"The Organization of American States selected our President as its Man of the Year. That selection was applauded by *Time Magazine.* It was proposed that a study be made of the way we had solved our problems. We offered technical assistance to Peru. The Queen of England, at a press conference, let it slip that when she retired she intended to move to our lake country in the south.

"There were no busy signals on our telephones."

The announcer slowly stood up. In that darkness, the tears in his eyes could scarcely be seen. "But what can I tell you. It was almost paradise. The closest we've ever come to paradise."

For a moment no one wants to interrupt. Then, the colonel makes a signal and the lights are turned on, one by one; nobody looks at anybody else. The bartender and the waiter go over to the entrance to the bar. They begin to lower the metal curtain. Slowly the street and the black face of the low mountains in the distance are erased from the mirror. The sky over Chile is no longer visible. The bar is closed.

"Very good," says the retired colonel.

"Now you've heard what our country was like back then." He stands up. "Now that you know, you must realize they lied to you."

The Argentine doctor does not lift his head to look at him. He makes no attempt to stand up.

"So you're going to Chile?" says the blond youth.

"Of course he's going to Chile," says the voice behind him.

"He's waiting for them to clear the tracks," says the announcer. "Tomorrow he'll continue his journey. By tomorrow you'll be back on the national territory, right?"

The Argentine doctor reaches out his hand and picks up his drink. Without tasting it, he replaces it on the table.

225

"Fine, now you know our opinion. No doubt it's been an illuminating experience. You've had the chance to hear the other side."

In the mirror, in the narrow space that's left through which to see the mirror, the bartender and the waiter fumble with the lock on the metal curtain.

"Now maybe you feel like telling us something about Chile," says the announcer. "I mean it's been years since any of us was there."

The cashier receives the key to the lock. The bartender steps into the space through which the mirror could be seen.

"Dialogue is good," says the retired colonel. "It's good to be able to exchange impressions."

The Argentine doctor says nothing.

"We're waiting," says the announcer. "We'd like to hear your point of view."

"It's probably an accident that one of us is the intersection," says Juan, the protagonist of the novel *Which of These Roads Leads to Rome?* by Renato Fardo (pen name), recently published by Process Publishing Company, "while the rest of us are the roads."

A question asked by any man who, against his will, has found himself in difficult straits: Why me? Why not somebody else?

Juan is an innocuous employee of a distributing company. Socialist by conviction, he always comfortably posed the need for another kind of society and a profound change of structures. I say comfortably, because having such ideas never meant that he felt any compulsion to change his own way of life. When Unidad Popular came to power, it disturbed his peaceful existence. Now he, along with some other colleagues, has to keep tabs on the management of the company, to prevent any tax evasion, confront the black market that's just beginning to flourish, demand greater participation from workers and employees, prepare for eventual nationalization, or, in the case of a counter-order, to put on hold any attempt to speed up the process.

But Juan doesn't have the personality for that kind of thing. All he's ever wanted, ever since he was a child, was to live in peace with his friends. The possibility of being someone else, which sometimes teased him from afar, was never more than an abstraction: he didn't have the motivation, the opportunity, the energy or the drive.

Juan is too much of a "good ole boy" to get caught up in the life-or-death political struggle that hangs over him. A good drinking companion; a soccer buddy; always standing by, ready with his attention, his money, or advice; he's a naive and good-natured friend to half the world; always ready to believe in the good intentions of those around him; he can't live without giving and receiving love.

"The only thing that matters to me is for people to love me," he confesses to a stranger in a bar, toward the end of the novel. "That was the only thing that mattered, I swear."

So Juan is the worst possible person to be a political activist: he suffers from an excessive ability to put himself in the other man's shoes and to see things from that other perspective, and is therefore too ready to see truth in what his adversary proposes.

But he can't just remain aloof from the struggle that surrounds him either, as much as that might be desirable for his own peace of mind. Strictly educated by a father who was an evangelical minister, under the weight of his memories of a family always obsessed with justice (an abundance of lawyers and judges), he can't accept any deviation, however small, from an irreproachable moral conduct.

So the Unidad Popular victory threatened what was already a precariously split personality, whose contradictory facets had always been difficult to reconcile. From the moment of Allende's victory, every political decision Juan makes will mean undermining the foundation of his own emotional balance. An example: Juan's benefactor and teacher, the one who brought him into the office, instructed and protected him, is working for management, has become an enemy to the revolution. But he's also a personal friend. What is Juan to do?

The person who writes under the name Fardo concentrates on this kind of dilemma. What matters from a literary point of view in a social process is pulling together all the psychological alterations that are brought about by any profound change, examining a poor devil who, like so many others, wanted to live on the fringes of history, peering into it from time to time, like any good tourist, but who suddenly finds himself hurled into the implacable eye of the storm.

Around Juan is a group of other human beings who, confronting the same situation, by the direction they take, reflect a solution that he was unable to adopt. They are faces he could not put on, no matter how much he might want to. Tomás, for example, is a political activist who never experiences a moment of doubt. As far as he's concerned, Juan's vacillations are foolish; a complete waste of time when there's so much to do. Pancho Carrasco (Carrasquito), on the other hand, joined the political crusade along with Juan, but soon concluded that that kind of life was not for him. I'm poisoning my life. I've had it with indigestion. If I can help, fine. But this business of working twenty-five hours a day and never seeing my kids is out. No way.

Juan can't be like Tomás, but on the other hand...

The cop should ask the truck driver. The truck driver knows more than I do; even if he didn't take off his shirt, his green plaid shirt, with its faded brown lines and short sleeves. Ask him. As for my shirt, there it is: it was white; now two red shadows are spreading. I can tell you a lot about the shirt, but not about the dead man.

The cop doesn't believe me. He thinks I'm a friend, that I just don't want to get involved. He takes out a pencil, a pad. My license?

The medics are taking the body away. They're efficient, real professionals, and polite. I realize my license isn't in my trouser-pocket. The medics, who are now opening the back doors of the ambulance, step back when I suddenly appear before them.

Maybe they expect me finally to admit my relationship to the victim and to identify the body. But I just point to my shirt pocket and by some miracle, one of them understands and takes out the license. He hands it to me with a smile.

"Keep on moving, keep on moving," says the policeman.

Nobody moves.

One of the medics pushes the doors shut.

Once again that voice asks me how to spell my name. You can hear somebody shutting the front door now, and the motor starting. The ambulance pulls away, soon it'll be nothing more than a white spot in the distance, down the avenue bordered by flowering trees.

"What did you say?"

"We'll call you if we need you." He returns the license.

I can hardly keep myself from making the automatic gesture of putting it in my shirt pocket.

"Can I go?"

229

"We'll call if something comes up."

I just stand there, feeling the heat increase. I'm no athlete. My underarms exude the pungent odor of someone who leaves home at seven-thirty and doesn't get home until nightfall, someone who refuses to use deodorants because they're not natural. I have a couple of moles, and my girlfriend likes to bite me when we make love. The cop looks behind him once or twice, without moving away very far, as if he were still trying to come up with the exact question that would trap me. I don't feel like explaining at home; when I get home with no shirt on and need to give some explanation, I don't want to have to spell out what happened the way I just spelled my name. I just want to be up there in the ambulance, riding along with that guy and my shirt, holding on to his dead hand. I could've lied - he's my best friend. That way I'd be with him now. I'd never get out of that ambulance, like when you're riding a bus on a hot summer night and the window's open and the cool, fresh air is blowing in.

I don't move until the crowd disperses, until there's not one of those spectators left who saw me take off my shirt. It's only when I'm surrounded by strangers, by hostile passers-by, who snarl indignantly at my presence, only then, do I start to walk. An old man smiles, and raises his hand to his mouth, saying something to the one walking beside him. Other people look at me too. A young girl points at me. There's a chorus of whispers. So the husband finally found out and caught them in the act, and he had to run out so fast he forgot his..., training for the Olympic Games, huh?... A good deodorant commercial, it must be some kind of new hippie style. They're all so sure of themselves in their shirts. White, blue, pink, with simple or eccentric designs, and their clean-scrubbed, Ivory-soap faces, without a trace of a bluish stain, not even a memory of a stain on the pocket above the heart, but they've all gone now; nobody's left; it's time to go home.

I step off the sidewalk; there's a little kid beside me. He's not wearing a shirt either, his pants are worn and he's barefoot. Hey, mister, hey, just enough for the bus, just a few pesos, what about it? I don't say anything to him; I don't look him in the eye, I just speed up my pace. He speeds up too, trotting along beside me. I'd like to see the ambulance, but I can no longer even hear it, I long for the sight of its speeding whiteness up the avenue, the blur of the ambulance carrying the man who is perhaps not dead after all, up the avenue that is beautifully alive with trees, awash in the shimmering sunlight, maybe he's not dead, maybe he's alive after all.

not like Carrasquito either. He can't even be like his friend Muñoz, who understands there can be no change without pain and that, even though it's hard, he's ready to change neighborhoods and even interests. "Look," Muñoz tells him, "sure I had time to go out to the mountains before. But you know I enjoy three minutes now more than I did three days back then. As long as we can guarantee that those trees will be there for everyone and not just for a few who can pay for the privilege, I'm satisfied."

But Juan is not satisfied with that. He was so happy, living with the hope that every day would be a never-ending birthday party. It was so easy for me to be one of them, one of you. Roads pass by me, within reach of my eyes, but not my feet, and I find myself more and more alone and isolated.

His life is crumbling around him.

"Help me."

"You're too old for us to be changing your diapers. Everybody has

231

problems, Juancho."

Juan is beginning to think that what's happening to him is because he's a coward. And it's not because he fails to act with courage; what he does, in fact is far more significant than what Tomás or Muñoz do. It's just that he does it grudgingly, almost as a way of giving the lie to his own cowardice, probably as a neurotic way of forcing himself to break with that other side of his personality which anchors him to the past and attracts him. As the novel advances, this gentle, kind man begins to fall into behavior that is cruel and even borders on fanaticism, as if he were trying to burn the bridges that connect him with his former friends, the only way of assuring that there's no way back for him.

We expect Juan to explode. The other characters, who do not have access to the protagonist's rich individuality,

Everything turned out perfectly. After all, I had organized the whole thing. I called all the people, planned every move, kept an eye on the distribution of the pamphlets, gave instructions to those responsible for security. It's all like clock-work for you, they told me. That's right; that's the way I was, Peters the clock, the blond guy who's always been a good organizer, the one who never failed, who never came to a meeting late.

This way I'm sure, if I do everything myself. Soldier-boy Peters, that's what they called me, the one who's always punctual, even when he's breathing. It's all those years in the army, that's what they whispered to each other, they trained him well. So what! Let them believe that, if they want to. I, on the other hand, knew perfectly well that it wasn't the army that made me this way. If I had managed to adapt myself to the armed forces during those years, it was because with them everything was laid out like a map of a city that hasn't been built yet: Sergeant Peters, the blond guy who's good at giving orders. If I let up for a minute, everything fell apart. Sure, they complained about my strong-arm tactics, but then they'd turn around and beg me to take over the ship. Peters the Tyrant, they called me, but affectionately, because everybody in the Party knew that they needed people like me; you make a revolution with discipline and responsibility. Even Juanita threw that tyrant business in my face once in a while; she was probably pissed off, because everything I did always turned out perfectly; I never made a mistake.

That blond guy's really lucky. Lucky? No way. I'm just Peters. Ever since I was a kid they taught me to deal with responsibility. My dad worked in Internal Revenue, and got a medal for never missing a day. Mom was an elementary school teacher, and the first memory I have of her was her hand correcting the twisted letters of the alphabet in the kids' notebooks. Pedro Peters, my old man called me, the day you get to an appointment late is the day you're really screwed. When that happens your whole day goes wrong and nobody will ever believe you again. Sure, Dad, I said. Son, added Mom, use ·your responsibilities to do what's right. Sure, Mom, I said to her too. I dare anybody to accuse Peters of having his hand stuck in any dirty business. When it comes to building Socialism, hell, I'm strict, because we can't set a bad example here in our country.

It's not that I'm a leader. They've never told me I should be the leader. It's not that I don't have my own ideas, I talk to people, read the texts they give me. But all they have to do is wait until there's a meeting to schedule and organize, and I'm off like a shot, or a communications network to set up among all the *compañeros,* great, that's all I need, whether it's the Party, or my own life, it's the Peters schedule, at your service. Just do what's best for everybody, son, my mother told me. And years later, Juanita has to admit, what luck, Pedro, what luck that the Socialists have you. It would be terrible if you were with somebody else.

That's not luck, I answer. It's my destiny. It couldn't be any other way. But Juanita's insistent, it is luck, Pedro Peters, she says, a flash of light in her tender eyes (I really love Juanita). The day you wake up, Juanita tells me, the day you come down with a crash, that's when I want to see you, Pedro, that's when things are really going to start, Pedro, Pedro Peters.

they don't know what's the matter with him. They're just passing travellers that flash across the horizon, like a mountain storm. They don't have time either to understand or to analyze Juan. He's just a factor they count on for the...

"No, sir. You're not taking the seeds out of here."

changes being proposed. We hope something will happen, but miraculously Juan doesn't

"Just one minute, Mr Dorfman," asked the reporter.

explode. Juan just goes on, in spite of all the indications that he will inevitably explode.

Which of These Roads Lead to Rome? had to have the same use of formal counterpoint that, ever since Con-centrations, seems to have come into vogue among young Chilean writers. Suddenly, just before we reach the middle of the novel, there is an extremely long chapter which seems to have nothing to do with the action being developed. We know that Juan experiences his share of immediate problems beginning in July of 1972, with the novel ending on the last day of the truck drivers' strike in October of that year. On the other hand, this second sequence, which is not parallel, but rather appears only once and never reappears, is situated, one would think, during any period of time, although, since it makes no allusion to Salvador Allende's electoral victory, we must suppose that it occurs earlier. Nor do we know in what city or what country it occurs. We are submerged in the dense consciousness of one Diego, a young high school student, who is participating in a take-over at his school in order to throw out the director. The student movement fails, in large measure because Diego, at a given moment, refuses to go on participating.

There is no direct relationship between Juan and the teenager

"Old woman," he told her, "tomorrow we all get up at five o'clock."

"Fine. At five."

That's how she found out about the bus drivers' strike that October day. Now all hell's going to break out for sure, Holy Mother! And what if he was the only one who walked to work? What if everybody else stayed? But everybody would walk to work at the same time, without really planning it together, each one going toward a different place in that immense city, joining other workers as they left their neighborhoods early, recognizing each other on street corners, forming small groups that would divide and separate again, bidding each other good-bye on other corners, and if they were lucky, climbing aboard packed buses.

"I'm glad I work in a shoe factory, old woman. Because people are wearing out lots of leather walking to their jobs. And when they need new shoes, we'll have 'em ready."

What about Enrique? Why hadn't he come back yet?

"Your brother stayed there overnight. He asked if you could add an orange to his lunch, if you have one. I'll take it."

"That Enrique's really lazy."

"Lazy all right. Doesn't like to walk."

They both knew that wasn't true. Enrique wouldn't sleep a wink tonight. With an enormous stick in his hand he would walk from warehouse to warehouse, to make sure the fascists didn't come to burn the stock, and from work area to work area, keeping an eye on the night shifts, and then he'd go back to the phone to check on

235

whether more *compañeros* were needed to guard the ALMAC supermarket, the one that was three blocks away. Enrique was tireless.

Lord, don't let anything happen to my men. Keep my hothead brother away when the fight begins, when the thugs and the scabs take out their guns. Don't let my men be paralyzed like the country is being paralyzed, Lord. Keep my husband, dear God, from running into one of these high-society smart-alecks in a car, who'll crawl along beside him for a few miles insulting him, asking him if he isn't tired of walking all the way to Socialism. And keep the kids off the streets, even if the teachers don't make it tomorrow to school. No more trouble, Lord, but if there is, if it does come down to that, let me show some of those rich gossips in their fancy dresses what's what, let me aim a stone and get 'em right where it hurts, where it bleeds, like I did when we ran 'em off when they came to buy the chickens we were distributing in the neighborhood. If it comes to the worst, Lord, give me a steady hand. Just do me that one little favor.

Diego – who must be half his age. They don't know each other, neither one of them ever refers to the other, they don't inhabit the same physical or temporal space. There's no reason to suppose that Juan's acts are in any way predicated upon what Diego has done, is doing or will do. Nor do we know who came first, although we suspect that Juan, being older, must be living at a later time.

What the reader cannot doubt, it would seem, is that we are dealing with the same person under two different names. They have the same tastes, are caught in the same dilemmas, and are surrounded by friends who seem to be exact copies as far as their attitudes and their conduct are concerned. Though the central problem they share is the conflict between cowardice (or, if you prefer, peace of mind, bonhomie, accommodation) and an incorruptible moral imperative, they develop in opposite directions: Juan becomes more and

236

more committed and breaks all ties, even though this means that he's lost his peace of mind. On the

"Just one minute, Mr Dorfman."

As in Caballero Muñoz's other works, the world in *But You'll Do It/Tomorrow/Yes, If...* is divided between "inside" and "outside". The inside part should not surprise us. It's a Pullman bus, peaceful and full of passengers, who are dozing, playing cards, calmly conversing or looking out the windows, while they travel toward an uncertain destiny. Meanwhile, outside, just a few inches away, around the bus, all kinds of atrocities are being committed, some of them with a particular date, country and names, others of a more general nature. Bombings, rapes, shootings, concentration camps, burning of fields, massacres of strikers, evictions of people from their homes. As the bus advances, scenes from every imaginable geography in the world, and from every imaginable epoch, flash by in that external landscape, the on-going history of exploitation and of horror. All of this transpires in a chaotic fashion, jumping from one incomplete scene to another, as if "the bus were the only ride in an amusement park created by a sadist", as if it were trapped inside a movie projector full of celluloid fragments of scenes, and that's the way it goes on, spinning, ever farther down the road, toward another injustice, perhaps another century, this time with black slaves, later the extermination of Mexican Indians, then the stench of the textile factories in England in 1830, Christ as a poor carpenter on a cross like the ones he himself used to build, a medieval serf called Peter, a nameless Hindu outcast dying of hunger.

237

Throughout this endless, monstrous story, whose vicissitudes were never collected by any official text, the only recurring motif is the history of Chile, interwoven at regular intervals with full chronological rigor - the foundation of suffering and struggle that is this country's true reality.

Meanwhile, inside the bus, nothing. Nobody reacts; everybody goes on calmly as if they were watching lakes, beautiful mountains, fields, cattle grazing in peaceful meadows, gray cities and neon lights pass by on the other side of the windows. With just one exception: the young and anonymous protagonist who is occupying the last seat at the back of the bus, astonished that no one else - or so it seems - is seeing the same spectacle he is witnessing.

Caballero Muñoz takes the typical anti-hero of the contemporary novel, therefore, and confronts him, for good or ill, with a struggling, agonizing humanity. An interesting evolution. In his previous book, *No, There is Not, Not Today, Noah,* to look no further, that writer had also created an inside - Noah's Ark besieged at the end of the Twentieth Century by an old beggar woman, trying to get in to save her skin. It was the typical split between the refuge (equivalent to the conscience terrified by change, the womb that refuses to be opened) and the destructive forces which surround that refuge and try to hurl humanity out into the cold, naked world of confrontation with history. It is a split that occurs in many western literary works, not a few from Latin America, during the second half of the present century. But in the case of Caballero Muñoz, his previous works presumed that the outside was not made up of an objective reality and its historical specificity, but rather was basically the projection of the protagonist's own terrors; his conscience was punishing him with the most dangerous, repellent, criminal images, as a way of demonstrating the falsity of the life in which he had enclosed himself, the habits with which he was dying every day, the lack of contact with his neighbors, showing, in fact, how he had become a ghost even before he died, that is, dying in the act of being born.

But the protagonist of *But You'll Do It/ Tomorrow/Yes, If...* cannot escape the need for commitment; he must convince himself that everything he sees is something more than a deformed and ravaged image of his own ego. From the moment the novel begins - when he witnesses a youth being machine-gunned, apparently in Vietnam, and watches him drag himself toward the road at the moment the bus passes, the moment when the eyes of the dying man meet the eyes of the one passing by, at that very instant it is already decided that that witness can no longer go on living as if nothing had happened, that he'll have to construct a life which takes into account what he has just seen. There's no going back.

But first Caballero Muñoz explores the easy confines of the rhetoric of indignation. The thread of the arguments by which the protagonist asks himself what he should do becomes at the same time a linguistic bus confronting an external narrative that is more and more oppressive and undeniable. The independent weight which is gradually taken on by what is happening outside becomes a critique of the conscience of that individual who, at the same time he moves along like a voyeur of one horror after another, is awash in a quagmire of alternatives, overlapping statistics, historical and legal studies, searching for a solution which will not bring about his own death as the final result.

We'll never know, in fact, how the novel ends.

When the protagonist finally tells the driver to stop the bus, it's so good throwing so much masturbatory subtlety to hell, and from out here I watch the bus move away and I turn around to join all history's other forgotten ones - when we hear those words, we have no way of judging whether they're true or not. Because right away we hear another mocking voice, which shatters that apparently very effective and transparent linguistic windshield, speaking in the second person singular: So, this is all it takes to console you, the heroic dream demanded by everybody who's nauseated by his own inability to act. It's like the delirium of the cat who thinks he's a bird at the moment they throw him out the window of the moving car. You fantasize that you're getting off the bus when you're only approaching that pretty girl in one of the front seats, calculating how many moves you'll need to make to seduce her.

Therefore, we don't really know for sure whether the protagonist gets off the bus or not. As readers, we can't choose between the two versions and decide which of the voices is telling the truth; we can only conclude that both of them are roads opened up by those who can no longer deny the suffering they witness. Some - I - will join the exploited of the world; others - you - will become more and more cornered and conciliatory; and both exemplify the perennial instability of a class, the petit-bourgeoisie, which is historically condemned to disappear, historically condemned to be important, very important, in fact, before it disappears.

CESAR ROCCAFITTO

Words of Roccafitto that nobody really believes. He wrote a critical review of *But You'll Do It/Tomorrow/Yes, If...* in the journal *Tiempo Indefinido,* as if anguish were no longer possible in the face of the revolution - And then what does he turn around and do? The very next month he publishes *The Hero's Nightmares.* The great literary scandal of the decade.

Everything is not easy-going in *The Hero's Nightmares.* Its title is not *Home Delivery.* The protagonist has two sides, his daytime side and his night-time side - which are portrayed in alternating chapters. Beneath splashes of sunlight the hero is portrayed carrying out his daily activities, almost all of which are political, in his slow but sure march toward liberation. His advance is constant. Whenever a problem has him boxed in, he solves it. He improves his relations with other people, his conscience is sharpened, he's always ready and willing to speak up and to learn; humble, but strong when he needs to be. He changes his approach to his work, joins a party, gets himself organized and moves to a new neighborhood.

But this man, plugged into the high fidelity of Socialism twenty-four hours a day, has another side: a nocturnal side...

other hand, Diego becomes more of a *gusano* and prefers to hold back at the decisive moment. He discovers something which Juan will find out to his great sorrow many years later: that he wasn't cut out for

241

that kind of fratricidal fight. He'd rather withdraw and watch both bands tear themselves to shreds. Maybe some day he can be a referee - some kind of conciliator will be needed in the future.

Simultaneously, successively, in a circular and cyclical fashion, though they are one and the same person, they are nevertheless different. Juan, living an ordinary life, in a specific period, has a sense of belonging, one could almost say a reality, which Diego lacks. It is as if Diego were the memory that surrounds Juan, a tormenting fear, a white shadow, his own son or father. Diego could be Juan's remote grandchild; he could be any young man who at that same instant is choosing another road; he could be that silent, youthful reason because of which Juan cannot go back (because he's already betrayed his ideals once). Perhaps Diego is the real, although secret, source of Juan's moral obsession.

But, in any case, Diego's touch of irreality, his lack of immediacy, paradoxically universalizes his experience, makes it transcend his singular and limited life. It clarifies the perspective from which one must judge Juan. The reader is left with the notion that a unique human being (man), as an adolescent, lived Diego's experience and later,

They'll tell you you're very young, they'll say you're crazy, they'll say if you're so brave, you get off the bus first, they'll say that with all their unbridled and unhealthy violence that you're serving the interests of the oligarchy; they'll say why don't you listen a little, OK, and then you'll know what to do; they'll tell you to get organized first, to think before you act; they'll call you an extremist, a reformist, a bureaucrat, a traitor; they'll say, just wait a minute, test the water, study the situation; they'll tell you it's not a matter of principles, just goals; they'll say you ought to talk less; they'll call you crazy; they'll say you're too young, too impatient, too slow, too rational; they'll say we're wrong, we have to beat a retreat; they'll tell you to go ahead; they'll say it's time to take a breather, consolidation is the watchword; they'll say you have to search out the weakest point in the wall for the final blow; they'll say you have to read more; they'll say there's no better book than experience; they'll say how great it is to see a real idealist in this day and time; they'll tell you to wait until you've had a few kids; they'll say your intentions are good, but your methods stink; where are all these beggars you're talking about, they'll say; they'll say Rome wasn't built n a day; they'll say everybody's free here, anybody can leave the country whenever he wants; they'll say a bird in hand is worth three in the bush; they'll say let sleeping dogs lie; they'll say how much longer are they going to go on singing that same old Vietnam tune; first you have to change people, they'll say, then you can change society; they'll say you're not just going to screw yourselves, you're going to fuck up the next generation too; they'll call you a fool; they'll say it's not my fault these children are starving; they'll say you don't even have time for your wife, it's always the Party first; they'll say you're too old to be caught up in all this; look how it's raining out there in the garden, they'll say; they'll tell you, I admire them, but I'm too old to change; what's going to replace the copper industry, they'll ask; they'll say whoever comes late, loses two brownie points; don't use that tone with me, they'll say; I don't love you anymore, they'll say, now I'm really going to leave; they'll say charity begins at home; they'll say we're getting there; they'll say last night I was crying all night, it was cold and you hadn't gotten here; the cops caught us, they'll say; all the red paint spilled, they'll say, and I was like Dracula going up Recoleto Street; they'll say look at page 35; they'll say I wouldn't even go to church with you; I'm dying to go to bed with you, they'll say; I'm tired of being used, they'll say; they'll say a new humanity dawns every day; they'll say, eat your mashed potatoes and remember the children in Biafra; let's have more dues starting with the ones from September; they'll say, hey, what about Prague, what about Stalin, they'll say; they'll tell you, we're going to have a baby; you're too young, too impatient, too old, too foolish, too impulsive, too patient, they'll say; they'll tell you flies are the malaria of the soul; they'll say I'm really screwed, man; help me, they'll say; they'll tell you conditions just aren't right; they'll say you're bourgeois; they'll call you a poverty-stricken intellectual; they'll say you're partial to the working class and call you crazy and a blackmailer; I give up, they'll say; they'll say life's not worth a plug nickel if you don't have a single minute during the day to gaze at the stars; they'll tell you the masses are blind without leadership; they'll say you're too young; but they'll also tell you, sure, man, we're doing great, sure, man, everything's cool.

as an adult, almost overcame that trauma under the identity of Juan. Because Juan succeeds where Diego failed: he makes a commitment to his own moral truth and sticks to that commitment, come what may. But that doesn't mean that Juan has become another human being, or has cast all his doubts to the winds, defeating Diego's problem. That is the basis of what we could call Juan's "tragedy": he's still the same as

"Just one minute, Mr Dorfman," the reporter insisted. "You have repeatedly affirmed that this was not the book you wanted to write, that you'd change the ending. Now that we're talking about *The Hero's Nightmares,* and approaching that end, could you refer to those changes?"

"I don't think so. You'd better talk to Roccafitto."

"You're the one I'm interviewing."

"If you insist. Toward the end of the novel the intrusions that have already been introduced - as we well know - at isolated moments of the narrative, were supposed to begin to intensify. An acceleration of the fragments, like mad satellites, bits and pieces extracted from books previously commented on or from the *Final Project.* It would be a deliberate attempt to sabotage the development of the reviews. The commentator's voice would become incoherent in the face of this offensive against logical order, he would be incapable of placing limits on the fragmentation."

"And the reasons?" asked the reporter.

"Numerous. On the one hand, to allow literary sensuality to take over that exclusive access to the reader which the parasitic reviews had monopolized."

"And is it true that you intended this to serve as a metaphor for the way in which the real situation with Chile and its working class would erupt into the lives of those parasites who control the country?"

"Well, not exactly a metaphor, but something like that is what I had in mind."

"Quite a mechanistic thesis," said the reporter.

"Maybe. But those intrusions had other advantages, as well. Those narratives provided some narrative relief."

"So it's true you had planned to write another work, a - how shall I put it? - more conventional work of fiction?"

"So true, in fact, that I had even asked for a sabbatical from the University, where I was working, to write it. They refused. So I took a leave without pay. I'm about to begin, and along comes the September crisis. I find a few days to go on with the novel - then along comes the strike of October '72. So I sent the novel packing; after all, everything was at stake if our enemies won... So here it is the middle of November and I have less than two months left to write the novel. I couldn't go back to the University, you understand, and I had to have something to show after having given up my salary in such a dramatic way. I no longer had time to write that other book I had planned. Besides, it was pessimistic."

"Pessimistic?"

"Yes. It portrayed a savage dictatorship in our country - one that lasted some twenty years. How could I write something like that - when I knew we'd win, that we'd never have that sort of tyranny in our Chile. So I started writing

245

Hard Rain. At first I intended to call it **Reviews**."

"**Reviews**?"

"For obvious reasons. I changed the title several times.
Farías suggested **Cross Out What You Don't Like**, and
that's where things were until Skármeta offered the title
Hard Rain as a New Year's gift... There was no problem
putting in all those fragments, because if the readers didn't
like them, they would end up blaming poor Monreal or the
nun Teresa de León. I washed my hands of it."

"And this...uh, experiment, that was supposed to be the
work's apocalypse, how was it to be carried out?"

"The idea was, little by little, to start mixing the fiction in
with the reviews, only fleeting, inexplicable appearances. The
reader wouldn't be able to identify the passages. Maybe they
were from one of the novels being reviewed or they might
even be from a work that was never mentioned, like **The
Secret Memoirs of Father Hasbún**."

"Father Hasbún? Is he another of your inventions?"

"Nobody remembers him now, but he really existed: he
was the manager of TV Channel 13 and he persecuted
people on the left, always invoking a whole calendar of
saints."

"Could you give me specific examples?"

"There was a sequence, let's say, from the struggle in the
countryside. All of a sudden, in the middle of a review of
But You'll Do It / Tomorrow / Yes, If..., the voice of an
anonymous peasant would intervene, saying: 'No, boss.' Then
fifteen pages later there'd be another intrusion from another
part of the book: 'No, boss. You're not taking any calves out
of here.' You see, the landowners stole everything before
expropriation, and when production declined, they blamed
the agrarian reform. And still later: 'No, boss, you're not
taking this tractor,' and so on, in crescendo."

"Were the narrative intrusions always political?"

"Well, almost all the reviews had political implications,
so...but, actually, there was a little bit of everything. Just as

there were a lot of people in the country who were just bench-warmers. Of course, fundamentally, it was a matter of a delayed revenge on the part of fiction for not having been allowed to extol itself in literary language, for having to experience everything second hand."

"And, if every little fragment was taken from a much longer work, didn't it bother you having to break that work's artistic unity?"

"Of course. There was one story, 'Come Home, John Wayne', written, I think, by Juan Menguant. All I was going to use from it was the last sentence: 'The projector. You can shove it up your ass.' I was going to put that phrase in just like that, all of a sudden, right in the middle of nightmare number eight. A sad fate - to write an entire story just so the last line can be cited. And that's the way it was going to be. All of a sudden, a dialogue involving a marital squabble. And the reader wouldn't know if something was starting there or ending, if it was foreplay or an abortion."

"What about elements drawn from the current reality?"

"Those too. If you recall, **Hard Rain** ends with **Nightmares** and with the **Final Project**, mixed together. In that hypothetical project, the group of writers who appeared earlier were going to tell about the October crisis. I chose some twenty or thirty situations, mostly dialogues, that would float freely, without anchor, in which priority was given to revealing how the crisis was overcome, the way our people forged ahead. That was the great army (as much in literature as in reality) that would end up taking the book over, displacing the other fragments, as well as the other reviews. I still have the fragments here. Look. One about a nurse they called La Rata who stole anesthetics from the private clinic of a Doctor Alonso, the Parisian Clinic. She took them to hospitals that were undersupplied. Great woman, right? And here's another one - take a look - about the workers' march, from their neighborhoods to their jobs, the day the bus strike was declared. If you want, I'll read you

247

some later. . . "

"Sure. Later."

*"For the reader, the origin of those fragments could only be a mystery. Not even once they knew the scope of the unrealizable **Final Project**, could they really know for sure where each intrusion came from, since the source could be a real event and not a book."*

"How could the reader confuse those fragments with reality? It's impossible."

"On the contrary, of course it's possible. I'm telling you most of those fragments consisted of dialogues I gathered in the street. Just a few, plain words: 'Fucking fascist.' Like that. Or look, no, I'd better read this to you or else you won't understand. A voice coming from who knows where: 'Just talk to me about the new man, about Socialism and our comrade President. My fool of a husband goes around spouting that gibberish, trying to persuade a bunch of jerks and idiots, and here I am standing in line to buy cooking oil, and maybe, if I'm lucky there's soap so he can wash behind his ears. Holy Mother, let's see if he comes to his senses. There's nothing to buy, but I don't see him cutting down on his appetite. I'd like to see him standing here for hours - and then he had the nerve to ask for my vote. They're not going to take me in again.' You see, we have no way of knowing who's saying that. We no longer know what's real, what's fiction and what's testimonial. Here, for example, a construction worker . . . "

"Perhaps later."

"You'll have to forgive me. I get carried away. It was a mosaic of Chile, a sample of what had remained outside the book. And it made one anticipate that at any given moment an insignificant fragment of reality - a word, or a snail or a newspaper headline - might erupt infinitely into the middle of the novel, into the middle of any novel. A progressive rhythm would be gradually attained. Between each review; then between each nightmare described in Roccafitto's book;

248

then between each paragraph. Until, when we reach the **Final Project**, every three lines, then every two, and finally every line, until finally there would be an intrusive passage between every word; and the only thing being narrated, without rhyme nor reason was October, 1972, with a distant excuse from some lost and pale commentator."

"Here we are again and we can't be stopped, we can't be stopped. The epigraph: Was that the idea?"

"The book became its own negation. It existed to be substituted."

"And, nevertheless," said the reporter, "you decided to eliminate those intrusive passages."

"My damned critical sense. After the first few attempts, I realized the book was becoming a bunch of illegible garbage, it was losing - how shall I put it? - its beauty. It was going to become something ugly and misshapen."

"But wasn't that precisely the joke? To kill off the novelist?"

"Kill him, yes, but not after having tortured him and the reader for hours. I at least wanted a relative to be able to identify the body. I confess, I'd always dreamed of doing this: that Bach would have composed the **St. Matthew Passion** with the sole purpose of introducing a dissonant element at the end which would refute its full realization and esthetic effectiveness. You've got to have guts to kill something into which you've poured all that love."

"Were you in love with your creation then? With the fragments, I mean."

"Let's just say I felt a certain amount of affection for them. But that plan was excessive, even for a crazy fellow like me. The intrusions didn't destroy the book as a work of fiction. They destroyed it in the area of its potential publication, in the real story of the life of Ariel Dorfman. The theoretical conception of the book was fascinating, having the world of the senses shove it to the world of ideas, having Empedocles fart on Plato's head, having all those self-destructive tendencies which had been set forth earlier in the reviews verified right there in the novel that contained them. Sure. All that was great. But putting it into practice was something else altogether."

"Were you afraid you'd become... Do you remember Hernán Iriarte?"

"I don't remember. The fact is, the literary work never freed itself from the reviews, never succeeded in driving them out of the novel; the reader never extended that model to his own cloistered existence; and for my part, I simply dreamed of escaping my role as critic, with any luck I'd be participating in working class newspapers, producing comic books, writing soap opera scripts and looking for ways to use images to increase agricultural production in CORA, as well as gathering testimonials from survivors of the nitrate miners' strike. But I didn't. I just went on being a writer. I refused to destroy **Hard Rain** - and if I had, no one would have known it, because there wasn't anybody around who would have dared publish it - not even good old Alberto Hinostroza. When somebody commits suicide for love, the least he can hope for is that the woman will know he did it for her."

"You insist on comparing the book to a woman."

"You can interpret that however you want. What I can assure you of is that I was afraid of the reviews that were going to be written about my own book. What would they tell me? The critics, I mean. The commentators."

"So something good came out of all this after all," murmured the reporter. "You at least learned the limitations of your own intentions."

"Yes. I discovered that I'd rather produce a successful novel than be faithful to my own artistic theories. Success was real and tangible, beyond all rhetoric. That's the way things are in Chile; we do everything half-way."

"But, in any case," continued the reporter, after thinking for a moment, "you could have had faith in the reader."

"I could have. That's true."

"Because otherwise, and I say this from my own experience, there's no way to understand that abrupt ending. How is one to understand all that foreplay and a coitus that never comes? Something real was needed, something that was more than words, something that would be a touchstone, a witness to your sincerity."

"That's true," said Dorfman. "But I didn't dare."

Diego, with the same terrors, the same need for peace and family life; but, in fact, he has lost all of that and has not yet found any replacement for it. His belief in the revolution is sufficient to make him act, but it offers no fulfilment after he has acted.

Whereas, Diego feels relatively happy: he didn't have to fight with his girlfriend, he keeps his friends from both groups; he finishes a chemical experiment that interested him; he plays a game of touch football, goes camping, and enjoys excellent health. Diego has everything Juan will wish for, although it's also probable that ahead of him he will have everything Juan has lived through and decided on. Years later perhaps another situation awaits him, a situation from which he may not be able to escape so easily - when the conflicts are no longer local, but are instead projected on the entire country and all its reality.

The problem of Juan and Diego is that they're tied up in themselves, that final barrier against which all good intentions are battered and rise up again, that irreducible foundation which everyone is, his ego; and it's here that the author shows his talent. He throws us head-first into that universe, makes us dizzy, grinds us to a pulp, sucks us in again, persuades us, draws us in, until we can no longer doubt that Juan, but also Diego, yes, also Diego, unfortunately, is a little bit ourselves, in fact, a great deal ourselves, a little bit and a lot and too much what all we readers are.

JORGE CABALLERO MUNOZ

Letter to the Editors of the *Revista Tiempo Indefinido e Infinito*:

Dear Sirs:

I've had it with all this idiocy. As a reader, I protest.

The central theme of *Which of These Roads Leads to Rome?* is not cowardice. It is courage.

That's the way history is made. With people like Juan - who, in the present, redeems all the past mistakes of his adolescent alter ego. Farías' novel is pristine and clear: you're either for the revolution or you're against it. If there's any ambiguity, it's not in the text. Instead, it's in the reviewer who projects his own timidity onto material that is unequivocal. As a critic, Caballero Muñoz is incapable of choosing between the new material that Chile offers him and that old, presumptuous literature wherein one man is every man, the traitor is the hero, and a character can become his opposite. It's no accident Mr Caballero Muñoz dedicated his own book to "a man who probably doesn't exist and is certainly impossible, the Jorge Luis Borges who supported Fidel and professed to be a Marxist".

Juan dared go out into the rain and take the risk. Diego - and the critic - stayed in the house so as not to catch cold and - if you'll pardon the expression, since we're dealing with literature - all for what? To end up drowning in their own bathtubs.

Hell, you have to choose.

You, Mr Caballero Muñoz, be Diego. If you feel like it.

As for me, as a reader, I choose to be Juan.

But this man, as I was saying when they so rudely interrupted me, this man plugged in 24 hours a day to the high fidelity of Socialism, has another side: a nocturnal side. In the predawn hours he is visited by nightmares, some of them extraordinarily real, others disconnected, but all of them derived from a single premise: the revolution has failed or is about to crumble. If the hero constructs the nation during the day, before the tribunals of the night he constructs projects and maps of a future that threatens him, what could happen, what is perhaps already happening somewhere. It's as if he were dreaming a second monstrous history of Chile whenever he closes his eyes. He is being punished in the progressive circles of a hell that he cannot destroy with the librium he takes from his night table before he goes to bed.

There are those who criticize Roccafitto severely. They say the author created an insipid Socialist daytime hero only as a pretext to smuggle in what really interests him: attacking the revolution. They mention nightmare number two as an example: the hero, exiled by a strong-arm government, boards an airplane, but no one will grant him asylum, and he ends up spending his time in customs offices, dealing with passports and safe-conduct forms while countries play with him like a golfball in a game being played entirely in the dark. That, according to Roccafitto's detractors, would not be what the protagonist would fear temporarily, but rather it becomes his reality, from which he dreams the possibility of a distant and non-existent Chilean youth who, almost effortlessly, experiences a radical transformation in his life.

Such an interpretation seems to us unfair. The fact that the writer refuses to turn his back on the weaknesses and deficiencies of the revolutionary process does not mean that he embraces them. The central line of the novel is the way in which, during the day, he in fact overcomes the trap or the temptation which was proclaimed to be unavoidable in the nightmare from which he has just awakened. That's precisely why he is a hero, because every morning he goes on trusting others, he moves on, certain they are waking up together in eyes that are not, after all, alien. No one could suspect that in the nightmare with which he was struggling just a few hours before, a member of the Party's security forces approached him and advised him of the need to infiltrate the Nationalist Front to get information on an impending coup d'état, and that, in order to do so, they are going to pretend he is being expelled from the Party. The hero accepts that mission and undoes the fascists' plans. But when the revolution triumphs, it turns out that the member of the security forces, who was his only witness and contact, has been killed and now no one believes his treachery was fabricated. No one will even hear any explanation. His case is not set down in any document; they burned the local headquarters where there might have been some evidence; and now his own comrades are searching for him and want to kill him. He has to leave the country. He'll end his days condemned to the fringes of history forever, watching American TV series in a Miami hotel. Series in which, of course, everything always turns out perfectly, where the witness who can prove the celluloid hero's innocence is alive and ready to help him. *Happy Ending.* The hero realizes that the face on the screen will never be his.

Whom are we to believe? Whom can we trust? What happens when there's someone who wants to take advantage of the revolution for his own purposes? And, of course, there's always more than one. How can we go on being spontaneous, how can we still be pure, if we happen to find ourselves beside that kind of person, as in nightmare number ten? The answer is found in the real actions of the hero. In the next chapter, during an emergency, someone trusts the hero, instead of playing a dirty trick and extracting a small revenge that might be deserved, and he, in turn, places himself in the hands of another comrade, and so the three of them risk their lives, just out of a sense of solidarity. There's not a sign of egotism in any of them.

That situation has brought on another kind of attack by the critics, who say that Caballero Muñoz is in fact an extremist who doesn't appreciate the fact that you have to move slowly. By placing everything bad in one zone and everything good in another, all the complexity of the struggle is being deformed. Of course there's bureaucracy, say these adversaries of Roccafitto - but never like the one in nightmare number thirteen. There the hero imagines himself as the section chief of the Civil Records Office. He sets out to correct that agency's inefficiency. There'll be no more influence peddling, no more false documents and no more illicit intermediaries in matters of retirement pensions. At the beginning of the dream, everything is going well. Fired up by their boss's enthusiasm, the employees start to help him. But in a short while the outside world begins to undermine his efforts. That office is the only island of light in a polluted universe and it can't hold out against the pressure to go back to its usual, underdeveloped rhythm. You can't move so fast - first you have to educate employees and public. One day no one shows up for work. Another day it's the public that rebels, suspecting that behind all that unaccustomed courtesy there must be something fishy. All his most intimate friends come in asking him to steal documents, to change files or to hurry along some request. The protagonist ends up drowning in a sea of paper.

Typical, proclaim the critics: he takes an incomplete and negative aspect of the revolutionary process and distorts it.

Esteban Monreal thinks we can't answer Roccafitto's critics by pointing out that day defeats night in the end, because the proof of who wins in this battle is not found in the novel's contents. Monreal, a faithful disciple of Josefina de Leon, believes that the peaceful music, which provides a refreshing and sensual backdrop to the daytime segments, is the best answer to the overwhelming turbulence which darkens the night. Therein we see the author's irrevocable intention. "If he didn't dream of making mistakes," adds Gerardo Trabata, "then we would know that something was wrong. We'd know he was lying to himself."

Very comforting judgements. But they don't stop the flow of nightmares that weigh more and more upon events, not on some dim and uncertain future, but upon the day to day life of Chile.

The party to which the hero belongs needs money and needs it fast, for some unspecified activity (arms, propaganda, a newspaper, salaries for activists?). Get the money any way you can, even if you have to blackmail some industrialists. He doesn't know what to do. That action could, in effect, compromise the revolution's effectiveness; it could muzzle his own voice in denouncing internal corruption whenever it appears. He awakens from nightmare number seven at precisely the moment his secretary calls to say that an industrialist is waiting to see him.

"Have him come in."

But all the attacks on Roccafitto don't come from the left. "What he wants to do with this impossible character," meditates Enrique Lafourcade, "is excuse the mistakes of Unidad Popular. There are all the problems, quotas, bickering, betrayals, shortages, but, of course, don't worry, ma'am, they're just little nightmares, pure fantasy, mere accidents. What is real and what you should trust is that messianic, exemplary hero who will easily banish all these problems from his real life. You don't have anything to eat, ma'am. The hero will create a food distribution agency in his imagination and you'll have a banquet. A vaccine for Marxists: to prevent the disease of criticism that buries them like an avalanche. Just a small inoculation on the arm. Later the nightmare is answered by the seraphic protagonist, and good night, ladies - or better yet, good morning. It's too bad for literature's Leninist bureaucrats that we've all grown up. Not even all the tricks of a magician of fiction can save the country from the real, physical debacle into which we've been hurled by these nightmares that, unfortunately, are all too real."

But Lafourcade, as usual, is wrong.

To begin with, not all the nightmares are political. There's one, for example, number six, in which they're searching for the protagonist because he's a criminal, not a revolutionary. He loses his identity and all he has left is his terror of fog. It's as if Roccafitto had made his hero touch rock-bottom: there's no connection with daytime life. This "ordinary" dream is the one that will cause the protagonist the greatest anguish, as it will the readers as well, because it turns out to be almost impossible to answer it in daily practice.

Caballero Muñoz, Roccafitto's most important defender, uses this novel as a model of his famous theory of "Socialist Irreality" (in *Art Engagé in a Dependent World*). "We don't deny," he writes, "that men are phantoms. But we have to turn the screw on Henry James himself: we have to show how men, with their very bones and muscles, gradually take control from within of what is unreal and bury it, frightening away the ghosts. We can defeat this phantasmagoria if we take it into account, if we confront all the myths in the light of day."

But not even Caballero Muñoz knows how to interpret the last of the nightmares, where we are caught up in a whirlwind of simultaneous events, the thousands of elections that were held or will be held during Unidad Popular's six years in power. He pokes fun at the time Chileans devote to the selection of those who will represent them: parliamentary representatives, union officials, municipal officials, CUT, workers' representatives to the Committee on Production, university plebiscites, reams of petitions, strikes, votes of confidence or no-confidence in leaders, ratification of salary raises, an eternal flow of referenda, polling booths, papers, petty frauds, alliances, conversations to get somebody's vote, lists of supporters, campaign outings, fundraisers, distribution of flyers, negotiations to form alliances, court appeals, quotas on the Electoral Council, attempts to convince a candidate to withdraw, stealing an opposition vote, checking out voter identification, petitions to have political ads withdrawn from polling booths, keeping an eye on that shithead poll-watcher, insisting that the names of those who are absent be read twice before closing the session in hopes that Matas will get there in time to vote, putting one more vote in the bag, denying someone's right to vote after the polling place has closed, multiple, eternal, rotating elections, with pencils in an infinite variety of colors, and inclinations of the equinox, the first Sunday in February, the third Sunday in August, the first Sunday in April, asking the presiding officer at the polling station to please verify the gentleman's name, thousands of names, numbers, lines, cigarette butts, warnings, now I'm going to vote if they'll let me and marking the fresh, clean, pure-as-a-dove ballot, not like that guy who messed up his ballot and then created a fuss by asking for another chance, and memorizing all the regulations, elections in every union, in youth centers, in sports clubs, in JAPs, cooperatives, Neighborhood Councils, special elections for a member of Congress, they bring a gigantic French bread sandwich to the rest of the members of the polling committee, but nothing for me, the others invite him, jokes when the heat is unbearable and there are no curtains in the school where the voting is taking place, handing over the results at a vote-counting center, victory embraces, hey old man, come take my place for a while, demanding credentials from the one in charge of the polling station, until finally the nightmare's over, all the elections become one, the last one,

Among all the phenomena with which that minority called Unidad Popular have laid waste to the country, the one that has perhaps produced the greatest dismay among the select spirits of our race - and there are not a few of them - has been the attempt to introduce chaos and consciousness-raising (words whose cacophony would repel any educated person) into the novel.

Not content with having destroyed a healthy economy with their obsessive and erroneous reading of our reality, inflicting incalculable suffering upon the population in the process; not satisfied with having unleashed a partisan persecution which they themselves denounce but against which they do nothing; not happy with having seriously compromised our national interests with those of a totalitarian, foreign power, undermining the ties of mutual tolerance and help which linked us with traditionally friendly countries that were more in tune with our own idiosyncrasies and our intellectual development, and perverting, therefore, the independence and non-intervention of our armed forces, and not content with the distortion of our laws, applying them in a slanted and discrimina-

tory way, and, in addition, negating the police power and intimidating the courts, when demagogic excesses attempted to take by force what other citizens, rightfully, are not willing to surrender; not only celebrating all this, but much, much more, those "individuals" who support the regime have systematically curtailed the people's freedom of expression. We have repeatedly written in our editorials about the attempts to smother the democratic media and to take over the Paper and Carton Manufacturing Company, but insufficient emphasis has been placed on the new literature which these new men propose as reading material that, we must remember, will no doubt be obligatory in the future.

Before 1970 there were also attacks upon our cultural patrimony, attacks in which the edifying function of art and its use to express the depths of the perceptive spirit, gathered and transcribed in a solitary act, were also denied. But those irresponsible people had no power; their very tendency toward exaggeration isolated them from the conviviality that was common here. And it's not that our newspaper considers it illegitimate to use literature as a vehicle of

260

protest concerning the state of the human condition or as a means to criticize certain unhealthy tendencies in society. We've even accepted the fact that the search for new formulas must perhaps inevitably disturb the reader's sensibility.

Now these self-proclaimed writers' groups would like to make a clean slate of it and start off at point zero in the field of fiction. And they have the means to carry out their objectives. Reinforced by an abusive publicity machine, with influential contacts in the Ministry of Education, closely connected to those who are vomiting out all their bile in films from Chile-Films and in series scripts and news broadcasts on Communist-controlled TV stations, drawing our youngest readers in with eroticism and heretofore unheard of violence, infiltrating various organizations, under the pretext of extending knowledge, when what they actually want to do is to bureaucratize the legitimate voice of the people, and promoted internationally by misguided Latin American writers, they are now in a position to impose their own concept of reality.

At first they appeared to be rebelling against stifling norms, giving the impression of an outburst of creative energy. But now they declare themselves independent, they misunderstand Neruda and squander the heritage of Gabriela Mistral; they play around with words, scorn careful meditation and the objective (and therefore more impassioned) eye of calmer artists;

they celebrate the doodlings of the illiterate as examples of the most elevated lyricism; anything that falls outside their blinders they label as "bourgeois", "reactionary" and "retrograde". And they mock our most sacred values. It's the first step, the hook, the undoing of any concept of Beauty, so · that, later, when fatigue reigns in the suffocated minds of Chileans, they can replace it with the gray monotony of a pedestrian realism, the ceaseless construction of banalities, thus politicizing even the leisure moments of our citizenry, setting themselves up as representatives of sectors of the population that never elected them to such a position, so that in the end, in the name of the very dogmas that earlier justified their supposed liberation and anarchy, they will demand the chaining of all human creative power to the postulates of the commissars.

The day will come when all the designs of their political masters will have been defeated and the reconstruction of our nation and its industries will have begun. That will be the moment to apply sanctions against those who tweaked the nose of a constitution they had sworn to defend. At that moment of settling debts, there will no doubt be naive citizens who will ask that these so-called writers be spared any judgement or condemnation. In the opinion of this paper such writers, almost all of whom have foreign names, who did not respect the sacred temple of letters and who profaned the tradition of autonomy that always surrounded them, cannot at that moment turn to that tradition for aid. They cannot seek the support of the very laws they themselves violated.

The literature which they despise will not protect them when the people of Chile demand an accounting for their words and their deeds.

. . . that terrible day, the fourth of September, 1976, when Eduardo Frei Montalva was once more inaugurated as President of the Republic. That is the fear that devours the protagonist - the fear that all those elections have in the end served no purpose other than to entrap the revolution and bring back the Christian Democrats.

Even though the hero responds the next day with the successful take-over of a factory, that chapter on electoral nightmares is the one that has attracted the attention of readers. "There are ways other than an opposition victory at the polls to put an end to the revolutionary process," muses Venezuelan Arístides Ulloa, who ought to know something of these matters. "I'd explore what they are."

As an answer, Roccafitto lifted his eyebrows slightly. "You don't know us," he told him. "We're different here in Chile."

They had that conversation, according to Poli Delano, on the night of the *Final Project.*

FINAL PROJECT

To give an example, one of them had decided that his character, a provincial cab driver, would sign up as a volunteer truck driver during the truckers' strike, promising his girlfriend back home that he'd be back in a few days. Then he had thrown himself headlong onto the highways with a load of raw material for a textile factory, which would grind to a halt if he didn't get there.

"Something like *The Salary of Fear,*" said the writer. "But I'd rather call it *The Salary of Hope.*"

He got involved in the whole thing without knowing exactly why. He'd never developed a very sharp political conscience, but no doubt he was spurred on by a vague sense of guilt for having been the driver, during the previous two months, of a truck that was being used for hoarding, speculation and the black market. With each mile he drove he erased that past deed, which was painful to him and was not his kind of job; yet at the same time he brought it up in his memory. His progress, the delays along the way, the fights he confronted, the solidarity he discovered. "He's a lot like the character I've been working on," said Farías. "He's one of these fellows who plays a street Santa in the Plaza de Armas during the month of December, you know, so people can have their kids' pictures taken with him, you know what they're like, squalid, skinny, with a cotton beard and..."

"It's October, Farías. Not December. The theme is October."

"Yeah. I know that. He recalls that job, while he's throwing a bunch of baby bottles into the canal. I think I'm going to have him rebel."

That journey becomes not just a personal adventure,

but one that involves the people as a whole. The repairs on both truck and driver on the second night, while he's talking to the truck as if it understood him. The moment when he curses himself for having taken a detour. His arrival at the textile factory, leaning on the horn. All this interspersed with the narrative of his past life, the way he had been dominated by the power-brokers of that area, always guided, as he was, by the hope of buying his own truck so he could be independent, all the scraping for a few dollars, more or less. That's what he gradually overcomes and, toward the end, we sense that when he goes back to his home town, he'll be very different from when he left.

Each one went on explaining his own project. But it wasn't enough. They felt dissatisfied.

Besides that, they could choose themes by lot. First, you write a theme on a little piece of paper, then you put them all in a hat and everybody chooses one. It was a matter of outlining the essential, prototypical cases.

So the people would be completely portrayed, just as in *The First Forty Measures*: the neutrals, the fascists, the doubtful, the indifferent, the ones who were getting married, the ones who were dying, the ones who where throwing themselves into the struggle as if someone had sounded a gong, the ones who were holding on to their little reserve tank, those who talked a lot but worked very little, the ones who wore out their backs carrying sacks of potatoes . . . all of them together until we had a complete picture. But they weren't satisfied with that either. With a story about a peasant, and a list of dismal statistics that would show an exact replica of what a peasant should be, you accomplished nothing. You had to tell the story of every peasant, each one by itself, and then all of them together.

And that was enough to give art as they had practised it up until then a real heart attack. They had to somehow transcend that false illusion. An attempt to include everything, in which every point of view would be exhausted in a magnificent juxtaposition which itself would form a more universal and repetitive law. The collective effort might make it possible to go beyond what one isolated individual could accomplish. Meaning would be born out of the senseless piling up of data, just as it was in everyday reality.

"But what about my truck driver," protested the one who...

One truck driver would never be exactly like another, however much they both might objectively represent the same interests and ideas, and that in itself was by no means certain. No life of an old woman waiting in line was going to be a mathematical copy of the old woman who earlier was complaining about the scarcity of powdered milk or the one who later told them both to shut up, talking like that about her handsome President, just let him do the governing. It was a labor for essayists to discover the exact configuration that would include that trio of old women and many more, all of them standing in some line, ranting or resigned or committed Allende supporters. The way to create an artistic nation was to show all of them, even if the differences might not be noticed at a first reading, even though the string of secondary school students who would vote, let's say, for the Christian Democrats, would end up driving the reader to despair, because of their endless and obvious repetition, even if all the gardeners who worked in the ritzy part of town pulled up the weeds and stooped over to admire the gladioli at the same instant, nevertheless, it was the mandate of the new art to show all of them. That was Chile: all these individual wills, thoughts, journeys, betrayals, acts of generosity, acts of faith, obscenities, evasions. So choose one, just one, specific moment that the country had lived through during that strike, any moment, that would catch men, women and children in all their fleeting clarity, in their best or their worst incarnations, making love, harvesting carrots, apologizing to Dad, wiping off the bar counter, putting a bomb on the railroad tracks, endorsing a check, making shoes, and then without the author's arbitrary and merciless intervention, one could come close to the nation's reality, where it was headed, why, what its problems were, what the citizens really thought; it was like letting them vote and, in the process say everything they thought, like a public opinion poll taken simultaneously on ten million television broadcasts, that was the only alternative if you really wanted to achieve the oft-touted purpose of fully discovering and showing our world the way it really was.

Not even the right could have come up with a more sinister plan against the revolution. To carry it out, every Chilean would have to stop working and start recording his own experiences or transcribing those of others; you'd need an army, an entire country and more, if you took into account all those who couldn't even read or write; we'd have to import tons of paper, typewriter ribbons, pencils; we could never do that with the kind of foreign debt we had; you'd have to freeze time and bring every life to a halt so that no one would forget what had happened at that precise moment; you'd have to re-organize the economy completely, based on the new slogan, let Chile finally know herself; the mere formulation and planning of the assault on the national conscience would mean a disaster of epic proportions; we would never recover from that kind of art, not even with the help of a Marshall Plan.

"Do you know what else?" said Inibata. "I'll never write another word as long as I live. Never. I swear it."

Unless some day we'd all be making poetry the way we worked and lived in this country; unless some day our story would be merely reality without words and without paper, unless . . .

It was getting late. The curfew would be lifted at six in the morning; tomorrow could be decisive for defeating the counter-revolution, tomorrow or maybe the day after. All the brothers had better get some sleep. Slowly the conversation began to die down.

Someone else, on the other hand, without anyone seeing him, started to write inside his head; he couldn't help it. Some magical afternoon would come when there would be time, when there would be no right wing to threaten us; so he started to spell it out here along the road, where's your body, my love, when everything made me believe that today, Sunday, we'd be under some tree whispering the sweet nothings lovers tell each other, but the road, sweetheart, is so glorious and savage and clean, and this truck that's not my own is an animal that right now I control, and tomorrow . . .

So when the protagonist gets off the bus (or dreams that he gets off) and they kill him, the last thing he sees (or dreams that he sees) is that somebody's leaning over his bullet-ridden body, and he's become that youth who runs toward a bus that's carrying a face looking out a window, the youth with whom the novel begins; someone approaches and covers him with a shirt and the shirt has a bluish stain on the pocket, a shirt he had taken off years ago to cover an unknown man hit by a car on the street. We don't know if this act of getting off the bus and this death and this gesture of incomprehensible love are true or if they're fiction. We don't know whether the vicious circle, into which falls the conscience not fed by action, is being broken or not. We don't know what personality, what course, he took. We know only that in the last sentence the protagonist ceases to be you or I and becomes he; perhaps dead, perhaps alive and still vacillating, he becomes an integrated human being and enters history.

267

But you'll do it, and you always say tomorrow, whether it's out of hope or simply postponement, you always answer tomorrow, although, in the final analysis, instead of the conditional "if", if I can, if I feel like it, if it occurs to me, if they support me, if I want to, instead of that "if" that's always being brandished by the johnny-come-lately's, the opportunists, the anguished, the fearful and the sons-of-bitches, instead of that "if", we're going to answer with an affirmative, emphatic "yes, I will", the yes that lovers use for love, that the writer uses for the written word, the yes that men and women use for the revolution, yes, I will.

**So you see, in spite of everything,
I have after all advanced.
We have.**

December 31, 1972

About the translator: Professor George Shivers teaches Spanish in the Department of Modern Languages at Washington College in Maryland, USA. His translations include several works by Ariel Dorfman: *The Last Song of Manuel Sendero, My House Is on Fire,* and *Someone Writes to the Future* (forthcoming from Duke University Press).